The Man Who Loved His Wife

FEMMES FATALES

Femmes Fatales restores to print the best of women's writing in the classic pulp genres of the mid-twentieth century. From mysteries to hard-boiled noir to taboo lesbian romance, these rediscovered queens of pulp offer subversive perspectives on a turbulent era.

The Man Who Loved His Wife

VERA CASPARY

THE FEMINIST PRESS
AT THE CITY UNIVERSITY OF NEW YORK
NEW YORK CITY

Published in 2013 by the Feminist Press
at the City University of New York
The Graduate Center
365 Fifth Avenue, Suite 5406
New York, NY 10016

feministpress.org

First Feminist Press edition

Originally published by G.P. Putnam's Sons, New York.

Cover and text design by Drew Stevens.

Library of Congress Cataloging-in-Publication Data
Caspary, Vera, 1899-1987.
 The man who loved his wife / Vera Caspary.
    pages cm
Includes bibliographical references and index.
ISBN 978-1-55861-846-6 (alk. paper)
I. Title.
PS3505.A842M36 2014
813'.52—dc23
                                        2013035186

1 THE DIARY WAS STARTED, PROPERLY, ON JANUARY
first. More than merely the beginning of another year, it
marked a new phase in the life of a man. Fletcher Strode
had always known quick satisfactions, easy delight, and the
exercise of such teeming energy that if one of his many projects
failed, he had at once plunged into more extravagant activities.
The written word had neither dazzled nor distressed him; the
only books he had read all the way through were detective stories. There can be no doubt of their influence on the purpose and
content of his diary.

It was a good thick book, beautifully bound in dark green
morocco stamped with his initials. He had got it as a Christmas
present, one of many useless, expensive trinkets elaborately
wrapped to make a show under the tree. Together he and Elaine
had selected the Douglas fir, trimmed it, admired their work but
there had been no surprise in it and no one to help them cel-
ebrate. Over an abundant Christmas dinner at a charming table,
merriment was pretense. They had hoped on New Year's Eve to
recapture some of the old joy, wore New York clothes and drank
Cordon Rouge '59. For a short time, dancing to a tune that had
driven them half out of their minds that first whirlwind season,
they had let themselves believe a miracle would bring about a
return of that delightful fever. They hurried out of the nightclub,
leaving half a bottle of champagne.

On the hilltop their house was as lonely as a ship far out at sea. The night was silent, the world exclusively theirs. In the hall Elaine dropped the fur-lined cloak, left it crumpled on the floor. Before they reached her room, Fletcher had jerked down the zipper of her dress and kissed her back, inch by inch. The chiffon fell about her feet. She stepped over it grandly and, with a fine disregard for things treasured by colder women, tossed upon the dressing table encumbrances of gold, jade, and pearls. Long legs shining in misty stockings, thighs round and female, a narrow strip of satin girdling her hips, she teased and pranced before him like one of those naughty French girls on posters. Fletcher played at the game of pursuit until he had caught her and performed the ritual of the bra, unfastening the single hook, pulling her to him with rough joy, circling her torso with his heavy arms, cupping big hands over her breasts. They kissed like new lovers. This was how it had been in the beginning; they followed the routine for luck.

Out in the dark an owl hooted.

Fletcher cursed, but silently, because Elaine actually liked having an owl screeching on the telephone pole near the house. It was *amusing* (Shakespearean, she said) to hear *to-whit, to-who* in the night. Fletcher regarded the owl as an enemy. A city man who had learned to live with crickets and night birds, he could not tolerate the mockery of the raucous tones. In the pause between the cracked cries, Fletcher lay tense, waiting for the unbearable repetition.

Elaine kissed him with many small kisses, touched and teased in a way that would once have aroused superior power. "Be patient, darling." In aborted groans Fletcher cursed the earth and heaven, himself, the owl. "Try, darling, to relax. Just a bit longer, dear." Into Fletcher's mind hobbled the memory of a boy whose unequal arms trembled, whose drawn legs jerked at every step. Sick at the sight of deformity, Fletcher had admitted the poor cripple to his office to offer an unsteady tray of pencils and shoelaces. A dollar had brought tears to the animal eyes, spittle had caked loose lips while, gulping and winking, the poor fellow had spewed out gratitude. Fletcher's generosity had been the easy penance of a healthy man. He did not like to

2

remember this, but the spastic ghost came to haunt him during those fragile, important moments when he could least afford to be tormented by memories.

"Patience, dear."

Her voice was like a breeze sweeping his cheek. A man's patience could not hold forever. Her whispers grew fainter, endurance flagged, the owl hooted. Worn and disgusted, he left her.

"Sorry, darling."

The owl hooted again. "Damn you!" Fletcher cursed the owl because he could not curse a wife who pretended the failure was her own. She had no right to remorse. Alone in his bed he thought of Elaine alone in hers, and became resentful of her suffering. Had she been older, less lusty, merely performing her duty toward the husband who kept her, he would not need to have tortured himself with the concern of her. He lay and listened to the faint stir of her restlessness, heard the click of a light switch, the sound of running water, the clatter of a cupboard door.

Neither slept much. At half-past seven on New Year's Day Elaine found Fletcher in the den with a cup of instant coffee grown cold at his elbow. She wore a smile. "Oh, darling, you're writing in your diary."

He covered the page with his arm.

If she had noticed the gesture of concealment she gave no sign of it. "You'll enjoy keeping a diary," she said, finding some pleasure in his using her gift. "Don't have any inhibitions. About anything. Just put it all down, your craziest notions. Later when you read it over, you'll find it terribly amusing."

Elaine had a lot of favorite words. The way she emphasized and thrust them at him sometimes annoyed Fletcher. He found *amusing* a reproach. A man who could not satisfy nor be satisfied ought, at least, to be amused. His first entry would never amuse anyone:

Happy New Year, Fletcher J. Strode. Oh, yeah. A lousy lot you have to be happy about. Just another 365 days to wonder

3

about what FJS is doing here. I would be a lot better burning down there and so would my wife. She knows it. I know it. God knows it. She is getting to despise me and I do not blame her for it. I would not blame her for anything she might do.

"What have you written?"

He looked up sheepishly. His eyes, in spite of all that he had gone through, were still childishly wide and blue, fringed by lashes that women remarked upon enviously. His wife laughed at the secrecy, swooped down to kiss him. His covering the diary did not displease her because she felt that Fletcher ought to have something, if only the diversion of recording secret thought, to reawaken the spirit of that vital and impetuous man with whom she had fallen so vitally and impetuously in love.

IT WAS NOT that love had died. Quite the opposite. Circumstance had reshaped their lives and emotions. Elaine had become softer, more mature, in many ways, maternal; Fletcher more dominating and willful. He had to possess her fully. She was the ether and the substance, the strength and the ornament, the reason and despair of his life. In this lay their tragedy.

Five years earlier, a hearty man of forty-two, Fletcher J. Strode had fallen so profoundly in love that he felt that he would die unless he won the darling creature. At this time Fletcher had been boisterous, given to impulse and high living, easy laughter and hard work. In Elaine Guardino he had found more than a desirable girl. She had, as he had, a madness for living, spent her energy and her earnings with a zest that had been due not simply to youth but to a freedom of spirit which he had never before found, nor expected, in a woman.

At the time of their marriage all of their friends had predicted early disaster. An unlikelier couple could not be imagined. There was a difference of nineteen years in their ages; their tastes were incompatible; every element of character, background, and education was dissimilar. Her friends considered him the stereotype of the self-made man, a show-off who expressed himself by conspicuous spending and loud talk. His cronies were sure he would never be able to live contentedly with a highbrow who talked about ambivalence, Shostakovich, existentialism, and Martha Graham.

They met in New York at Sardi's restaurant after a play opening. One of Fletcher's associates had invested money in the show. Elaine had come with a young actor who had a minor part. The place was thronged, too many people crowded on the banquettes along the walls. Perhaps it was for the benefit of the graceful girl beside him that Fletcher Strode boomed out startling, boastful statements; perhaps it was not an accident that upset a bowl of marinara sauce over her dress.

His apologies had been overwrought. While waiters dabbed at her with hot water, she had tried to comfort her unhappy neighbor with assurances that the dress was unimportant, inexpensive, and would probably come back from the cleaner's good as new. Fletcher had not asked her to send him the cleaner's bill. This would have been too mean. Instead he had found out that she was a photographer's model, Miss Giordino, traced her address, and sent a new and costly gown. She had refused to accept it. Her dress, she told him on the telephone, had come from a cut-price shop, the spot was almost invisible, and he was too, too generous. They had argued for half an hour, and she had finally agreed to discuss it with him at dinner.

"Is your name really Elaine?"

"Why shouldn't it be?"

"Elaine, the fair, Elaine the lovable, Elaine, the lily maid of Astolat." He had offered this proudly. Tennyson's poems, like Emerson's essays, had been a chore for him in school.

She told him that her mother had been working on illustrations for a children's edition of *The Idylls* when she met Professor Guardino. "It was a pickup. At the Tate. Mother had gone to London to study the pre-Raphaelites and set up her easel before Burne-Jones, and Papa was a refugee from Rome waiting for his American visa. He had thought of translating Blake into Italian and was looking at the lithographs. But he never did. Blake, I mean. He always said Mother took his mind off the project. You see, it was inevitable that they named me Elaine."

Fletcher had not seen it at all. Her smile and the ivory pallor of her flesh, cheekbones, pointed chin, and her sweet habit of blushing made the names Tate, Burne-Jones, Blake, more important to him than the day's stock market quotations. Fletcher Strode had never before met a girl who could be, at the same time, so refined and so lusty. Three weeks after he spilled the marinara sauce he had asked his wife for a divorce.

On the first date Fletcher had told Elaine that he was married, technically. His wife and daughter lived in an exclusive New Jersey suburb while he kept a bachelor's apartment in New York. Mrs. Strode always explained that her husband was too busy in the city and too restless for commuting and added that his devotion never flagged. The truth was that they loathed each other. He gave her a good allowance and kept up the appearance of marriage to guard himself against designing women. He had been sure that he would never remarry.

Kay Strode had put up a bitter fight. She was content to live without her husband, but not without the legend of devotion. There were tears and arguments, countless meetings with lawyers, exorbitant demands, endless haggling over the will and the insurance. All of this delay had heightened Fletcher's impatience. Twenty-four hours after the divorce papers were signed, he and Elaine were married at the Maryland farm of one of his business friends.

In spite of dire predictions it had been a good marriage; more than this, delight by day, ecstasy at night. Elaine had shown herself to be a female of such fiery talent that her delirious husband had looked back to earlier exploits as mere rehearsals for the endless fulfillment of love. There was never a moment's doubt of her sincerity. No half-contented woman would have responded with such rapture. The difference in their ages had been no bar to her emotions. Adoring, she had let flow upon him her rich stream of feminine skill in making a man feel supreme, the hero, the god, infallible. Nor did the husband suffer because she was his superior in education, a college graduate, a daughter of a professor who had written books in two languages. Instead, she confessed awe of his business mind, listening like a child while he explained deals and schemes.

Looking back, as he often did nowadays, it all seemed too romantic, unreal in its perfection, but he liked to think about it that way. There had been, of course, small clashes. Every marriage has problems, disagreements, bursts of temper. Elaine could be wayward and childlike with a man who had probably become the image of her dead, adored father. Elderly doting parents had spoiled her somewhat; thwarted, she could become a vengeful imp. But the fights had been brief. There was no malice. Elaine's reproaches, her tricks of revenge, could not be compared with the stinging refinements of the first wife. Kay had criticized endlessly, sneered at Fletcher for showing off, complained that he was vulgar and loud. "Do you think I'm too noisy?" he had once asked, humbly. Elaine had answered that his big voice was appropriate to his big body and lusty nature. Everything about Fletcher Strode had this quality of power; even his graying hair grew thick upon his large head.

In both fun and business he had been noisy; sung bass, led the cheering at games, shouted commands, hurled retorts, yelled with anger, boomed out bawdy jokes, won arguments by sheer vocal authority. Fletcher Strode had shouted his way to the top, confounding competitors and frightening creditors by screaming secrets that others would whisper. Today he saw his past as a jubilant vocal exercise and attributed all of his gains to the supremacy of his voice. This power was gone now, never to be recovered.

To save his life, the doctors had said when they took away his voice. Carcinoma of the larynx, when discovered in time, is one of the most curable of all cancers. Although he had been informed of the effects, he had believed that the operation would affect no more than the vigor of his speech. The rest of his body could live as it always had, in full and pleasing exercise of its demands. The loss of his vocal apparatus would be compensated for by different mechanics of sound production. His voice would be stilled for a time, but when the wound was sufficiently healed, he would learn to control a different set of muscles and would be able to speak in an altered voice. Examples were quoted to him, statistics read, stories told of patients who had overcome trauma and gone on with their work, enjoyed sports, eaten heartily, and made love to women.

During the mute period after the operation, he had been eager and positive that he would soon acquire a new voice. A breezy, self-confident man entered his hospital room to tell him, hoarsely, that many of those who had suffered the same operation had been able to return to work within a few weeks. This man, who had lost his voice box several years earlier, promised that with patience and practice, Fletcher would be able to speak as well as he did. *Hell, I'll do a lot better,* Fletcher told himself. Thinking of the success he had achieved in business, the money he had made, the obstacles overcome, he knew himself the better man. He was both contemptuous of and amused by those sympathetic friends who, visiting him at the hospital, shouted at him or whispered, using their lips extravagantly as though he were deaf.

I'll show them.

After he left the hospital, optimism collapsed. There were too many changes. Smell and taste returned slowly and were never as keen as they had been. He had to breathe through a hole in his neck, a wound that could never be allowed to close now that his windpipe had been removed, there was no connection between the mouth or nose with the lungs. He had to cough, sneeze, and blow his nose through this opening. There would be no more swimming for him, nor could he step into the shower carelessly. His loud and boisterous laughter was silenced forever. Every action required adjustment. Encounters with old friends left him morbid. Strangers appalled him. Going out became a nightmare.

When the voice therapist had been introduced, Fletcher had welcomed an angel. For months this hideously cheerful woman tried to teach him to belch aesthetically, but from the first day, he so loathed the processes of learning to lock in his breath and speak through the esophagus that he became fixed with the idea that he would never conquer stubborn muscles. Never before had his body failed him. Form and competence had been readily acquired in every sport he had bothered to learn. But the voice exercises were not sport. Repetition bored him. For years in business he had been able to leave petty detail to employees. Patience was not one of Fletcher Strode's virtues. Wearisome practice drove him to despair. Unable to progress at a satisfying pace, he often lost his temper. Fury and frustration robbed him of what little voice he had acquired. When he forgot himself and tried to shout in the old, authoritative manner, he could utter nothing but a string of unintelligible sounds.

"Don't listen to yourself," his teacher said. How could he help it? His ears had not been cut off. It was far worse when he used an electronic device. To his oversensitive ear the tones were like those cute TV characters whose echo-chamber voices extol floor wax, pancake mix, and pet food. With or without the machine, he heard too acutely. Offensive tones echoed in his mental ear until he felt that he would go mad. One day, he smashed the instrument and discharged the therapist (with an unforgivable letter about her ability, her clothes, and complexion).

The man who had visited him at the hospital, the breezy fellow whose soft, hoarse voice he had sworn to surpass, suggested group therapy. Fletcher and Elaine attended several classes. Advanced students happily conversed, recited poetry, sang huskily. Elaine went about saying that she was thrilled by the indomitable spirit of people who had won the battle against disability. But Fletcher, who had to join a beginners' group, could not bear his classmates' squawks and hoots and efforts to sound human. This, too, was abandoned. He said he could do better alone. Elaine worked with him, using the therapist's manual. At times Fletcher was hopeful and industrious, practiced, noted improvement, but one bad session, one unconquerable sound, and he would quit for days.

Several new electronic devices were purchased, each hopefully, each a magic machine which would give him a clear, smooth voice. The latest invention, the costliest, was little better than the others. At home he never used them, but would never go out alone without the crutch. In time he became better able to communicate, but never without self-consciousness. Lesser men, those who had not made fortunes, learned with patience and humility; economic necessity drove them to speech. Fletcher had no such incentive. He had made himself secure, could give in to impatience and bad temper. His ego had been permanently maimed; there was no cure for lost pride.

New symptoms developed: spasms, excess mucus, dryness of the mouth, temporary paralysis. He was certain that the cancer had returned. This time I will die, he thought, not unhappily. But the surgeon showed him X-ray plates with a benefactor's smile. Nothing more, he said, than neurosis and prescribed psychiatry.

Fletcher was horrified. The wife of one of his business friends, a rich man who could give a woman anything her heart desired, alternated between the analyst's couch and the booby hatch. No headshrinker could give him back a lost voice, for God's sake. He retreated farther into himself, fled when visitors came to the apartment, and in public places let Elaine speak for him. She ordered meals in restaurants, cashed checks, performed every chore that demanded speech with strangers. Through his lawyer and broker, both old friends, he sold out the last of his business interests and arranged investments that would permit him to live on his income.

They moved to Los Angeles because it was far away and reputed to have a good climate. An unseasonable heat wave . . . in February! . . . destroyed that illusion. Blistering desert winds dried the air so that crust formed on the stoma which had to be kept open so that air could be drawn into the damaged trachea. Every breath became painful. The specialist recommended by his New York doctor suggested that he live near the ocean. Elaine found a house upon a hill in Pacific Palisades where fog kept the air cooler and moister than in the city. He let her furnish it as she liked and spend what she pleased, but would allow no visitors. Nothing mattered to him except the concealment of disability.

For a time Elaine was carried away by the excitement of decorating a house and reviving a garden. Inevitably boredom set in. Elaine was completely of this world, gregarious, used to city excitements, a whirl of activity and friendships, passionate involvements. She had hoped to draw Fletcher into her world. "You can't become an island," she told him.

"A what?"

"An island unto yourself."

"What's that mean?"

No man is an island entire of itself; even man is a piece of the continent, a part of the maine; if a clod to be washed away by the seas, Europe is less, as well as if a promontory were, as well as if a manor of thy friends or thine own were—"

"Oh, poetry," he interrupted.

"It's famous," she told him loftily.

Since he had given up smoking he sucked fruit drops. Purposely he rolled one against his teeth. "Who wrote it? Longfellow? Tennyson?"

"John Donne."

"Never heard of him." In the voice of the gullet there is no inflection. Gesture and facial expression announced scorn. A great poet's name ought to be as well known as Shakespeare or Cadillac.

Elaine did not remind Fletcher that he knew very little about poetry. His self-esteem had become so frail that she could not utter a word that he might interpret as criticism. She left a book of poems on a table in his den and noted with pleasure that he had secretly looked into it. One day he came to her with the proud news that he had found another great poem, opened the book to a stanza he ordered her to read aloud:

Yet each man kills the thing he loves,
By each let his be heard;
Some do it with a bitter look,
Some with a flattering word;
The coward does it with a kiss,
The brave man with a sword!

Evidently he had memorized the lines. His lips moved as Elaine read. For a time then she allowed herself to believe that a new life had opened to him. She sought other interests, unsuccessfully, for Fletcher had never learned to lose himself in quiet pursuits nor to accept the consolations of art. The books she brought home—volumes of history, philosophy, science, essays—were untouched, the poetry anthology returned to the shelf. He preferred a game of gin rummy, taught her to play pinochle, but found her such an unsatisfying opponent that he soon returned to his games of solitaire, his detective stories, and the flashy accounts of murder featured in the best newspapers of Los Angeles.

It was during this period that she gave him the diary.

IT BECAME HIS obsession, a guarded secret, the man's private life. Like every amateur writer, Fletcher considered each sentence immortal, every turgid idea daring and original. In the way of those who establish new religions and accept their own beliefs as the ultimate word of God, he saw revery as reality and fed bias with every trifle of every uneventful day. Time and time again he returned to his favorite entry:

> Evil is in the air around us. Look at those nearest you. Every soul contains every sin. In the hidden self the murderer waits. I have seen the change in E. From love to pity, from pity to disgust, from disgust to evil. Guilt shines right out of those beautiful eyes. When she is the sweetest to me she is most deceitful. Is her kindness a way to hide her wish to get rid of me? She is a devious woman.

He had written and rewritten this entry on pages of old memo pads marked: FROM THE DESK OF FLETCHER STRODE. When finally his prose had satisfied him, he had copied the paragraph into the diary. In his active days Fletcher had scribbled notes on the memo pads, dictated the complete thoughts and messages to educated secretaries who had corrected errors of syntax. Now he found value in words and became committed to thought. Had he lived longer he might have developed some kind of philosophy.

Words which he had never spoken (devious, obsession) became as valuable to Fletcher as his gold Patek Philippe watch or platinum and pearl cufflinks in his safety deposit vault. The diary was also kept locked away. To show that she respected his privacy, Elaine asked no questions, never remarked that he shared none of his secrets. It was beyond imagining that into this secret volume he was writing her doom. *Obsession. Devious.* The words gave him strength. Exercise of the imagination nourished belief in what he had written. Labels fastened to his wife's character and activities fixed upon her a wealth of guile that would have served a Borgia.

Nature and habit had shaped Fletcher to compete, surpass, exhibit strength, enjoy public triumph. Without these he did not care about living. The thought of suicide was inevitable. He pondered it constantly, considered various methods, suffered the pain of poison, the terror of drowning, the stink of gas, the dizziness of the long plunge, the shock of gunfire. He also thought about the availability of the various means, the quantity of pain, the matter of time, even the untidiness; he anticipated the drama of the discovery of the body, heard exclamations of shock, counted messages of condolence, envisioned the floral offerings, attended the funeral. Life held little attraction for him; he knew greater pleasure in the contemplation of death. All in fantasy, of course, conceived and carried out on goose-down pillows or behind the wheel of a car. Thus far he had satisfied the urge by rehearsals played out in the theater of revery, but there was never any doubt of his intention.

These vacillations were not caused simply by the urge for self-preservation. He had a wife. He foresaw her future too clearly. Aware of the frustrations of a young woman tied to an afflicted man, he recognized in her every sigh and silence the needs of a young woman's passionate nature. When he had been able to satisfy her, Fletcher had enjoyed the spectacle of her charm for other men, had relished his triumph over her younger admirers. Now there was no solace for castrate pride. Several doctors had assured him that there was no physical reason for his loss of power. It was a block, mental and emotional. These learned opinions were of no help. How could theoreticians know the hopelessness of effort, the sick shame of failure?

Elaine was damnably tactful. In bed she protected his manly pride, just as in shops and restaurants she used little ruses to save him from the pity of clerks and waiters. Her patience embarrassed him. He suspected the tenderness with which she embraced him and the gallantry which pretended that mere physical contact could fulfill her. She was now twenty-eight, lovelier in ripeness than in girlish promise. Her husband could not fail to notice the jets that sparked out of men's eyes at the sight of her rounded limbs, the rise of her breasts, the delicious curves of hip and buttock. The thought of her heat spent upon another man, the vision of her unclothed flesh close to a naked male body, tormented his days and made night unbearable. He was determined that no other man should possess his lovable wife . . .

Nor the fortune accumulated through his years of hard work. As a rich widow Elaine would be even more desirable than the working girl he had married. Prophetic specters haunted him. He saw another man, young and robust of voice, in his house, his car, his bed. Day by day these images grew sturdier. He had only to see his wife shake hands with a man and he was possessed by the will to destroy her.

There had come into his mind, nourished as it was by ghoulish newspaper photographs, the thought of a double death. He saw as through a lens the two bodies on a disarranged bed. Impossible. Every man's strength has limits. His ended with the vision of damage to the beloved body. He wanted only to make certain that she would never know fulfillment in another man's arms. With such assurance could he die peacefully.

Out of nightmare and brooding, out of newspaper sensations, out of the contrivance of detective stories, he made a plan of devilish ingenuity. He would commit suicide so that his death should seem the result of murder. The plot was devious and irresistible. A wealth of devices sprang to mind. With the

14

zest and care he had once given to big business deals, Fletcher Strode planned his death. Schemes were shaped and reshaped, details altered. His mind became a theater in which the drama was endlessly rehearsed. The perfect murder: revenge and self-destruction. Evidence would be circumstantial but convincing. He did not want Elaine to be executed as his murderess; he convinced himself that her charm would save her this fate. He preferred to foresee her future in a woman's jail where her beauty would fade, her sparkle dim, where she would grow old and stale before, if ever again, she lay with a man.

At times he weakened, rejected the whole idea, enjoying freedom from obsession until some incident . . . another man's delight in Elaine's grace . . . would spark the scheme to life again. With exquisite cunning Fletcher worked out tricks and ruses that would seem part of her plot to kill him. Into his diary went paragraphs of suspicion, phrases of fear, suggestions of the ways a woman would kill, nuggets of information gathered from newspaper reports and crime fiction. Begun as a means, the diary became an end, Fletcher Strode's work of art, obsession and legacy:

> One who looks for opportunity finds it everywhere. The smallest weapon, something right under your hand, could be a weapon. When I see her with a kitchen knife in her hand or turning on the gas heater at night I wonder. It would be easy for her to say that a man in my physical and mental state would take his own life. I see this in those dreamy eyes when she does not know I am watching her. When she is shocked out of one of those dreams she shivers and shakes at seeing me close to her and hearing the hell . . .

The entry was unfinished. Fletcher could not write down words that described the hellish horror of his voice.

2 "I WANT YOU TO DIE? WHERE DID YOU EVER GET AN idea like that? It's weird. Sinful." But Elaine had to turn away to hide the burning shame of her face. Over her

shoulder she continued to scold, "As for my dreaming of free-dom"—she turned toward him again, her face faintly pink—"why should I? Freedom from what? As if this place weren't so devastatingly beautiful and I"—she paused to stretch her long body on the long chair and give attention to a family of quail going through their ritual movements on the grass—"weren't in love with you."

The garden was alive with the scents and sounds of early spring. Freesia and narcissus sent out strong perfumes, the grass glittered with dampness left by morning fog, bees and hum-mingbirds pondered the rich choice of blossoms. Elaine closed her eyes to recall the past and Fletcher when she had first known him, a man totally committed to life.

"I don't deny that I said that freedom's the most wonderful thing for a girl, by why did I say it? You've got to consider the circumstances. When your best friend weeps over long dis-tance after getting her divorce, you've got to think of some way to console her. Freedom's great for Joyce, but Fletch, really!" Since he had lost his vocal authority Elaine had tried to control her own speech so that he would not know the passion of her pity. "Darling, please don't take everything so personally."

Fletcher turned to study the rosy countenance. They were in the small trellised pavilion that had been added as a con-ceit by a previous owner of the property. Their garden was out of all proportion to its neighbors', just as the Mexican ranch house was too mellow and simple for the district. All around them, the trees had been cut down, gardens cut up into building lots upon which stood pretentious, sterile houses surrounded by cactus and broad-leafed tropical plants set into patches of colored stone.

"I'm so happy here, honestly, I dote on the place. And the garden's getting better every day, don't you think? Next winter I'm going to plant more azaleas, huge, expensive plants, Fletch, under the pines. Pinks and deep rose color, don't you think it'll be beautiful? And so amusing to work out."

The quail continued their odd dance, Elaine dreamed of costly shrubs, a plane buzzed overhead, and Fletcher smiled at her enthusiasm. The movement of indulgence was not to last. A truck had entered the driveway and stopped at the kitchen door. "Oh, heavens, I've forgotten!" and Elaine ran, long legged and supple, toward the house where the milkman waited.

Fletcher, following less frantically, came upon them as Elaine with a devastating smile told the fellow, apologetically, "Of course it's not your fault, but I do think at the prices they charge, your company could deliver fresher eggs."

"I'll take it up with the board of directors."

Elaine laughed immoderately, her husband thought. The milkman was young and blithe. With all of these sturdy trades-men she made a ceremony of selection, asked questions about each item, discussed family habits. "I ought to take that disgust-ing non-fat, but we hate it. My husband, especially, and he's the one who can't afford to put on another ounce."

His weight, thought Fletcher, was not the business of the youth who stared flagrantly at Elaine's long legs in cream-tan trousers, at hips and breasts whose curves were not entirely con-cealed by the loose overblouse. As always when she passed the time with a man, Fletcher was plagued by unendurable visions.

Later that day he went shopping with her. At the supermar-ket he suffered fiercely, pushing the cart in her wake as she exchanged greetings with clerks, selected washing powder and stood reflective before counters of fruit. "Do you think this melon is ripe, Fletch? I have no talent at all for melon-pinching." She darted after the fruit clerk, addressed him a look so engaging that the fellow must consider himself infallible in judging melons. At the check-out counter a boy greeted her like a long-lost love. Fletcher stood behind the odious cart while the cocky kid held her in discussion of the weather. At once Fletcher saw her, lively and unclothed, in the boy's arms. The vision, more real than the labels of Marvel-Bleach or Vigor for Stubborn Stains, remained while her packages were checked; changed its male protagonist when a muscular package boy ran to offer service. Sweating, but with self-control, Fletcher allowed the boy to push the cart to the parking lot and load their bags into the car. Elaine offered thanks as though the kid had won an Olympic medal, turned back to wave as Fletcher drove out of the lot.

In the convertible silvercloud Lincoln Continental, Mr. and Mrs. Fletcher Strode made a picture as handsome as a color advertisement, the man big and rugged, deeply tanned, the young woman sleek and lovely, her dark hair careless in the wind. She chatted about the dinner menu, about the absurdity of her pleasure in a ripe honeydew, her indignation at the tastelessness of California tomatoes. Earlier these ardors would have been roused by the works of Chagall, Bernstein, and Balenciaga.

Fletcher sighed.

"You're bored," Elaine sighed, immediately regretted the word, asked hastily, "Why don't we play golf this afternoon?" As though she liked the game! If she had been as companionable as she pretended, she would have learned to play; but no, she refused to yield body or mind to the tyranny of athletic form. "I'd rather watch you." She rode around with him in the caddy cart, called out greetings and answered questions shouted by other players. Her show of interest was mere lip service. Privately, Fletcher thought, his wife believed it absurd for a man to care about knocking a ball around the links. Before he retired he had played weekday golf with the zest of a schoolboy enjoying hookey. Now that the game had become a time-killer, he found golf another form of impotence.

As they drove along Elaine studied young men in passing cars. "Darling! Did you notice just now? It was Manuel." She waved wildly at the gardener. Manual was slender, dark, romantic in a sweaty Mexican way. Another disturbing vision clouded Fletcher's mind. "Manuel's a gentle person but he will keep that nasty stuff in the shed. He says it's necessary for bugs and slugs and stuff, but I wish he wouldn't. He says there are no children in the house and the boxes are plainly marked, but I told him," she laughed slyly, "I'd hold him personally responsible for accidents. Fletch dear, why are you looking so somber?"

A grunt was his answer. He turned a corner swiftly. She slid along the leather seat. "Oh, Fletch, please! Don't drive so suicidally."

When they were back at the house and Elaine busy with her groceries, Fletcher investigated the garden shed. Later that day he wrote in his diary:

> Today she talked about the poisons in the garden shed. Has she honestly warned Manuel and has he told her that a package labeled POISON is not dangerous to adults who can read? Maybe it is just suspicion or one of those persecution complexes, but there are so many signs of danger in this house that I do not think I am just giving in to imagination. The thought of death is in her mind all the time. I wonder if she keeps talking about suicide to prepare the ground. I am sensitive to signs of danger. They say that the loss of one sense sharpens the others, that deaf men see more, the blind hear whispers in the distance. I used to shout, and now I listen. And learn.

Early in the marriage, when they were so crazily in love, Elaine would wait on edge for the sound of Fletcher's key in the lock, his "Hi, lovable!" in a shout that shook the walls. Now that he had retired from work and life, she had too much of his passionate possessing. Every hour of every day his vast, useless curiosity was spent upon her. No movement was too trivial for his attention, each chore was supervised. When she bathed he came into the room and perched his big body on her spindly dressing table stool. She had to curb temper and humor, give every moment to the protection of the man's poor pride. Restraint charged her nerves. Electric tensions quivered like wires in a high wind. She became overcheerful, considered every word, smiled too often. The mask stifled her. Once in a while in sheer rebellion she would prolong her conversation with a headwaiter or bestow charm outrageously upon a boy in a parking lot.

Once a week she had an afternoon to herself. Fletcher's Thursday appointment with the barber and manicurist, sacred to a man who had nothing else on his calendar, took him into Los Angeles. He could easily have found a more convenient shop, but he had started with this barber and manicurist when he and Elaine had first come to the city and stayed at the Ambassador

Hotel. He said the shop was the best in the city; his real reason was that they knew his disability and spared him the ordeal of speaking before strangers. He often lingered for a walk on streets where there were other pedestrians, tourists no doubt, whose presence gave the streets a slight sense of belonging to a city. Sometimes he drove down to the seedy center of the town to move with a crowd or listen to the street orators.

On one of these Thursdays Elaine's treasured loneliness was interrupted. Kneeling on the garden path, digging up and separating irises, she heard wheels on the driveway, thought that Fletcher had come home early. From the path came a voice, whole and masculine, "I hope I'm not disturbing you. I just want to look at your garden."

She turned with loam in her hands. From where she squatted, the man seemed very high, a long stretch of gabardine and tweed. "You haven't changed much in the garden."

"You know this garden?"

"I grew up in this house."

"Oh." She stood up to see him better. A narrow-brimmed hat shaded a narrow face, bony and sparsely covered with transparent skin, freckle-spattered. His eyes were shielded by close-fitting dark glasses.

"I haven't been on the hill for a long time. But today . . . I had to see a patient on Geranium Drive so"—a long, freckled hand covered the grounds in a wide arc—"I came to see whether the new owners had ruined Aunt Cora's garden."

"New! We've been here more than a year, and why," she challenged, "should we spoil your aunt's garden?"

"Everyone else does. How could I know you wouldn't pull out all the plants and put in those bestial-looking plants set in white pebbles? All around here," the long, freckled hand moved in an arc of eloquent contempt, "they hire landscape *specialists*," scorn underlined the word, "to make gardens ugly. I'm glad she isn't here to see it."

"Who?"

"Aunt Cora. My foster-mother. She planned and planted this garden."

"It's lovely."

"You wouldn't know the neighborhood. When I was a kid there was a grove of eucalyptus where that horror stands." He jerked a nod toward a Greco-Roman contemporary with Regency urns on the roof. "And over there were two enormous pepper trees, male and female. I used to wonder how trees made it." He laughed; Elaine offered an echo. The man paid no attention. "Modern gardeners don't go for pepper and eucalyptus. They shed too much." Uninvited he strode to the shade garden where azaleas and camellia shone pink and rose and white among polished foliage. "I used to resent it when she asked me to rake and carry, but in the blooming season . . . by God, it *is* the blooming season." He took off his hat in obeisance.

Dusty red hair curled above a tall brow.

Elaine thought him too ardent but said gently, "I'm grateful to your foster-mother. Her garden's one of the reasons we bought the place. And the privacy, too. It must have been pleasant to grow up here."

He was too thickly wrapped in memories to give attention to a stranger. Elaine followed while he strode along the path to the pool. Suddenly, "I laid these stones. The path was originally gravel. How well the dichondra's done. What a job to pull out all the crabgrass. I got twenty-five cents an hour. But why should you care?"

"I do. You made it lovely for me. At twenty-five cents an hour."

"You haven't spoiled the house either."

The stranger's compliment pleased her. Elaine valued mellowness and texture, thought the Mexican farmhouse architecture perfectly suited to the climate. The neighbors were always remodeling their houses, turning Tudor mansions into French chateaux, Cape Cod cottages into ranch houses with picture windows. Dazzling white stones and marble pillars transformed Mediterranean villas into buildings like funeral homes, and California bungalows were capped with mansard roofs. "Abortions," said the visitor as they walked the paths he had laid.

"Why don't we sit down?"

"I don't want to keep you from anything."

"I wasn't doing anything in particular, just transplanting irises."

"It's the wrong season," he said, and he held a chair for her. He asked her name, learned that she was married, that her husband was retired and generally at home, but always went out on Thursday afternoons. "That's my free day, too," he said. "I do my hospital rounds in the morning but unless there's an emergency or necessary house calls, I try to keep Thursday afternoons for myself. Usually there are emergencies and necessary house calls. By the way, I'm Ralph Julian."

They shook hands formally. Elaine listened edgily for the sound of her husband's car. Dr. Julian's visit would not be hard to explain, but there would inevitably be taut moments when the introduction would have to be acknowledged and Fletcher suffered the exposure of his infirmity. Just the same, Elaine was enjoying the unexpected visit and asked the guest if he would like to see how she had done the inside of the house.

He liked her furniture and hangings, noted the crammed bookshelves in the room which had been his foster-father's library and enjoyed, after proper protest about not wanting to bother her, a cup of tea. Elaine said she always made tea for herself in the afternoon, and he said it was like old times with Aunt Cora pouring Tibetan tea and serving cookies on a silver plate.

After he had gone and she had put the tea things in the dishwasher, she bathed and dressed in a bright hostess gown to greet her husband. She told him all about the visit of Dr. Ralph Julian who had grown up in this house as the son of Dr. Harry and Mrs. Cora Julian, who had adopted him after their son had drowned in the swimming pool. "When he came to live here he was eight and this seemed the most beautiful place in the world. He's sentimental about it."

Sentiment brought Dr. Julian back after two weeks. He brought bulbs of a new tuberous begonia for the shade garden which he still considered his foster-mother's. Elaine happened to have baked chocolate brownies that morning. Once more the spirit of Aunt Cora joined them. Eulogies were devoted to her cooking. Ralph had her recipe books somewhere in his apartment and promised to look for them. The next week he brought the books, which Elaine refused to keep since his future wife (on the second visit she had discovered that he was a bachelor) would surely want them. All week she copied out recipes and on the following Thursday tried her hand at macaroons. Fruitlessly. It was three weeks before he turned up to collect the cookbooks. There were no explanations as there were no formal dates. He came or did not. Elaine bought three new summer dresses and two pairs of bright slacks.

It was inevitable that her husband would meet the new friend. Ralph had been prepared for the maimed voice and showed neither the layman's offensive tact nor a doctor's clinical interest. When the subject was brought up . . . by Fletcher himself . . . Ralph praised the Los Angeles specialist recommended by Fletcher's doctor in New York.

A few weeks after this Elaine had become ill with the flu. Fletcher's specialist was certainly not the doctor to attend to her, and while he might have given her the name of a good internist, Fletcher suggested that she call Dr. Julian. Elaine was not so ill that she required that much attention, but Ralph came for daily visits, usually after all his other calls were finished so that he could linger with the patient and her husband. She was a healthy girl and recovered quickly. Nevertheless Ralph suggested a checkup. Fletcher drove her to his office and read magazines in the waiting room while she was with the doctor.

After her heartbeat and blood pressure had been recorded Ralph said, "I'm not coming to visit you anymore."

Elaine hugged the coarse white examination gown tighter around her nakedness. "Oh dear, I'm sorry," she said.

"So am I. I've enjoyed coming to the house again, but I don't think it's good for your husband. Lie down on the table, please."

She had thought she would shrink at the exquisitely personal examination. Austere in his white coat, Ralph Julian studied her with the detachment of an engineer concerned with the working of a familiar machine. "Nothing wrong with you except tensions. You must try and relax."

"Don't I need vitamins or a tonic or something?"

He suspected the cause of her nervousness, but was not licensed to ask about her relations with her husband. She would have liked to speak out, but could not say aloud that she lived in the constant dread of her husband's suicide. In Fletcher's every sigh and whim, his frequent rages, his sudden bursts of tenderness, she saw the compulsion. When they were alone and Fletcher croaked out his ideas and opinions, she listened for words that might reveal his intentions. It would have relieved her to relate these fears to Dr. Julian. She could not. They shook hands in parting and the doctor came out to the waiting room for a word with Fletcher.

Months passed before she saw Ralph again. She thought about him endlessly, held long conversations . . . in her bed, in the bathtub, swimming in the pool, digging in the garden, while she tended the kitchen machines . . . poured out a stream of fear and evidence of the increasing danger. In this harmless way a certain portion of her fear was absorbed. A shade, never clearly seen, Ralph became not a lover but a compassionate listener.

"How Fletch adores that diary of his. Isn't it awfully good for him to be so interested in *something?*" No response, but none was expected. "Don't you think that means that underneath everything, deeply, he wants to live?" In finding words for the question she had framed her own answer. "He hides the diary like a priceless treasure, a guilty secret. If I come in when he's writing, he sneaks it into a desk drawer. With a new Yale lock. And the look on his face! An anarchist hiding his bomb." She laughed at the simile. "Fletch is such a child, really. Have you ever noticed that wide-eyed look? So unexpected in a big, tough, successful business man. I fell in love with that little-boy look." Facing the absent confessor she dared hope. "I believe, I honestly do, that the fatal mood is dwindling. He can enjoy himself. Did I tell you we went to the movies? It was a good comedy for a change and then we went to a Chinese place to eat. He had such an appetite, like the old days. Almost the same, but . . . " Here she faltered for she could not, even in revery, permit herself to play out another one of those teeth-clenching climaxes, the failure and remorse. She changed the subject. "That doctor! A good man, they say, in his field, but specialists can be too special, People aren't all bone and flesh. Doesn't he know what's *underneath?* Fifty sleeping pills! Can you believe it for a man in Fletch's state? I have the prescriptions filled myself and keep the pills hidden. He gets two a night, never more. I don't want him getting the habit, first two, then three, and so on. Fletch pretends to be amused, but I wonder. Perhaps it's all in my own mind; do you think I'm worrying uselessly?" As though the man were talking she answered herself hastily, "Of course it is. My own crazy imagination. There's really no danger." And finally like a prayer repeated as self-hypnosis, "I worry because I love him so much. I do, you know."

ONE NIGHT IN a dream, a sleep-dream rather than revery contrived as appeasement of an unborn wish, she walked with Ralph Julian on the deck of a ship. A band played, banners fluttered, her hand was locked in a firm warm palm. Suddenly, with the angular movement of nightmare, the mood changed. Shame chilled her like a sharp wind, and she knew she was not properly dressed for the journey. The chiffon nightgown did not half cover her breasts and the flimsy material whirled about her bare legs. Horrified strangers stared. She knew that dozens of lovely dresses, colored slippers, jackets, and sweaters had been packed in her mother's old wardrobe trunk, which she could see clearly on the pier. The ship moved off, faster and faster. She trembled and perspired in the cold wind, cried out, and woke to find herself locked in shivering tension. At once, in another fruitless fantasy conversation, she asked Ralph Julian if the dream had significance. Was there evil in her unconscious mind? "Do I want to be free? Do I, down deep in me, want Fletcher to die?" The question was as shocking as the nightmare.

At once she forced herself out of bed and walked on bare feet to Fletcher's room, saw that the man-made mouth at the base of his neck was uncovered, heard the click of his breathing. Like a criminal reprieved she hurried back to bed. As punishment she gave up the talks with Ralph Julian, vowed to forget him, and on Thursdays tried not to listen for his car. And from this time on, it became her habit to creep into Fletcher's room once or twice a night to listen to his breathing.

He noted in the diary:

> At night she visits my room to watch me sleep. What does she hope to find? How easy it would be to end it all with a man who breathes through a hole in his neck. Is she trying to work up the courage?

And again he wrote:

> She is so dreamy nowadays that she does not always know I am in the room with her. When she comes out of it she will look at me in a sly way and wonder who the stranger is. Then she will suddenly smile and kiss me and get all girlish and flattering. I wish I did not enjoy it so much when she is sweet to me. Oh, my God, to love a woman who dreams about being rid of you. I live in hell.

3 SEPTEMBER IS THE INTOLERABLE MONTH. GRAY mornings and cool nights of early summer become memories of the improbable; soothing fogs are burned out by relentless sunshine. Heat as solid as metal strikes like a blunt instrument. Nerves are unsteady, energy unthinkable, lethargy ill-tempered. In the Strode house the tensions were aggravated by the presence of visitors.

Fletcher's daughter and son-in-law had come to spend their summer vacation. This is how they wrote of it when they announced their intentions, and the way they spoke of it when they arrived in the white Jaguar. "*My* vacation," said Cindy almost daily. Since nursery school she had been taught that special conditions—*my* graduation, *my* school, *my* holidays, *my* debut, *our* neighborhood, people of *our* sort, *my* engagement, *my* wedding, *my* vacation—deserved special privilege. Six years younger than Elaine she seemed, by contrast, a child, for she had never taken responsibility of any sort, never held a job, never even finished college. Before her engagement the great event of Cynthia Strode's life had been a debut, along with fifty-nine other girls whose parents had contributed to a charity whose board of governors sponsored a dance at the Hotel Plaza in New York.

In her father's house she accepted the double privileges of bride and visitor. "No maid?" she asked when Elaine went into the kitchen to prepare their first meal.

"Your father doesn't like having anyone around. We have a cleaning woman once a week. She's very thorough."

"Doesn't Daddy object to her?"

"We usually go out that day, drive someplace, or he plays golf. Your father loathes these women chattering at him. Besides," Elaine hated herself for using the tone of apology, "there's very little to do with only two of us in the house."

As though bestowing a favor, Cindy offered to make the twin beds in the guest room. Often they were left unmade until late afternoon. Did it matter that she and Don liked to sleep late? After a very few mornings under her father's roof, Cindy learned there was not much to get up for. No parties were given for the visitors, no introductions offered, no invitations sent by people who dutifully entertained friends' houseguests. Instead, the young people endured long drives with Fletcher and Elaine, went on sightseeing trips to the few unexciting places that contrasted so drearily with the glowing advertisements of the California All-Year Club. Over endless dinners in overdecorated, overpriced, high-style restaurants, Fletcher sat dumb while Elaine made conversation, laughed at Don's jokes, hastened to answer when Cindy forgot that she was not to ask Fletcher direct questions in public places.

"I think you're hurting Daddy more than helping him with all this privacy stuff," Cindy said when she was alone with Elaine. "In my opinion he'd be a lot better off if you'd make an effort to have some kind of social life."

"He doesn't want it."

"He may tell you that, but believe me, a man of his sort, always so lively and social, with so many connections, I mean! Not even belonging to a country club."

"He prefers the public course. He doesn't want a lot of people getting chummy and compassionate."

"The right sort of people wouldn't make him feel so badly," Cindy argued. "No wonder he's so desperate, doing nothing but mooning around this gloomy old house. It's not at all healthy, psychologically."

"It's the way he wants it." Elaine despised herself for the tone of appeasement.

Cindy would never give up an argument. Even when she was proven wrong she exercised the right of reassertion. Elaine grew more and more strained in conversations, which she tried to keep Fletcher from hearing. Cindy's voice, as modern as her tastes, was hard, emphatic, and loud.

One of the girl's school friends was the daughter of a millionaire whose name was printed in gold on the plate-glass windows of loan and trust banks all over the city. Nan, who was exactly Cindy's age, had been married for three years to Rex Burke, a young man who had become almost as famous as his father-in-law. When Don and Cindy arrived, the young Burkes were away on "a private yacht." Cindy was sadly disappointed and could not help showing that she considered the first two weeks of the vacation a sad waste. When Nan returned, Cindy and her husband were invited to spend Sunday at her house at Newport Beach. Cindy's rapture at the invitation was trivial in comparison with the ecstasy of her return.

"If I ever saw gracious living! Three in help, at the seashore."

"They've got a honey of a cruiser, eighty feet," Don reported with slightly less frenzy.

"Two Rollses. She and he both drive them."

"It's a deduction for Rex," Don hastened to explain. "He's executive assistant to Nan's father." Don's eloquent dark eyes fixed themselves on his father-in-law's face.

Cindy's father did not need an executive assistant. She announced, reproachfully, "They've promised to introduce Don to their lawyers."

"Anderson, Lord & James. You must have heard of them, sir."

"Never did," barked Fletcher. Having no business in California he needed no lawyers. Cindy tried to impress him by telling him how famous these attorneys were and how much they would, in Nan's husband's opinion, welcome a bright young man trained in New York. "And besides, Daddy, you owe it to yourself to have a legal representative in the city you live in."

"Why?" croaked Fletcher.

"Everybody does, and especially a man of your standing. I mean . . . in a city like this there are all sorts of fabulous opportunities. I want you to meet Rex Burke, he's a perfect darling and so successful—"

"Not interested." Fletcher's rejection came out like a belch.

"It'd be food for you. Psychologically, I mean. And if Don went into that law firm and you'd have a member of the family as a contact, you'd know your interests wouldn't be neglected."

"Cindy!"

Don Hustings's nod and frown indicated that he and Cindy had an understanding about this subject. He had asked and she had promised not to bring it up crudely. Don did not want to be looked upon as the son-in-law in search of favors.

"My husband's too much of a gentleman for his own good."

Cindy's laughter reminded Fletcher of his first wife, who had somehow believed that an inappropriate or unwelcome remark could be softened by the appearance of levity. Without bothering to excuse himself, he marched out of the room.

This was by no means the end of Cindy's efforts to promote Don's career. Nothing was said about his getting back to his job in New York. Either he had been given an extraordinary holiday or he had been fired. Fletcher became irritable. Behind closed doors he and Elaine discussed their visitors. The air of the house had become conspiratorial. "Please try to be patient," begged Elaine. "After all, Fletch, she is your daughter. And it's sort of lonesome here for a young girl without a car of her own."

Don went off nearly every day in the Jaguar. He spoke mysteriously of "important contacts." Cindy sulked. She would have enjoyed driving the Lincoln, but Fletcher did not care to be left without a car. He did not go out a lot, but did not want to be kept at home if he felt the sudden impulse.

"Daddy, just this once," she begged on a blistering Thursday morning. "I wouldn't take your car away from you if it weren't just too vital. I've got to do some shopping before Saturday—"

"Your father's going to the barber this afternoon. He'll need the car."

They were in the kitchen, Elaine preparing lunch, Cindy pressing a dress. Fletcher answered, but no one heard. Even a normal voice could not compete with the clamor of household machines. Water splashed over rinds and peels of fruit, which were being sucked into the clashing maws of the garbage disposal, the refrigerator grumbled like an upset stomach, the stove's exhaust roared as if in an airplane engine had been set into the wall.

"What did you say, Daddy?"

"He's using the car this afternoon," Elaine said for the second time.

Fletcher's throat tightened. Elaine was always too swift and ready to answer for him. Even here at home with only his own daughter to hear his efforts at clear speech. Dependence upon his wife had become for him an abominable need, and for Elaine an important habit, damn her. Of late when she answered for him with her smug tact, he suffered the sense of strangulation.

Elaine looked at the clock nervously. "Do you think Don will be on time for lunch?"

"Don's always on time. Unless people keep him waiting."

People in California were always keeping Don waiting. He had gone to see another friend of Nan's father, a person whose importance made it unimportant to be prompt with a man in Don's situation. This made Don very late for lunch. As a result the broccoli was overcooked, the hollandaise sauce lumpy. Elaine apologized too extravagantly. Fletcher merely tasted the food and pushed away his plate.

Don praised every mouthful. "You're a lucky man, sir, to have a wife who cooks so magnificently as well as having a great many other feminine talents." He offered Elaine a compassionate smile.

She thanked him coolly. Fletcher's scowl warned her that she must not show pleasure in the young man's compliments. She tried to turn their attention to Don's business. "You haven't told us what happened at your meeting this morning. How did it go?"

"It didn't."

"Didn't you see Mr. Heatherington?" wailed Cindy.

"For five minutes. After he'd kept me waiting all that time, he shook hands with me and said we'd have to arrange another date."

"People out here are impossible. No manners at all," Cindy said.

"He had a board meeting. But he made another appointment."

"How soon?"

"A week from Tuesday."

"Not till then? He's impossible."

"He's flying to Hawaii tonight. For a week."

Cindy looked toward heaven. Fletcher rumbled out a question. This time they all understood and wished they hadn't. The attack was direct. Didn't Don's bosses in New York expect him back on the job?

Cindy answered quickly, "They've given Don a leave of absence. They don't want to let him go permanently, but if he finds something better out here, they won't hold him back." She tossed an arch smile at her husband, tilted a shoulder, let out a crescendo of laughter.

Fletcher looked grim. At the time of the engagement both Cindy and her mother had assured him that Donald Hustings had brilliant prospects and was considered indispensable by his employers.

"Well, sir," Don said glibly, "they've been decent enough people to work for, but a man has to consider his future. And, frankly, they've got too much family in the firm. All the important cases go to nephews and grandsons, and if you're not related you get nothing but minor cases. So I decided to look around out here."

Cindy removed from her mouth the stalk of celery she had been sucking like a stick of candy. "After all, Los Angeles is supposed to be the coming land of opportunity, and with all of Don's connections out here, we thought . . . " Confused by her father's frown she giggled again.

"What connections?" croaked Fletcher.

"Nan's father," Cindy began. Don cut her off with the statement that he had excellent contacts of his own. Cindy interrupted with stubborn authority. "Nan's father couldn't have tried harder to help us if Don were his own son-in-law."

The fact could be questioned. His own son-in-law had been made executive assistant while the only help the banker had given Don was introductions to certain friends. Before this could be stated, Don told his father-in-law, apologetically, "We know you're not active now, sir. We didn't expect anything." Expectancy shone out of his clear, bright, undergraduate face. At twenty-nine, Don Hustings had the docility and easy charm of a boy who has gone to the correct prep school and college. Spiritually he had never got out of either. He continued to wear the deferential garments of the schoolboy who knows his place in the company of older, wealthier men. Good breeding and background were as obvious as his Maryland accent and fresh complexion. He had many notable ancestors but the family had been impoverished by a series of historical events that had begun with the Civil War and continued through a century of panics and depressions. Don could recite these misfortunes like a catechism.

He had dark, deep-set eyes and the prominent curling lips of a classical statue. Adoring him, Cindy could never forget that other girls' fathers poured benefits upon less worthy sons-in-law. Vehemently she declared, "Don isn't the type to depend on relations. And he's had a couple of very good offers in case you're interested."

Fletcher rumbled out another question.

Don understood well enough to answer, "I couldn't accept that sort of money, sir."

The money people offered was never satisfactory to Don and Cindy. The ten thousand dollars that Fletcher had sent his daughter as a wedding present had simply gone with the wind. Don had been deeply in debt when they married, and was now in danger of being engulfed. Both he and Cindy felt it important to keep up appearances.

"Couldn't accept that sort of money!" The voice in Fletcher's mind was clear and scornful. The young man's lack of humility irritated him. He would have liked to remind the complacent fellow that he had made his money without asking favors of anyone. Aloud, "What the hell do you think you're worth?" he bellowed. Caught up in anger he forgot the therapist's instructions for producing sound and controlling breath.

"What did you say, Daddy?"

Elaine had understood but did not try to interpret Fletcher's wrath. She felt sorry for Don and did not wish to see him humiliated again. Her mouth closed stubbornly, and she pressed herself back as if her body were part of the chair. Don caught her eye. A swift glance flashed between them. Fletcher, watching warily, saw these two in the familiar vision, unclothed, embracing. On the table his big hands lay curled in frustration. His skin itched with impotent rage.

Elaine started collecting plates. Sighing, Cindy followed. The two men sat like strangers on a bus. Fletcher's silence embarrassed Don, but his conversation would have been harder to take. If it had not taken so much effort, Fletcher would have let him know what he thought about a generation that believed the world owed it a living. Had he succeeded in expressing himself he would not have been so sensitive to a swift exchange of smiles when Elaine returned with the dessert. Again the vision flashed across the screen of consciousness. What Fletcher saw was not a girl in a flowered dress and a young man in a neat summer jacket erect behind his plate, but the guilty pair—faithless wife, worthless son-in-law—naked in a shadowy place.

"Why are you looking so impatient, dear? You've got plenty of time. Didn't you say you'd put off the barber until four today?"

Fletcher had told her, but she had apparently forgotten, that he was to see his dentist that afternoon. He spoke angrily, too fast and without giving thought to breathing and the control of abdominal muscles. Sounds like animal grunts struck his ears with fresh agony.

Before Cindy could chirp the usual "What, Daddy?" Elaine translated with her loathsome tact, "Oh, darling, I forgot your dentist appointment. But you've got plenty of time still. Look, I've made you a chocolate mousse."

For no reason Cindy giggled, Don stared at the centerpiece as if he hoped to find some mystic answer among the asters. Elaine set the plate before him. Once more they looked at each other, heat welled up in Fletcher, and he flung the dish of chocolate mousse at his wife.

"Daddy, what are you doing?"

Under blond curls Cindy's face glowed with delight. She had good features and flawless skin, but was too solid to be noticeable among all the pretty girls who did their lips and eyes and hair in the same fashion and wore clothes from the proper stores. She had never been so lovely as at this moment of witnessing her father's cruelty to the woman who had taken his daughter's rightful place in his heart.

AT THE RISK of being late for the dentist's appointment, Fletcher lingered in the house until Don drove off to meet a fraternity brother who had good contacts. Cindy took one look at the untidy kitchen and decided to drive into the city with her father.

Elaine set about her chores briskly, eager to be done. Even housework came easier when there was no one to watch, interrupt, demand attention. To save effort she stacked dishes on the tray and carried them to the kitchen. At the threshold she paused, struck anew by the clutter, confusion seemed symbolic, her life a mess of untidiness, disappointment, and futile chores.

The tray trembled in her hands. She thought of herself cringing, a victim without dignity or self-respect, while her husband assaulted her with pudding.

Her tray fell. Porcelain clattered and broke on the kitchen tiles. Plates, cups, saucers, glasses, everything. It was no accident. She had willed the destruction. So many broken dishes! Fletcher would be furious.

For an instant tears threatened. Elaine thought of excuses, confession, soft appeal. These were immediately rejected. Defiance hardened her. Deliberately and in malice she walked to the counter and, one by one, hurled every dish upon the tiled floor. One plate rebelled, rolled into a corner, remained whole. She picked it up and flung it down with sturdy malevolence. When every soiled dish and glass lay in shards, she collected all the dirty pots and utensils, carried them to the garbage cans, covered them securely and returned to the kitchen.

She had no idea that she was being watched.

Next she set about the task of sweeping up the wreckage, gathering broken bits into the dustpan, emptying it into the garbage tins. On her third trip she saw the man, recoiled and instinctively hid the guilty dustpan behind her back.

"Didn't you hear my car? I didn't see you in the garden so I came to find you here."

It was Ralph Julian. After all of her confessions to his invisible shape the solid man seemed unreal. Her hand trembled. He took the dustpan from her.

"Accident?"

"I broke them on purpose." Defiant, as though he had provoked the destruction, she laughed spitefully.

"So many dishes?"

"Just the ones we used at lunch, Service for four. We've still got eight of everything. Haviland." She laughed again at the extravagance. "We bought the set, a dozen of each, when we moved in here."

Ralph helped her with the rest of the clearing up. "Don't say anything to your husband until he's in a better mood."

"What makes you think he's in a bad one?"

"Something must have caused the havoc. Or do you break dishes just for the hell of it?"

They stood under the olive tree. Leaf shadows darkened her face. She had changed from the soiled dress, so that there were no visible signs of the assault. For all that she had ached to tell Ralph, she could find nothing to say except that it had been a long time since they had seen each other. Ralph had wanted to visit her, he said, but had kept away because he thought her husband did not approve of him.

"It's not you, it's every man. The way he watches me, you'd think the supermarket was a bordello." She had learned the word from her father. Once she had said it to Fletcher and he had laughed, telling her that she was too genteel. "In this country we call it a whorehouse." The recollection brought a faint smile.

Again there was silence under the olive tree. Hot afternoon sun pierced the shadow. Elaine asked him into the house. He reached ahead to open the screen door. Her body brushed against his, so that she stiffened and hurried ahead. There was still a clutter in the kitchen but she made no apologies.

In the living room harsh light lay in yellow rectangles and sent up cruel blades of brightness from the polished tiles between Oriental rugs. Elaine hurried to draw the curtains. At once the mood softened. A dimmed mirror threw back her image. "I ought to comb my hair," she said, but threw herself upon the couch, stretching her long legs and resting sandaled feet upon a cushion.

Ralph stood above the couch and looked down upon her body. "I've thought of you every day." His tone was too ardent. "I couldn't stay away any longer."

She sat up abruptly, asked for a cigarette, moved to the far edge of the couch after he had leaned close to give her a light. His hands smelled of antiseptic soap. Elaine held herself tight to show indifference. He sat at the couch's other end. The curtains blew out like inflated balloons. Elaine and Ralph watched as though this were some strange phenomenon.

She thought of the meetings in daydreams, the conversations carried on in silence, the relief of confession. *My husband wants to die.* In every revery the facts gushed out; in the man's presence she felt a cowardly fool. *Some day he'll do it.* Perhaps, she told herself, it was all a product of her inflamed imagination; or worse, a guilty wish. No, no, no, her heart protested, she did not want to gain freedom that way. Her hands flew to cover the shameful color that flushed in her face.

Through all the weeks that he had denied himself this visit, Ralph had thought about Elaine, cherished many images, tried to capture the elusive delight of her changing expressions, recalled the modeling of bone, the coral tint which often and unexpectedly brightened ivory flesh. He had tried without success to exorcise the spell by making love to a handsome nurse, had told himself severely that he did not approve of involvements with married women. "I've got something to show you." With a tense hand he took out his wallet and from it took a clipping mounted on cardboard.

"Recognize the girl?"

"Me. But years ago."

Professional dignity slipped away. No longer self-contained and superior, the doctor became a diffident boy. He had found the picture in an advertisement in an old magazine given to him by a patient who had wanted him to read a story he had written. "The girl looked like you, and then I remembered that you told me you'd put yourself through college working as a model."

"That's ten years ago. I was a sophomore and missed an ancient history class to pose for that picture."

He returned the picture to his wallet carefully while his eyes were fixed upon her. The scrutiny was almost contact. Elaine became nervous, left the couch, sought protection in deeper shadow. There was the smell of challenge in the room, in the scent of flowers, in the hot wind. Ralph's body was long and spare, his head narrow. Fiery red hot sparks shot from his green-tinted eyes. Not daring to let him see that she recognized mood and masculinity, Elaine bustled about the room in the need to avoid contact of eye or hand. She talked in a nervous, flutey voice about the years when she had worked as a model, rushed from class to photographer's studio, from studio to date. Her days and nights had been too crowded, she had studied when she came in after theater and dancing, had got along with three or four hours of sleep. Excitement had carried her along, she had lived in a whirl of fascinating activity. Ralph saw her as she must have been before her marriage, a gay and popular girl, teasing and enchanting the many men who had surely been in love with her.

"But you wouldn't have liked me then. I was too frivolous." Recollection of frivolity brought out a stream of laughter, "I'm sure you were much more serious when you were at college."

"Too serious." There had never been a moment in his life when Ralph had doubted his dedication to the profession of his foster-father. Above all in his life he had wanted to prove himself to the generous pair who had treated him as their own son.

At last she settled down again, hands folded primly in her lap. Ralph chose the far end of the couch. In the dim room they sat like sedate children waiting to be sent out onto the floor of the dancing school. Presently Ralph moved closer and reached for Elaine's hand. The kiss caught them both off balance.

For months she had been thinking about this man, but not in this way, not *physically*. He had been her confessor, the vessel into which she had poured her fears for her husband; certainly not the instrument of relief or revenge. Surprise made her vulnerable. She clung to Ralph, accepted and returned the kiss. But only for a few instinctive seconds. With a shudder, recognizing weakness, she pulled away, pushed at his chest, made movements of rejection.

"Oh, no, please. Please not . . . "

He became fiercer, murmured that he loved her, that he had tried to forget about her, that no woman had ever moved him so deeply and completely. Elaine seemed not to have heard. Both trembled and shrank into themselves. They heard wheels on the dead-end street, became paralyzed at the thought of having to face her husband calmly. The car turned and drove down the hill. Elaine rose and once again sought protection in the shadows. Ralph followed. Overhead a plane buzzed. They listened like people waiting for a bomb to destroy them. She threw back her head and stroked her neck in a way that Ralph found unbearably seductive.

Having once rejected him, Elaine did not expect to be seized again. The second shock swept away all defenses. She grew limp, pressed her breasts against his body, arched backward, supple and ready. Ralph carried her to the couch. "Not here, not in this room," she whispered as though it were the place rather than the act that would betray her husband. Her mind had cleared, she knew precisely what she was doing and loathed herself, but she had been so long deprived that she had no more will to resist. Her body felt remote from mind and heart as Ralph lifted and carried her to her own room and there, upon her own bed, took her. They made love in silence with no words of passion, no moans of rapture. Her lover was ardent and experienced, but Elaine felt less delight than the cessation of throbbing need.

Poor Fletcher, she thought.

Afterward she lay still, neither fully released nor repentant, but only arid and indifferent. Ralph came alive to the situation and groaned, "What are we going to do now?" All Elaine could say was, "Hurry, hurry. Please get dressed and go quickly."

HELPLESS IN THE padded chair, his jaw weighted with clamps, pipes, and tubes, Fletcher became the most captive of audiences. Not even the consolation of revery was permitted. Dr. Gentian indulged in the conversational flux that is the occupational disease of dentists and barbers. Although Fletcher had become accustomed to muteness he found these sessions particularly irritating because the doctor could not restrain his admiration for Fletcher's wife. In the most jocular way he reminded the poor man of his tremendous luck in having won the devotion of a delightful girl.

"So much younger, too. You must have something on the ball to keep her so faithful. At your age and with your trouble." The dentist touched his own Adam's apple.

Medical authority gave Dr. Gentian special privilege. He

did not feel restrained in speaking of the laryngectomy and its physical and psychological effects. He always had tidbits of unpleasant information. While he drilled and hammered he gave dull, repetitious lectures studded with technical phrases. From this he went on to another painful subject. One of his patients had been sued by his wife for half a million dollars. The drama had been covered by the morning and evening papers but the dentist, having looked into the protagonists' mouths, had extra tidbits about their teeth and their passions. He knew better than any reporter why Mr. X had failed to hold the affections of his wife. "Not that you're anything like him," Dr. Gentian shouted over the whirring of the drill, "a big good-looking man like you. He's a runt, a regular Mr. Five-by-Five who goes in for these tall, bleached dolls. She's nothing, if you ask me, but a run-of-the-mill gold-digger while your wife's true blue, all wool and a yard wide. And a million dollars' worth of sex appeal."

Held prisoner in the padded chair, Fletcher thought of the chocolate-colored blotch on Elaine's flowered silk dress. He saw her startled eyes, the shocked and graceless movement as she backed away. A groan escaped.

"Am I hurting you?"

The patient, bereft of larynx and encumbered by a mouthful of instruments, could give no more answer than another strangled moan.

A moment of rest was permitted. Then Dr. Gentian went on with his drilling and his story: "And one fine day when he was out on business his wife packed her things, priceless jewelry and four minks, and left him flat."

Elaine had not allowed her husband to buy her a mink coat. She had handsome wool wraps of various colors, satins and brocades for evening and an ermine-lined velvet cloak for cold nights. He saw her wearing it in New York, a young woman who had left a brutal, demanding, and impotent husband to enjoy freedom. A new vision rose. Somewhere beyond the dentist's drill and cabinets he saw his house deserted, too bright and glaring without his wife's gentle shadow. The house was Elaine; she had selected and furnished it, fixed its proportions, determined its colors, arranged its routines, filled it with her past, the looks and ornaments that had belonged to her family.

At once Fletcher felt that he must leap from the dentist's chair, desert the barber, jump into the car and speed to her side. He did not. Dr. Gentian was allowed to finish, to spend galling moments in trivial talk, to consult his book and arrange another appointment. Again prisoner in the barber's chair, Fletcher listened to political and scandalous gossip, heard praise of women, boasts of male prowess. He allowed the manicurist to pick at his cuticle and thought of his wife speeding in a taxi toward the airport. At long last he was free to pick up his car.

Cindy was to have waited at the parking lot. It was absurd to have expected her to be on time. Fletcher passed the time by studying displays in shop windows. He was tempted to buy an enameled brooch for Elaine, a box of chocolates, a twenty-dollar art book, a Japanese kimono. Before the operation, when his voice was whole, he used to burst into the New York apartment shouting, "Hi, lovable, I've brought you a present." Recently he had brought her a pair of amethyst earrings which she treasured less for their value than the price he had paid in pride in letting a strange shopkeeper hear his mangled voice.

Today a gift would be a gesture of penitence. She would understand too well, offer tact too generously. Better let the whole thing blow over . . . unless she had already packed and left him.

At the parking lot he found Cindy waiting and reproachful, swearing that she had not been more than three minutes late. Her hands were empty. She had bought nothing, merely enjoyed looking at things too costly for her modest purse. Fletcher did not bother to comment. At the time of the divorce he had established a trust fund for his daughter. Cindy's income was around seventy-five dollars a week, secure and permanent. What had she to complain about?

"I think it's time we had a heart-to-heart talk, Daddy. It's impossible to say anything in front of Don, he's so proud."

Fletcher only half listened. Rush hour traffic, changing lights, heedless drivers, the glare of late afternoon sunshine, long lines of cars belching gas fumes, compounded his impatience. He drove too fast, cheated the changing lights in the urgent need to find Elaine at home, loving and unchanged. He framed the words of apology, heard her laughter and forgiveness.

Cindy talked on and on about Don's misfortunes, not only in the office where they gave the best cases to members of the partners' families, but in previous jobs. "He simply doesn't have the connections in New York. And it's too brutal there, Daddy, you don't know."

The boulevard climbed a small hill. A shaft of sunlight smote Fletcher's eyes. Elaine's laughter dissolved, the smile vanished. He saw her empty room, the dressing table bare of her jewel case, her jars and bottles, a note on the polished wood. She would say she had borne his moods as long as possible and that she was sorry, so terribly, terribly, tragically sorry. Hidden in a place where no one would ever think of looking for them, Fletcher kept a secret store of sleeping pills.

"We've never asked you for any favors. Or money either," said Cindy with a little grimace of humility. "Money doesn't matter so terribly much to us except that you've got to keep up appearances. People would never want to pay a man a decent salary if they think he *needs* it." The absolving stream of laughter mingled with the shriek of a passing police car's siren. "Not that my husband expected anything, but people did talk a lot about me having a rich father. I told Don the truth, that seventy-five a week was every blessed cent I had in the world, but still there was the impression. Could I help it that Mom keeps up that big house and all? It wouldn't have been natural if he hadn't expected some excellent contacts at least. And when we came out here . . . " The laughter fluttered indecisively. Since Fletcher gave her no encouragement Cindy went on, "We did think you'd need a legal representative. Or something. Of course Don would have to pass his bar examinations but he's been reading a lot on California law. It's not too different basically, he says."

They turned off the boulevard onto a shady street. In a passing taxi Fletcher noticed a passenger in a large black straw hat.

It was the kind of hat Elaine wore on sunny days. Fear stabbed at his heart again. He turned to look backward.

"Please, Daddy, watch where you're going!"

He had crossed over the yellow line. He pulled the car over and pressed his foot hard upon the accelerator.

"Daddy! We're in a twenty-five-mile zone."

He drove the rest of the way at thirty and felt like a cripple. The ascent of their hill seemed endless. In the driveway he sounded his horn. The signal often brought Elaine running out to meet him. The kitchen was empty, the stove cold and without the pots that ought at this hour to have been bubbling and giving out pleasant odors. Her bedroom was too tidy, but the jars were still there, the jewel box and perfume bottles. In the living room the cushions were plumped up and in place. No newspapers and magazines littered the tables of the den. Alone, deserted, voiceless, and spent, Fletcher thought once more of his hidden pills.

At the end of the corridor a door opened, "Are you back? Oh, dear, I'm late. I didn't hear you come in, the shower was on, I guess." Elaine ran toward him, sweet-scented and warm. Of their own volition his arms curved around her. She pressed herself close to enjoy his strength. Resentment and fear fled, he forgot frustration, believed himself the man he had been, pulled open the white toweling robe to feel her soft flesh.

Cindy appeared. Elaine, self-conscious when her husband's daughter witnessed the most ordinary caress, jerked herself away. Fletcher grunted, furious because the priceless, hopeful moment had been interrupted.

"What's this?" asked the girl.

"A hat," Elaine said.

Cindy held it aloft, a man's hat, high-crowned, narrow-brimmed. "Whose?"

"Dr. Julian's. He was here this afternoon."

Elaine moved backward toward the wall, as if deeper shadow could make her invisible. After Ralph had left, she had changed the sheets on her bed, stood under the shower, soaped herself in the hottest water she could bear, rinsed with a cold stream, seeking discomfort as partial penance.

"Who's he?"

"A doctor. He took care of me when I had the flu, and he's a friend, too. He asked for you Fletch." There was no response. Elaine's voice reached a higher pitch, was forced down as she added, "He used to live in this house. He stops in to see us sometimes. He was visiting a patient in the neighborhood."

In the redundant, shrill explanation Fletcher sensed disquiet. Visions flashed, nude bodies writhed, sparks shot high, miniature suns dazzled, a carousel of arms and loins, caresses, attitudes, breasts, positions, all at a giddy pace. Fury rose, phrases came to mind, savage anger stifled by affliction and helplessness. Elaine had disappeared. Her bedroom door was closed. She had shut herself away from him.

At the corner bar in the den he filled a glass with ice, poured unmeasured whiskey. The drink brought no solace. This day had been an endurance contest against trivial irritations. Tomorrow would be no better. To regain self-esteem he looked backward to a past seen as a flashing parade of challenges and victories. Setbacks and losses were forgotten, for in the end he had put across big deals, recouped losses, kept ardent faith in himself. Fletcher Strode! Better off dead than enduring this life of petty defeats; showing the spleen of a spoiled child, throwing food at his wife, sulking because she had talked to another man.

Elaine had never given him any real cause, his reasonable mind argued, to suspect disloyalty. On another level he ached to punish the faithless creature, to keep her forever from the pleasures of love. The diary was brought out of its hiding place, touched reverently like a secret scripture or a secret weapon.

Her doctor paid another call on a healthy girl. Is the redhead in league with her? Perhaps Dr. Julian is only her sucker being used to provide her with some pill or poison that will do the job on me. Maybe a pain-killer because she is soft and would not want to see me suffer. I do not think she would dare tell him about her diabolical plan. Maybe she consults him about the psychological condition of her poor husband. It would be clever if she told him she worries about me wanting to commit suicide. How little they know about me. As if Fletcher Strode would take the coward's way out . . .

He stopped to read what he had written, proud and somewhat astonished by his use of words. Elaine came into the room so silently that Fletcher saw her as a vision transformed to reality; not the jealous vision of a woman writhing in lewd love, but the specter of a living angel. She wore a long hostess gown of some filmy material that swayed as she moved so that soft womanly curves and youthful suppleness were happily revealed. To shield himself from the thrust of pleasure aroused by her presence, he growled without the slightest effort to overcome disability, "What's taken you so long?" and at the same time locked his diary away in the desk drawer.

"Sorry, dear, I dawdled. I'll have supper in half an hour." Moist eyes and a nasal huskiness gave her away. She had been crying. This was not like Elaine. She had cried prettily at their wedding, had given in to small, sporadic cloudbursts when she had sought the comfort of his arms the day her mother died, had once at the hospital, just after his operation, turned away with clenched fists and muffled sniffles of fury against her weakness.

Fletcher tried to find a comfortable way of saying he regretted his stupid gesture with the pudding.

"I have something to confess," she said slowly.

He was shaken by a sudden chill.

"I broke the lunch dishes, all we used today, the Haviland. I"—she raised her head and offered the sight of her moist and swollen eyes as a sacrifice of pride—"I did it on purpose. In a hideous tantrum."

In relief he offered broken laughter. She floated toward him, touched her gentle palm to his cheek. Caught by her fragrance, he could not control the impulse to pull her hand over his mouth and kiss it tenderly.

4 THE NEXT NIGHT, AFTER HE HAD FINISHED HIS HOSpital rounds, Ralph stopped to pick up his hat. This was the excuse he gave the Strodes. The reason was quite different. Those few minutes of unleashed love had not eased the pressure of his desire for Elaine. For eight endless weeks,

knowing her situation and her husband's temper, he had kept away. When he had stopped by on Thursday afternoon he had not consciously intended to start an affair. Both he and she had been swept off their feet. At the end Elaine had said, "We must never see each other again. Never." Ralph had neither promised nor protested. But a man is justified in reclaiming property left behind. His pale, freckled skin was sensitive to sunlight, the hat his newest.

The night was clear and unbearably hot. No fog rolled in from the ocean, no breeze blew. Sullen air lay heavy upon the earth and after dark, the heat rose and smothered the hills. The sultry air suggested rain, hopelessly, for it would be many weeks before a storm blew in. From hundreds, perhaps thousands, of barbecues drifted the smell of burning fat and from all the swimming pools the shrieks and splashes of night bathers.

There was a smoky smell in the Strode yard, too, and dark silhouettes against the blue brightness of the lighted swimming pool. Instead of ringing the doorbell Ralph walked through the garden. "Good evening."

They saw the visitor with amazement. His footsteps had not been heard. Fletcher grunted a greeting. Cindy looked up with bright interest. Don wrung water out of his trunks.

"I hope I'm not disturbing you. I left my hat here yesterday."

"You must be Dr. Julian. I brought your hat to your office this afternoon. Your nurse was just closing the office."

"Thanks. That was very kind of you."

"Elaine asked me to. I'm Don Hustings."

They shook hands. Don introduced his wife, who said she was delighted to meet the famous Dr. Julian, she had heard so much about him.

Elaine lay upon her back in the pool, dreaming as she floated. Her eyes were closed, her ears covered by a tight cap. She discovered Ralph as she started up the ladder. "Why, hello!" She could not let herself appear discountenanced and hurried to offer her wet hand as though he were no more than an old family friend who had dropped in for a visit. Fletcher watched. His scowl was for the two packs of cards laid out in rows on the metal table under the light. He played solitaire compulsively, and whenever a game demanded choice, pondered it as grimly as if his entire wealth were at stake. A man who breathed through a hole in his neck could not swim nor dive into the pool.

He had always excelled at water sports, won his lifesaver's credentials and many medals at the YMCA when he was a kid; cherished a silver cup earned in a diving competition; had later, in his country club days, been a member of a businessmen's water polo team. Now, on hot days when there was no one except his wife to witness his shame, he could walk into the shallow end and cool himself to the chest. Elaine had not wanted a pool, but in that area pools were as much a part of a valuable house as the bathtubs. She had suggested that they fill it in and make a badminton court. Fletcher had insisted that they keep the pool for her pleasure. "I like to see you in a bathing suit, lovable." As though he couldn't see her without clothes whenever he chose.

She stood at the edge of the pool. Water dripped down her long legs and gathered in puddles at her feet. Her toenails were tinted with coral enamel and her bathing suit was as green and shimmering as a mermaid's tail. Garden lights were reflected in drops of water on her neck and arms.

"How are you?" asked Ralph.

"Fine. And you?" she said.

"Okay." Ralph took an uncertain step backward, looked away, but could not resist the temptation to look at her again and make love with his eyes. "I'd better be getting on," he said diffidently.

"Why don't you have a swim? It's a big relief on a night like this." Don welcomed young masculine company. He had become bored with Cindy's squeals, Fletcher's moods, and Elaine's indifference. "Let me get you a pair of trunks."

This pool had been the focus of Ralph's growing summers. He dived into his past, heard the shouts of youthful cronies, the voice of his foster-mother begging for quiet and offering cakes. He swam dreamily, eyes closed, until he was recalled to the present by the voices around the pool: Don Hustings's eastern college affectations, his wife's nervous giggle, the mangled efforts of Elaine's husband. Perhaps the harsh notes were distortions of Ralph's conscious.

He did not relish the role of clandestine lover.

"You shouldn't have come here." Elaine had dived in and come up beside him.

"I had to see you again."

"I asked you not to."

"Damn it, I'm in love with you."

She swam away. With long strokes Ralph was beside her again. "What are we going to do?"

Fletcher watched them moving along the pool, side by side. He was irritable because no red king had turned up to relieve a row of cards guarded by a black queen. He muttered something that no one could understand. At the far end of the pool and with a rubber cap over her ears, Elaine—usually so perceptive—could not make out a word. "Yes, dear," she said sweetly, and swam toward him, but collided with Cindy who had dived in without looking to see if anyone was in the way.

Elaine camp up coughing and spluttering, hoisted herself out of the pool, pulled off her cap and, still coughing, danced up and down, tossing her head from side to side to drain water out of her ears. In a flash Fletcher was beside her, pounding her back. The sensation pleased him. His sense of power grew.

"Darling, please, you don't know how strong you are."

She had quit coughing so that there was no reason beyond pleasure for Fletcher to go on beating her back. He stopped with the air of a king granting clemency. Magnanimity did not end here. He would not allow Ralph to leave without joining them for a drink. The two young men had climbed out of the pool, and as Fletcher watched them shaking themselves like wet dogs, he compared their bodies with his own.

For sheer brawn neither could come near him. His torso was bare above his white duck custom-made shorts. Around his neck, knotted like a brigand's kerchief, was a silk scarf that concealed and guarded the stoma. Except for this small, hidden area his body was deeply tanned. Ralph Julian, as tall as

Fletcher, was as pale as a Victorian beauty. With neither the time nor complexion for sunburn, he allowed his flesh to stay as white as a ghost's. The pale, freckled skin barely covered the gaunt bones. Don was darker than Fletcher, sturdily built, but short.

The sense of size and masculinity restored Fletcher's temper. He told Elaine to get out of her wet bathing suit, sent Don to fetch drinks, ordered Cindy to quit chattering, bade Ralph sit there and amuse him. Everyone obeyed.

Don brought the drinks. The service was impeccable. His son-in-law, Fletcher reflected, would make an excellent bartender or butler. When Elaine came out, the three men were standing up, drinking, under the lamp. Fletcher wondered if she noticed the contrast in their bodies and appreciated his superiority. He pulled in his stomach, straightened his shoulders.

"Why don't we sit down?" she said.

They did. The patio lamps thrust bright artificial rays upon them. Cindy took a cigarette from the box on the table; Don bent over to light it. Ralph stretched back on a chaise lounge, trying not to look at Elaine. She recrossed her legs. Fletcher studied his drink in which small flecks of lime drifted like tiny fish under the glass of an aquarium. Conversation lagged. The group seemed as static as models in a color advertisement. Then Ralph turned his head and caught Elaine's eye. Both looked too hastily in opposite directions. He hurried to swallow his drink and to say that he must not outstay his welcome. No one was sorry to see him go.

FLETCHER CAME TO Elaine's bed that night. On a high wave of elation, the conquering male who had shown up two inferior young men, he had chosen his best pajamas, opened a bottle of French cologne, combed his hair, and in the mirror found a man. The surge of youth was strong. He strutted down the short corridor. This was to be the night of the miracle, the end of anxiety, the fulfillment promised by doctors, the reward deserved by his loyal wife.

He found her reading with such intensity that she neither

heard nor saw him at the door. He watched her turn a page with a graceful hand, enjoyed the rise and fall of her chest, the sheen of lamplight upon her dark hair, the lace falling off her breast.

"Lovable!"

The whisper was so light that he had no need of the lost larynx. Her smile acknowledged the first step of the miracle. She knew he would not have come to her room to risk failure. Fletcher did not speak again lest the broken voice distress the mood. Elaine made room in the bed beside her. For the first moments they lay quiet, a husband and wife loving and normal at the end of a day.

"You're such a beautiful man. You've got a wonderful body."

So she had noticed! Praise nourished his self-confidence. He played with her hair. From time to time she looked up sideways from her niche under his arm. Her brimming smile showed belief in the possibility of a miracle.

Nothing came of it. "I'm sorry," Elaine said, as always taking upon herself the blame for their failure. As always the damn owl sat on the telephone pole, squawking derision. Fletcher shuffled off to his room. In the closet, hidden in a riding boot he never wore, he kept a vial of jewel-colored pills as lovely as fruit candies in a crystal jar. Whenever he had the strength to forego one or both of the two pills doled out to him at bedtime, he added to his hoard. Elaine was firm about the pills. She would never give him more than two. "You mustn't get into the habit of taking an extra one. The habit grows," she told him. Often, in the tormented dark when sleep was denied and the fear of sleeplessness brought about panic, he had stolen from his hoard.

Inevitably on such nights he was haunted by the memory of the spastic shoelace vendor. The boy was young, had no experiences to remember; how had he faced the thought of hopeless days? Perhaps the boy had been blessed with dull wits. One could not tell from the sputtering speech whether the infirmity had touched his mind. Separate from life, the boy was spared the anguish endured by a man who yearned for a past he could not recover. Fresh agonies were born. Specters vomited nostalgia;

visions of virile years possessed him; he was visited by ghosts of long-forgotten women, recollections of high-spirited nights, of jokes and singing, of victories in business, of solemn board members shouted down and conquered by Fletcher Strode's vitality. Relived in sour retrospect, these pictures reflected only the glories, never the pain and struggle, of earlier years.

With the vial of pills in his hand, he walked in the garden. "Shut up!" croaked Fletcher at the owl. A hoot gave hideous echo. In the dark the man threw rocks at the telephone pole. "I want to die," he challenged, his voice ringing out in full deformity. "No hope, no hope," mocked the owl.

Back in the house, he poured a measure of whiskey. Two pills were already down, the vial in his hand. He had so often thought of swallowing the whole hoard, had seen himself forcing the last ones into his mouth, had grimaced at the bitterness of gelatin capsules, had gagged at the thought of so much swallowing, had felt a dark and lovely cloud descend. Once more he counted the pills. How many? In the newspapers he often read about sleeping pill suicides. Amounts were never given. Sometimes the poor slobs were saved. God forbid! No humiliation could cut deeper, no failure scar a man more cruelly, than the defeat of attempted death.

"No hope, no hope," the owl repeated. Fletcher's hand trembled, the vial fell. Pills were scattered over the carpet, rolled under the furniture, hid themselves in shadows. He turned on all the lights, searched on hands and knees, counted, found three missing, went down upon his knees again to run both hands over the thick pile of the carpet. He had grown tired, the dark and lovely cloud descended so that he had barely strength to pull himself together and totter to his bed. The fog had entered his mind. He could not remember if he had swallowed more than the two pills.

DEATH, LIKE MONEY, cannot be acquired by wishing. Fletcher woke drowsily and in a vile mood, knowing that he had to live through the irritations of another day. When Elaine said she had been surprised at his having slept so long and had twice come to his room, he flew into a rage and asked if she had hoped to find a corpse in his bed.

"Eat your breakfast and don't say such silly things."

Under the date of September eighteenth there appeared in his diary this item:

Last night R.J. came to swim with us. My wife was all hot and bothered and kept giving me looks that sent shivers up my spine because I knew what was on her mind. She must have felt very guilty because she began to flirt with me like a girl on the make. Later she came to my room in a new nightie that showed everything she has. She praised my physique and said I was more attractive than the younger men and asked if I remembered how we used to hurry home from places in N.Y. and throw our clothes on the floor. But she did not throw that expensive nightgown on the floor. She came to bring me sleeping pills, and when I tried to make love she let me know she was not interested.

He stopped to pace the floor while he pondered the subtleties of the falsehood. No one could deny the facts except Elaine, who would be believed by no one who read the diary after her husband's death.

Elaine came to the library to ask him something, saw the diary open on the desk, remarked that she was glad to see him occupied. Her voice was a shade too cheerful, her eyes darkly circled, her smile an effort. After she had gone he wrote:

Am I wrong to distrust her? Suspicion haunts the guilty mind. But what am I guilty of? I wait like a sitting duck and do nothing to protect myself from the danger that hangs over me. This is because my life has no purpose and the future means nothing any more. When the time comes and she does the desperate act I wonder if I will know and resist. I see into her evil heart but cannot make any move against her because . . .

Here the entry finished. He could not acknowledge love in a document designed to destroy her. And since love had been the only virtue left in his life, his refusal to admit its existence was also an act of destruction. With passion futile, with no activities to involve mind or body, the man was compelled to reject himself. He became indifferent in other ways, showed little excitement when his stockbroker telephoned from New York to suggest profitable sales or purchases. His only interest was the diary which he read and reread, not as in the first flush of literary pride, but hypnotically as converts read their special scriptures; and like the convert he found belief.

CHILDREN OF THE electronic age, Cindy and Don were unable to live with silence. They always had to have the TV turned on or the radio or record player going. They had a radio in the car and kept a transistor on the table between their beds. Cindy preferred ballads and sentimental songs from recent movies. Don called himself a cat and considered himself an authority on jazz. The walls of the house seemed to quiver with the blasts of horns, the beat of drums. Out of necessity they had to talk loudly.

"Daddy's not taken in anymore," shouted Cindy over a Thelonious Monk recording. "He sees right through her at last."

Don had not heard. She had to repeat the statement. This gave her great pleasure. Cindy treasured the memory of her father's assault of his wife with a dish of chocolate mousse.

"What's there to see through?" Don asked.

"Now really! You're not taken in, too?"

"You sound just like your mother."

"What's wrong about that? My mother's a smart woman. From the very beginning Elaine intrigued him with her body. The attraction was merely physical and poor Daddy paid the price."

Cindy sounded so like a tape recording of the first Mrs. Strode that Don stiffened as he always did in the presence of that lady. She must have told him fifty times that poor Fletcher's affliction had come as just punishment for the sin of the second marriage.

"If you want my opinion, he despises her."

"That's not our business," Don said and tried to concentrate on a sax obbligato.

"What are you getting so snotty about? If it wasn't for her, you wouldn't have to be running around like a racehorse, begging for jobs."

The drums joined in. Over the music Don shouted, "I'm not begging for anything when I try to make the right contacts. You know perfectly well I could go right back to my job in New York."

"For peanuts. Who wants to?"

"I'm not so sure," Don answered haughtily. But he was quite sure. Before they came to California, Don had foreseen a brilliant future in the rapidly growing Los Angeles area. Surely some of these executives new to wealth and power ought to value the services of a clever young Easterner with legal training. If he could get his foot in the door of some solid organization, Don was willing to sacrifice his career as a lawyer. Other men were offered all sorts of opportunities.

Since Nan and Rex Burke had returned from the yachting trip, the young Hustings had been entertained lavishly. New friends had asked Don and Cindy to parties, offered them seats in their boxes at the racetrack, remembered them when they were selling tickets to charity affairs. Many of these people were valuable as business contacts.

"We can't go on forever accepting hospitality without reciprocating. We've got to establish ourselves even if it costs a few dollars."

It was out of the question for them to entertain in a good restaurant. They simply hadn't the money. "We could do a cocktail thing in the garden. With those fabulous caterers everyone uses," Cindy suggested.

"What about your father?"

"If only he'd relax a bit. It wouldn't hurt him at all to mix with people . . . I mean . . . Elaine really ought to do something! It's her fault he's so morbid. But he sees through her, Don, I'm positive. Sometimes," she added with a squeal that topped the drums, "he just acts beastly to her."

"Let's not suggest a party now. We're stuck here and we've got to do things his way." Don had sensed intolerance in his father-in-law and did not want to be insulted with the news that he was no longer a welcome guest in the house. Beneath his suave and gallant manners Don hid a sorely troubled mind. Even Cindy did not know the full extent of the debts he had left in New York. His small supply of cash had dwindled tragically. Although he had no rent to pay, no food to buy, there were still cigarettes and gasoline, service on the car, barber and beauty shop bills; flowers, jars of caviar, boxes of candy and other tokens of gratitude to generous hostesses. When Nan or her friends asked Don and Cindy to buy tickets to charity affairs they could not refuse, and if a few people stopped at a bar, Don had to occasionally pick up the check. They could not afford to be known as freeloaders since Don's career as well as their social future would be affected.

Inevitably when Don and Cindy were trying to have a private talk Elaine would knock at their door. "Please turn down the radio a bit. Not all the way," she would say apologetically, "but lower. The noise makes your father nervous."

"If only we had a place of our own," fretted Cindy.

Quite by accident they found the house.

5 SUMMER HAD GONE AND COME AGAIN. IN THE MIDdle of October the heat returned, raging. A Santa Ana, the natives called the wind that blew in from the desert with such fury that even the seashore burned. There was no humidity, no decent sweat to relieve fever temperature. Fletcher's wound needed moisture; with every breath he inhaled pain. His temper became insufferable. Elaine suggested that they drive north to Carmel, fly to Hawaii, sail off on any boat that went anywhere. He stamped about the house, grunting, refusing comfort.

To escape the unbearable climate of the house, Don and Cindy drove down to Nan's place at Newport Beach. She had promised that her house would always be open to them, her pool available. They found the doors locked, the gate barred. Too late Cindy remembered that Nan had gone to stay at her father's Lake Arrowhead place while her husband was abroad, her servants on holiday. It was irksome. She and Don had met a few people with houses in that area, but none whom she could visit without invitation. The shore burned like desert sand, the ocean lay sullen in the glare, the sky was as blue as oxidized copper molded to reflect heat. Although they disliked public beaches, they had to get into the water just to feel alive. Like ordinary people whose friends do not own beach houses, they undressed and left their clothes in the car. After the swim Cindy combed her hair and did her face on the open beach. While their bathing suits dried, they could find no pleasant place to sit, no cafés with tables under parasols, not even a decent cold drink. They walked a long way in search of some place more inviting than the sordid shacks whose signs advertised bottled drinks and whose stoves filled the air with the stink of frying fat and cheap ground meat. A diamond is easier to find on the California shore than a glass of fresh orange juice or real lemonade.

The beach ended in a bluff. Pretending to be gay and beatnik and unconventional, they decided to walk in bathing suits along the highway where they might find an edible sandwich. They ascended a narrow street. A sign caught their eye: FOR SALE—UNUSUAL—A BARGAIN. The house was only a few feet up a narrow lane, tree-shaded and secluded; a perfect gem, adorable, divine, irresistible and not expensive; less than forty-five thousand dollars. Forty-four, nine hundred and fifty. A few miles up the coast, where Nan lived, a narrow lot cost seventy-five thousand. Without the house. This was ideal for a young couple, the sort of unpretentious place they could explain to people who lived in two-hundred-thousand-dollar houses as "cozy" and "completely private." It was only five years old, authentic California modern with a flat roof, two sun decks, glass walls all over the place. There was no pool, merely the ocean for swimming, but they could maintain status by reminding their friends that they had come from the East, had spent their summers on the Atlantic and preferred surf bathing. The house was offered at this absurd price because the owner, a young executive who was transferred to his company's Ohio branch, wanted to sell immediately. For a down payment of only five thousand dollars they could own the house. They were almost naked, Don in the trunks, Cindy wearing a few inches of a bikini, but the owners of the house at once recognized them as the right sort and said they would be happy to have their home occupied by such nice people. Don mentioned casually that Nan's father would arrange the financing. Cindy added that the famous banker's daughter was her closest friend. The effect was magic, the house practically theirs.

Hand in hand, like enchanted children, they raced along the beach to fetch their clothes and car. "Just think, a home of our own. We can entertain," Cindy said, "informally, of course, but with chic." She saw a dining table in an ell that faced the sunset; laid it with wedding presents of china and silver stored now in her mother's basement; clothed herself in a fabulous cotton hostess gown and welcomed guests who simply adored her new house. Don thought barbecue dinners a better way of entertaining. Over watery coffee and plastic-wrapped sandwiches they argued about the sort of parties they would give.

They had been too hungry and too impatient to look for a decent place, so had settled on a so-called beach café where food and drinks were thrust over a counter at barefoot customers who, if they were lucky enough to get a table, could sit down while they ate. At this hour only one other table was occupied. A pair of foreigners in dark glasses spoke an ugly guttural language.

"What's the soonest we could move in, Don?"

Don bit into his sandwich, grimaced, said, "Well, I guess that settles it. We're staying in California definitely."

Cindy's sandwich might have been of glue or caviar, smoked turkey or cardboard. She was too excited to taste mere food. "Do you think we can use the Hitchcock chairs and the hutch in a modern house?" She had inherited the antiques from her maternal grandmother.

"Maybe I can land that job with Carter Consolidated." Don rode his own train of thought. "I'll try to see Doug Third in the morning. He told me his grandfather was looking desperately for the right man, and promised to make an appointment.

There's a future in that outfit." He saw himself at an executive's desk in an air-conditioned office with wall-to-wall carpeting, a beautiful secretary, and his name on the door. A group of young Negroes invaded the shack, took possession of the empty tables, crowded their brown bodies into the narrow space. They ordered hamburgers. A greasy smog drifted from the grill. Laughter and guttural foreign syllables interrupted Don's dreams of executive importance and Cindy's plans for entertaining millionaires.

When they returned they found the house prettier than they remembered. Imagination had made it their own. The owner's wife suggested that they change their clothes in a bedroom where they had a private moment, a naked embrace in the lustful thought that this pretty chamber would be their own. While Cindy took her own good time to redo her hair and face, Don discussed details of the transaction. The owner's agent lived close by and had been summoned by telephone.

Arrangements were the usual ones. A deposit of one thousand dollars would put the house in escrow. When these proceedings had been completed, Don would pay the additional four thousand and the house would be his. "Unfortunately," he said gaily, "I haven't a thousand dollars on me, and I didn't bring my checkbook to the beach."

No one expected him to pay on sight. A house is not purchased like a cake of soap. Impatient to make a deal, the agent suggested that they meet the next morning at the escrow department of a bank in downtown Los Angeles. Don remarked that deals of that sort were simpler in the East where no escrow formalities were demanded, and people simply bought and sold without having to wait while a third party held the buyer's money and searched the seller's title.

"It's for your protection," said the agent piously.

"You won't find any termites in this house," the owner added.

"What time do we meet?" asked the agent.

Don assumed an important air. "I happen to have a rather full day tomorrow. A meeting that may go on all afternoon." Like a man of affairs, he shrugged off the dreary business, suggested that they get together in the morning of the next day. There was no doubt that he had made a good impression. The Jaguar and the Strode address in Pacific Palisades had not gone unnoticed. These were solid assets like cash in the bank. Donald Hustings seemed a man whose signature could command thousands. But he did not feel that he had made a commitment recklessly. He had given himself an extra twenty-four hours to raise the money.

"You think your father'd advance it?"

Cindy thought about it bitterly. They were driving on the freeway, and she noticed all the posters advertising houses that could be owned by veterans without a penny's down payment. Don had given two years of his life to the US Navy. Her father would probably suggest that a man without ready cash take advantage of some such drab opportunity. During their stay in his house her father had shown little generosity to the honeymoon couple. It was galling to contrast her fate with Nan Burke's splendid life. If Cindy had been a poor man's daughter she could have forgiven her father's ungenerous attitude, but she had so often heard her mother speak in angry reverence of Fletcher's fortune that Cindy had grown up believing herself an heiress. Nothing in Fletcher Strode's present style of living (except the absence of a servant in the house) suggested that he was not wealthy. What had Cindy to expect from such a father? His money was squandered on that second wife.

She looked up at Don. His well-cut features were deformed by a scowl, the sculptured lips pressed between his teeth. "I don't know. Daddy's been so dismal lately, he's in a sort of depression." She did not speak in her usual flat voice but wailed softly like a disconsolate child. "I'm kind of afraid of asking. It'd be easier with Nan's father. He likes you so much, Donnie."

Don turned down the car radio. At any other time the jazz combo would have delighted him, but with so many cars whirring on the freeway and Cindy using that affected childish voice, he could barely hear. His tones, still adjusted to the jazz band, were far too loud. "We can't ask him for the down payment. If he's going to finance us for forty thousand, we can't let him know we don't have the first five thousand."

"Why not?"

"We'd be poor security. I doubt that his company would accept us even with his recommendation."

Cindy was not informed about money. Don had to explain the transaction in words of one syllable. He became harsher as the reality of the situation became clearer. It had disappointed Don that Cindy's private income and expectations were not what he had been led to believe; but then he had also represented himself as a suitor with a solid job and brilliant prospects. The house might indeed be a bargain for a man who had a few thousand dollars, but for a man in Don Hustings's position, there were no bargains. "Maybe we oughtn't to buy now."

"I'll die if we don't get that house. Isn't there some way, Don?"

"We might borrow on your trust fund."

A transformation took place in Cindy. The plaintive little girl became a woman of iron. Her very skin took on a metallic hue. Once before Don had suggested borrowing on the principal. She had burst out with such an astonishing series of shrieks, accusations, and tears that for days he had been afraid to talk to her. The trust fund settled upon her by Fletcher at the time of his divorce was sacred, her only security against starvation in the streets.

"You know I'd never do that," she answered with surprising dignity. "But there must be some other way. For people like us. Daddy must still have plenty of money. Couldn't we just use his name?"

Don had become very tense. An idiot truck driver had slowed up just ahead. They were entering the city. Smog made breathing impossible. Heat lay upon the earth like an electric blanket. "Not unless he'd co-sign. That'd be no different from asking him to lend us the money."

"I don't mean asking him. I mean just being his daughter. After all," Cindy held her breath while Don swung out and passed the huge truck, "I am his daughter, and he's not so young and has had that terrible operation."

"He's done all right by you. Do you know how much principal it takes to earn a seventy-five-a-week income? We know nothing about his will, and besides he may live for years."

"I hope he does," Cindy said and added without thought of the contradiction, "but there are big insurance policies. He made them out for Mom and me before the divorce and it was in the settlement he'd keep them for us."

Don sighed. They could not raise money on hopes and promises. Their only chance was a direct appeal to Fletcher Strode. The prospect appalled Don. From time to time he turned to look at Cindy and saw the fear in her face. There were only two courses, either to give up and go back to his hopeless job and his debts, or to risk his father-in-law's contempt. Presently he suggested that Cindy appeal to her father. She answered that financial problems were his responsibility. For the rest of the drive they argued, weaving in and out between the speeding cars and breathing foul fumes. In anger Don drove faster and more dangerously until he was stopped by a traffic cop and given a ticket for reckless driving. This was not a good omen.

A MIRACLE AWAITED Cindy's homecoming. "Nan's here," she announced with the reverence of a herald angel. A Rolls-Royce was parked in the driveway.

"Don't say anything about the house."

"Why not? I'm dying to tell them."

"We've got to break it to your father carefully. He might not approve if he's not in the right mood."

In the living room they found Nan Burke chattering at Fletcher. Her simple cotton dress had cost two hundred dollars, if not more. "Darling!" she and Cindy cried simultaneously and hurried to touch cheekbones.

"I thought you were in Arrowhead," Cindy said.

"I was. I am," Nan replied with the accent and giggle she and Cindy had acquired the same year at the same school. "But after all, Arrowhead shops aren't exactly fabulous and I was desperately in need of shorts. Imagine forgetting to pack shorts! They're an absolute must in the mountains." Nan could go on like this for hours. About nothing important. "And with the place at Newport empty, there was no one to fetch them so I came to town for some new ones. And stopped in to see you. And met your famous father." She glanced toward Fletcher coyly. She had been told about his infirmity and warned that he was morbidly sensitive. "Actually I dropped in to bring you something." From a mammoth alligator bag that must have cost three hundred dollars (if not more) she brought out a pair of engraved cards. "With Rexie away I don't feel much like going out at night. The mountain air's so positively great that . . . well, really, you won't believe this . . . we fall asleep at nine. Isn't it fantastic? You really ought to come up there, Mr. Strode"—she favored him with a bright, apologetic smile—"it's so relaxing. Really! And you'd be welcome to use our bit of beach and sail one of my father's boats if you'd like." She gestured with a cigarette, brushed ash off her expensive cotton bosom. Her breasts were large, her waist filling out. Although she was Cindy's age and had so far only one child, she had begun to wear the bountiful air of a patroness.

Cindy cooed over the cards which were for a widely advertised movie premiere, a benefit sponsored by one of Nan's favorite charities. Cindy had heard the girls talk about it, had been aching to go but could not dream of paying fifty dollars for the cheapest seats. The tickets Nan bestowed were for the best box and had probably cost a thousand dollars, if not more. They also entitled the bearers to attend a midnight supper dance at the San Marino estate of an oil millionaire.

Ecstatic, Cindy contrived to show decent protest. "Are you sure you don't want to go, Nan?"

"Without my husband?"

"Why not?" asked Don with a provocative smile.

"Who'd take me?"

"I'm sure there are dozens of men who'd welcome the privilege."

"I'm not that sort of wife. Not yet."

Cindy joined Nan in gales of merriment over the innuendo. Don had pleased Nan, which pleased Cindy; and Don was pleased with himself. Fletcher's stomach rumbled. Elaine came in with a tray of iced tea and cookies.

"What about your parents? Couldn't you go with them?" asked Cindy, stretching the danger of self-sacrifice to its limit.

"They're too lazy. And my father's bored to death by those affairs. People make *speeches*." Nan made the word sound obscene.

"If you change your mind, just call up and you have your seats back," Cindy offered reluctantly as she tucked the tickets away in an amusing straw bag which cost only eighteen dollars at a sale.

"Why don't you use my father's seats, Mr. Strode? I'm sure you and your wife would enjoy the show." Nan addressed Fletcher in a slow, clear voice calculated to show compassion for the afflicted.

Fletcher grunted something inaudible and marched out of the room. He refused to stay and be spoken to like a deaf mute or a moron, and to be offered the charity of unwanted tickets. Did that fool girl imagine he'd burst with joy at the privilege of sitting through an affair that bored her father? Fletcher Strode! God knows, he could afford a pair of tickets if he wanted them; a dozen pairs. He would have liked to hurl the ashtray, stubs and all, at the complacent bosom. Most distasteful of all was Cindy's acting like a poor relation.

"I hope you don't mind poor Daddy, he's so morbidly sensitive," Cindy said with the frayed remnant of a laugh.

"I tried to offer him a bit of pleasure." Nan stood up. Her purse slid to the floor.

Elaine murmured thanks for the invitation and excused herself to go after Fletcher. Don hurried to retrieve the fallen bag. Sir Walter Raleigh could not have shown more gallant obeisance to his queen. Nan bestowed a regal smile. Don acknowledged it with a flattering eye. Nan walked out with a swinging motion of her hips. Don accompanied her to the car. Cindy started after them, but Don turned with a wink that bade her remain behind. When he helped Nan into the Rolls, he lifted her hand and kissed it.

"Wasn't Daddy awful?" Cindy whispered when she and Don were in their room with the transistor turned high and the door closed. "You don't think she was sore, do you?"

"I did my best to smooth out the ruffled plumage."

"You were adorable." Cindy kissed the tip of his chin. "If businessmen were women, you'd be a millionaire."

Don stripped off his shirt and flexed his muscles at the sun-tanned fellow in the mirror. "Never underestimate the power of a woman. Her old man may be clay in Nan's little hand."

"Wasn't Daddy terrible, though? Tomorrow, Donnie, I'm going to tell him what I thought of that performance—"

"Not if you want the house. Tomorrow you're going to ask Daddy for five thousand dollars. And one thousand of it right away."

"You're the man, darling, you've got to ask."

Implacable, the man said, "You're his daughter, the sweetest little girl in the world. Remember, daughter dear, it's only a loan you're asking for."

"He'll squawk at me in that voice. It makes me sick. I just can't take it."

The argument went on until they reached a compromise. Cindy would gird up courage and appeal to her father; Don would charm Elaine into using her influence with Fletcher. This seemed a brilliant idea. A couple of cocktails stiffened their courage. Fletcher drank a lot before and during dinner. After-ward they played bridge and he won. This seemed a good omen.

CINDY AND DON came to breakfast promptly. She explained prettily that she had decided to get up every morning at the crack of dawn, and do something useful. "After all, a vaca-tion can't last forever, you know." She kissed Fletcher on both cheeks and ran to the kitchen to help Elaine. Don explained that he had an early appointment with Douglas Lyman Carter III about an opening in his family's firm. Fletcher grunted some-thing that Don preferred not to understand. Since the day he arrived in California, Don had been talking about his frater-nity brother, the Carter heir. After several meetings and many martinis, Don had been introduced to the personnel manager of Carter Consolidated. An opening had been mentioned, but it was neither interesting nor remunerative enough for a man of Don's caliber. Young Doug had laughed at the very idea of his fraternity brother's taking a job on a junior-junior level and promised a personal meeting with his grandfather.

"Today's the day. Doug's done a top-selling job because the old man's giving me a half hour of his time." Don was never more blithe than in a spontaneous lie.

"Good luck," Elaine said.

Cindy wore a pink ribbon in her hair. It gave her an innocent look so that she seemed only a little older than the ruffled child in the photograph on Fletcher's desk. This picture was the one souvenir that Fletcher had wanted to keep after he married Elaine. It brought back memories of the days when his daughter had been adoring and adorable, and he had given her four Saturdays a year. They had gone off together like clandestine lovers, freed of his wife's heavy companionship; to beach or circus or rodeo or ice show; to overeat and laugh boisterously together. He had been looked upon as the king of happiness and had bestowed extravagant toys.

Cindy served Fletcher's toast and eggs. In the softest of little-girl voices she asked if Daddy would like to have her come and play golf with him. "Not that I'm good enough . . . I'm more of the tennis type . . . but if you'd want me . . . " She had dressed for the links in a misty pink and gray plaid dress and flat shoes.

She played deplorably, and the sun beat down like punishment. Fletcher tested her by going the full eighteen holes. She bore it valiantly so that he felt sorry and invited her to lunch. He suspected that she was out after a gift, perhaps a new dress for that shindig on Monday night. Why not give it to her? Fletcher Strode's daughter need not feel inferior. She had large blue eyes very much like his own, and her mother's pale skin, now prettily tanned. A good-looking girl deserves good clothes. He had not been generous to her lately, nor fair in judging her charms.

She imitated Elaine in suggesting his lunch menu, selecting things he liked, protecting him from the waiter. All through lunch she chattered so that people, observing them, probably thought the middle-aged man extremely patient with the prattle of his young companion. When they were drinking coffee she slid her hand across the table, rested it upon his and asked gently if he would like to help her and her husband. "We do so want a home of our own."

There were a number of questions in his mind but he did not care to expose his infirmity in the restaurant. He signaled the waiter, and Cindy, tactful today, announced that Mr. Strode would like the check. It was not until they were in the car that Fletcher spoke. Would she like a new dress for that party? Anything she chose at the shop. The price did not matter. Fletcher Strode's daughter could dress as well as that big-bosomed friend of hers. Ordinarily Cindy would have been ecstatic, not only having bought an expensive dress but wangled a wrap and a pair of slippers to go with the outfit.

"Thank you very much, Daddy. You're so wonderful but"— she slid toward him and rested her hand upon his knee—"my beige organza is just perfect for Monday night, and no one out here's seen it yet. There's something else," she paused for a deep breath, "money, Daddy. But only as a loan. Don will pay it back. He's practically been promised that Carter job, you know."

"How much?"

"We're not asking you to give it to us. Really. We've decided to live very economically so we can pay you back soon."

Fletcher barked out the question again.

Cindy hesitated. She was afraid he would remind her that the income from her trust fund was a lot of money for a young girl, that she did not appreciate the sacrifice it had cost to make this liberal settlement on his daughter. He had to ask once more before she tightened her hand on his thigh and asked tremulously, "Could you afford to lend us five thousand dollars, Daddy? One thousand Monday and the rest—"

A roar interrupted. That was a damn fool question, an insult, a slur on his name. Could he afford five thousand dollars? Did she think her father a pauper? Whenever he was angry and spoke too fast, neglecting the control of abdominal muscles and the rhythm of breath, he sounded like a defective machine. Cindy could not half understand, but experience had taught her that his rage would be increased if she reminded him of the horror.

He knew. A few blocks before they reached the house he parked the car, turned off the motor, and asked in painfully controlled syllables how much the house would cost and how Don expected to finance it. She told him all that Don had explained. Fletcher did not approve.

He kept her waiting. The suspense was unbearable. She was tempted to jump out of the car and run away from the sound of his breathing. She found a handkerchief in her bag, wiped her eyes, turned away and blew her nose. Fletcher pretended not to notice but was fully aware of her agitation. His blood ran faster, his pulse raced, the glow of power sent up his blood pressure. Fletcher Strode had become a man again. Others waited and feared his decisions.

His daughter eyed him timidly.

"Let me think about it." He had the voice of authority.

"You will, Daddy!" The girl was ecstatic at not having been rejected.

He switched on the motor, thrust his foot hard upon the gas pedal. The car raced up the hill like a creature freed from bondage, moving with swift and certain power.

"DON'T MOVE. STAY just as you are. I want to enjoy this pretty picture," Don said.

In spite of the warning, Elaine raised her head. Sunlight threw upon her face varied patterns of tree and shadow and the latticework of the pavilion. "Cindy went off to play golf with Fletcher. They're probably staying out for lunch so I'm enjoying the working girl's special." She had brought a sandwich, a glass of milk, and a book to the wicker table. "How'd it go? Did you meet Mr. Carter the First?"

"What a character!"

"Any luck?"

"I'm thinking over the offer." Don's sly wink could be interpreted in a number of ways.

"What about money? Will they pay you well?"

"I could do with more, but it's a hell of a lot better than what that bastard in personnel offered me last month." Don did not wish to admit that once again he had seen none of the Carters but only that bastard in the personnel office, that he had been told once more that there was a fair sort of job open, that several applicants were being considered and that Don's original application would be reviewed. All the bastard had offered was another appointment for Monday. Adding a bonus to the lie, "It was a tense hour with the tycoon," he said. "I could use a drink."

"Have you had lunch?"

Elaine enjoyed serving lunch to a young man with a hearty appetite. Don enjoyed eating with her in the charming pavilion. While he told her about the house, he watched her slender hands with the coffeepot and cream pitcher. His perverse mind caught glimpses of her, rather than Cindy, in the rooms and upon the windswept decks of the new house. Elaine had many talents that his wife lacked, chief among them the ability to listen. She asked for a cigarette. He held his lighter to it long after it had caught fire. Elaine backed away from the small flame.

"Sorry." Don moved off, too, stiffening slightly. "I was so busy admiring you that I didn't notice."

"Don't let your admiration set me on fire."

"I wish it could!"

Both laughed away the tasteless compliment. Elaine shifted her chair so that she was not facing him directly. Presently he moved around to see her better. Never, during his days as a lawyer, had Donald Hustings pleaded with greater brilliance. Elaine's attention excited him. Every word was cogent, every pause had meaning.

Elaine readily understood what he wanted of her. "Do you honestly think I can get Fletcher to help you?"

"Who else has such influence with him? He worships you like a goddess."

Her light died out. The lovely head drooped on the long stem of her neck.

"Please try, Elaine. I know he'll listen to you. God!" Don's fist struck the table with such force that cups leaped and saucers rattled. "A man needs a home of his own. Starting out the way I am, in a new field. A house is security. Especially out here in the West, if you don't own your home you're just dirt. White trash."

Though not quite honest, Don was completely sincere. Self-interest is a strong hypnotic. His heart was set upon possession of the house which, he believed with superstitious ardor, would finally turn his luck. No matter how heavily mortgaged, the property would be recorded in his name, adding the luster and solidity demanded of a young executive.

His urgency restored Elaine. She saw the eager spaniel eyes, the mouth more than ever sculpted by a boyish pout, the tremor of his hands. She could not remain indifferent to the tension, the anguish, and the frankness. "I'll try but I can't promise a lot. Fletcher makes his own decisions. He's a very positive person."

"But you'll try? Talk to him tonight."

"It depends upon his mood."

"I've got to have the first thousand on Monday. Otherwise we may lose the house. Bargains like that don't wait."

A bee flew between them, buzzing impudently over the dish of sweets. Elaine brushed at the air. Don jerked her arm away. "You'll get stung if you're not careful. Promise to help me, Elaine."

"I want to, but I can't argue with Fletcher. He's nervous lately and," she had become agitated and looked at the bee, studied the polish on her fingernails, toyed with the sugar tongs, "unhappy. He's very unhappy."

"You coddle him too much. He treats you brutally sometimes."

"Worshiping me like a goddess?"

"I often wonder why you put up with his tantrums."

"I love him." Defiantly, "I do," she declared. The bee flew around the pavilion, humming relentlessly. "Don't look at me so skeptically, Don. Probably Cindy and her mother have told wild tales about me, that I set a trap and caught Fletcher because he was rich. But I loved him. He was so wonderful."

"And so rich."

"Why must people always talk about money? I knew other rich men. Fletch was terrific." Memory kindled delight. She could no longer sit quiet behind the coffee cups, but had to get up and move around restlessly like the bee. "You can't imagine the man he was. So alive!" She wrapped her arms about her body, ecstatically. "I've never known anyone with such a capacity for living. Just sheer living. He enjoyed everything. Crazy!" She danced around the table with small springing steps that showed the way she had moved in that magic spring when she and Fletcher Strode became lovers. "How we'd laugh, you could hear him miles away, he was so hearty. His voice . . . " A curtain fell over the show of lost rapture. "Fletch had a very loud voice."

"And that made you forget that he was rich?"

"No. I don't want to lie. I like money. Perhaps without it Fletcher wouldn't have seemed so glamorous to me. But he wouldn't have been the same person either, there wouldn't have been such careless rapture. Money's wonderful not to think about. I love not counting the cost of groceries, I love charge accounts and expensive restaurants and beautiful clothes and . . . " She paused and thought about the present, laughed, and shrugged a shoulder to show the futility of her tastes. "Not that I have any use for them now. What good are pretty clothes if you never go anywhere?" The dancing mood was over. "It's wicked of me to talk like that. He's so desperately unhappy."

Don could not disagree. "It's tough. I feel sorry for him just the same."

"He wants to die."

There! At last she had said it. Fear, long contained, had escaped by its own force. Reality was less real than her imaginary conversations with Ralph Julian. Perhaps it was better this way; Don was a member of the family.

Fletcher's son-in-law was not shaken. "Wants to die? What makes you think so?"

Elaine sought protection in the pavilion's shadiest corner. "No. No, he hasn't actually threatened, but he thinks about it all the time."

"How do you know? He must have said something to give you that idea. Lots of people think about suicide, and some even talk about it. But they don't do anything so final." Don seemed to think the common formula would soothe her.

"Once," Elaine faltered and thought carefully of what she meant to say, "we saw one of those hysterical shows about mercy killing. Euthanasia, they say on TV, very fancy. The actor smothered his wife with a pillow. Like Othello." She looked through the lattice as though the drama were being played among the autumn flowers. "She was dying anyway, the wife. In ghastly pain. And the husband smothered her."

Don led her back to the long chair, drew his own chair closer, held her hand. "What did he say?"

"He asked if I had the courage."

"He was just talking. Probably didn't mean it."

Elaine shook her head. It had ceased to matter that she had told her secret to the wrong man. Speech solidified the horror. All of a sudden, remembering another time when Fletcher had talked about his death, she began, "One day last spring he said . . . " but could not go on. Right here in the pavilion while she lay upon this very chair and watched the quail; and she had turned away her flaming face as now she turned to hide herself from Don. Bees had been flying around the garden on that day, too. In the buzzing she heard echoes of the mangled voice: *You wish I was dead.*

Don held out a lighted cigarette. "Take it easy, dear. There's probably nothing to it. Probably it's all in your imagination."

Elaine shrank from his cigarette. Ridiculous, she had cried at Fletcher's recognition of a forbidden dream. In the daytime she tried never to think of freedom, but at night she sometimes woke abruptly and was ashamed because her dream had promised escape. Now that she had begun, she had to go on talking. "Sometimes at night, I'm frightened. I wake up . . . and go into his room to hear him breathing. Almost," she produced a shamed trill of laughter, "every night. It isn't only because I dream. I go before I let myself fall asleep. I think it will keep me from dreaming."

From a distance she heard Don beg her not to worry, say that she was building a mountain range out of a nonexistent molehill. It was easy enough for him, who had not been with Fletcher in the worst moods, to say that a man of that nature would never destroy himself.

"But if he should!"

"He wouldn't. He's too fond of himself."

This offended Elaine. Accustomed to protecting her husband, she kept up the habit when he was not present and in need of protection. "You don't know him at all. What you see today isn't the real Fletcher. Believe me. He's terribly sick, he's in misery. He doesn't like living, he's stopped caring about anything." She was shaken by her own vehemence, appalled at having shown passions that a decent soul would hide under layers of composure. The confession had not relieved her. And Don continued his arguments, offering reassurance like flowers in a sickroom.

They heard wheels on the driveway. "He's back," and Elaine was off to welcome her husband.

It was not Fletcher's silvercloud Lincoln but a white truck as antiseptic and glittering as an ambulance. A lanky Negro boy opened the back and brought out a bundle of clothes. "Top Drawer Cleaners, how you today, miss?" Like all other delivery men, he stopped for a chat with a friendly customer.

When the boy had gone, Don carried the bundle of clothes into Fletcher's room. Elaine opened the closet door. "Wait, let me make room." She cleared a space upon the pole and stood with her back to the door while Don brushed past. He kissed her. It was swift and shocking. Between them like a shield he held the bundle, plastic covers rustling delicately over Fletcher's suits.

"You're so damned lovely."

She tried to edge away. Don pressed her against the door. They did not hear the car stop nor the closing of doors. Cindy's voice came to them from the corridor. Elaine moved off like a jet. The bundle of clothes slid to the floor.

Fletcher came in.

"We're putting away your things from the cleaner's."

"Elaine was showing me where to hang them."

It would have been wiser not to offer excuses. Had there been anything between them, they would not have chosen Fletcher's bedroom nor been caught with a bundle of suits in plastic bags. "Your cashmere jacket," she said, "came back at last. I hope they got the oil stain out." As far as Don was concerned she had no cause for guilt, but the general burden was so heavy that the interrupted kiss, which she had tried to repel, added to the weight on her conscience.

Fletcher seemed to have noticed nothing unusual in their behavior. He helped pick up the fallen clothes. Later he invited them to the movies, then took them to a nightclub. Don had a way with headwaiters so that he managed, without reservations at the most popular place in town, to have Fletcher Strode treated as a frequent and desirable patron.

It turned out to be Don's lucky night. Had he gone to the men's room three minutes earlier or later, he would not have bumped into that important executive who, weeks before, had kept him waiting an hour for a five-minute interview, had promised another appointment and had never been heard from again. "Don't I know you?" Mr. Heatherington had asked. With exceptional tact Don had reminded him of the circumstances. Jocund and flushed, Heathington had offered profuse apology while Don had shown understanding of a position so demanding that a man could not remember his promises.

Mr. Heatherington invited Don to drink with him at the bar.

"To talk business, boy," he said with a nod toward the table where Mrs. Heatherington was entertaining cousins from the Middle West.

It certainly did not hurt Don Hustings to be seen in public with an executive arm around his shoulders. "What have you been doing with yourself lately?" the tycoon asked.

"I've decided to stay out here. Just bought a house."

"Fine, boy. Great. Where is it?"

"At the shore. In that new development below Newport Beach."

Mr. Heatherington approved. The area, he said, was bound to boom. And what was the young man doing with himself, business-wise? Don answered that he had been up to his ears in work. "Looking after my father-in-law's affairs. Fletcher Strode, you know, the man who promoted that Ark-well-BDU merger in New York. And Zeno, Incorporated, he put that on the map, too." Heatherington was impressed. There had been more revelations about Fletcher Strode's business and regretful mention of his illness and retirement. "But Dad's anxious to become active again. If he could find the right thing, of course." There was, Don hinted, far more than capital to be invested—although that was considerable, too—since it was vital that Fletcher Strode's business genius be utilized. Heatherington, drinking with zest, had encouraged Don to go on, and Don had implied, without making too much of it, that he acted as the voice of his afflicted father-in-law. Heatherington let drop word of a proposition that might catch Fletcher Strode's fancy. He would have liked to meet Don's father-in-law, but Don explained that a hasty, unprepared meeting would be the worst way of approaching the supersensitive man. "It might be more practical to give me the details first. How soon can we meet and talk it over, sir?"

"Free for lunch tomorrow?" asked Heatherington and signaled the bartender for another round of doubles.

"I'll make it my business."

Heatherington felt obliged to return to his wife's relations. Don went back to the table in high spirits. They were all in a good mood, the two girls reflecting Fletcher's pleasure. As a big spender he had always enjoyed privilege and in this nightclub he felt himself a man of importance again. In a place where loud music made conversation impossible, it was not necessary to talk. Don ordered food and drinks for the party, and although he hovered a bit too eagerly, Fletcher was pleased with the obeisance. Mr. Strode was functioning again, making decisions, exerting power over people who depended upon his favors. And his son-in-law was truly his mouthpiece.

6 "WE'RE GOING TO GET THAT MONEY FROM YOUR father," Don told Cindy the next morning. He had to shout because the radio was on at full volume.

"How do you know?" Awakened by progressive jazz, Cindy was sullen. "He said he'd think it over, he didn't promise definitely."

"I feel it in my bones." Don was at that exalted peak of optimism touched by people who believe in omens. "Elaine's on our side. Did you notice the way she danced with him last night? That means influence. What do you think I should wear, a suit or slacks and jacket?" For the moment his mood was shadowed by the necessity of decision. In New York he would instinctively have chosen the right outfit for a conference with a man of Heatherington's status. Out here in California there was a deplorable negligence in dress. Businessmen in downtown Los Angeles dressed conservatively, but Heatherington Industries was in one of those new broiling San Fernando Valley communities where people considered good tailoring Eastern and snobbish.

"You ought to know yourself," Cindy muttered sleepily.

He chose dark flannels and a worsted jacket that no one could criticize. "Which tie?" There was no answer. Cindy had gone back to sleep. After a careful search of his ample collection, Don wondered whether a striped guard's tie would make a better impression on Heatherington than a gray Countess Mara with a small blue crest. "Which would you choose?" he asked Elaine who was frying bacon in the kitchen.

"Both are very handsome."

"You're a big help."

"The stripes are more dashing."

"You think that's the right note to strike?"

Elaine answered seriously that the Countess Mara was a bit too subtle for the man she had seen with Don at the bar. As soon as the choice has been made, Don felt better. "Things are going my way, love. Today is definitely a turning point in the life of Donald Morton Hustings." He caught Elaine between the stove and refrigerator, kissed her lightly.

"Please, Don."

"It's only a family kiss. I like you better than my other mother-in-law." He sprang away when they heard Fletcher's step in the hall.

During breakfast Don talked airily of Mr. Heatherington's plans for expansion of his already vast interests, but carefully avoided mentioning the scheme to include Fletcher Strode in the business. The morning passed slowly. Don did not want to arrive too early, but planned to show that promptness was his habit. Exactly one and one-half minutes after the time set for the date, he walked into Mr. Heatherington's anteroom where, after being asked politely if he minded waiting, he spent exactly fifty-four minutes looking unruffled and leafing through *Time*, *Newsweek*, and *U.S. News and World Report*. At last Mr. Heatherington appeared, apologized for the delay, and asked if Don was hungry.

Don had expected to be taken to the best restaurant in the vicinity, if not to some Valley country club. Instead he was given an unforgivable meal at the company cafeteria where his host, to show a democratic spirit, ate among his employees in a cubicle only partially screened from the mob. There were constant interruptions by department managers, secretaries, third-class executives, all with excuses to make themselves important. If Don were Mr. Heatherington's executive assistant, he would make it his business to shield the boss from such intrusions.

"How much does your father-in-law want to invest?"

Don had been thinking in big terms about a deal which would

require many conferences before a figure was mentioned. At today's meeting he had thought they would have a preliminary talk about further negotiations. Mr. Heatherington pressed for precise figures. His judgment no longer diluted by alcohol, he studied Don warily.

Don floundered through, hinted grandly that there would soon be a change in his status and that he would be in complete charge of Fletcher Strode's affairs. To answer specifically about his father-in-law's assets was not at this time appropriate. Heatherington stubbornly refused to understand. The session ended with a cool handshake and Don's promise to give Mr. Heatherington a ring when Mr. Strode's decision was final.

At home he was subjected to another inquisition. How had it gone with Heatherington? "Fine, just fine," Don said, but without jauntiness.

"Didn't he give you the job?" asked Cindy.

"We're going to have further talks."

Elaine smiled sympathetically, and Fletcher raised skeptical eyebrows.

"That agent called about the house again," Cindy said.

Don had phoned the agent to say that the appointment had to be postponed on account of his important conference with J.J. Heatherington. He hoped, he had said, to get away in time to finalize the deal on the house. Cindy reported that the agent had asked her to remind her husband that the banks were open until six o'clock on Fridays, and that he would be free whenever Don could meet him and the owner.

"Call him back and say I've been kept out at the plant with J.J. And say we'll meet him at the bank on Monday morning," Don instructed. "No, don't say morning. In the morning Carter's man wants to see me." It all sounded very important and Don cast a speculative glance at Fletcher.

"Which of those big jobs are you going to accept?" grunted the offensive voice.

Don showed proper humility. "Whichever one is definitely offered to me first, sir."

This was the start of a hellish weekend. Although the banks

were closed until Monday, Cindy was sure that someone with a pocketful of money would buy the house. They waited feverishly for Fletcher to announce his decision. He entertained himself with their impatience. As long as he kept them waiting his power was secure. So much time had passed since people awaited the word of Fletcher Strode that he could not help but relish this small satisfaction.

Sunday was endless. At the breakfast table, beside the pool, over the cocktails Don mixed before lunch, during the meal and afterward, while Cindy, with a rush of domesticity, helped Elaine stack the dishes, and Don read the paper with one eye and watched Fletcher with the other, tension increased. The house reflected their mood: walls echoed whispers, electric appliances clattered expectantly, buttons waited to be pushed, plugs to be inserted, lights to flash. The air was heavy with the metallic odor of an approaching storm. No thunder boomed, no lightning split the sky, no wind brought relief. The sense of storm was there, and the brooding heat tightened every nerve.

It was late afternoon when Don, itching with controlled irritation, said, "I wonder, sir, if you've thought about that matter Cindy mentioned to you the other day."

Cindy lay sunning beside the pool. Taut fingers clutched the mat. She tried to woo her father with a childish smile.

"What matter?" croaked the voice.

"The house, sir. You told Cindy you'd think about it."

Fletcher was aware of the wary starts and nervous glances. In his active days he had watched buyers and sellers await his decisions, had kept them waiting until their fears swelled his profits. Such tactics had not seemed cruel to a practical businessman; they had merely proved the victor stronger than the vanquished. Now, with an air of unconcern, he watched a swarm of ants gather about a pool of spilled lemonade.

"Please, Daddy."

The voice, which seemed not to issue from the man but from a machine hidden in the shrubbery, announced, "I don't approve at all. You can't afford it."

"Then you won't help us?" Don tried to maintain the blandness of an accomplished executive.

"That's not what I said."

The leaves of the olive tree moved feebly. "Feel, a breeze," cried Elaine. The light wind drew another breath and died. Heat, victorious, increased its pressure.

They waited again. Fletcher spilled a bit of lemonade upon the ground, creating a second sugary pond for the excited ants. "Damn little fools," he croaked and tipped his glass again. A few ants drowned in the rain of nectar.

"Oh, Fletch, for heaven's sakes, tell them something," urged Elaine. "Say yes or no."

"Why are you so interested?"

Rasping, uninflected tones struck nervous ears with terror. Fletcher was not angry, but merely playing for time to keep hold of his precious power.

"It means so much to them, and so little to you." Elaine had not kept her promise to plead with Fletcher for the loan. Since the morning he had played golf and lunched with Cindy, he had, in spite of the dry heat and discomfort, been in a mood too rare to be destroyed by argument. She had adored him swaggering about as in the old days, sure of himself and powerful.

Don looked at her plaintively. Cindy sat up at attention. They watched Fletcher like suppliants before an altar. Still he kept them waiting. With decision, his game of power would be over. "Need a little more time to think about it."

"But, Daddy, we might lose the house. People always buy places on Sunday. We've got to give them some money tomorrow morning."

Don disapproved the whining tone. He tried to signal Cindy to quit begging. Fletcher scowled and moved his chair out of the glare. Acutely uncomfortable, Don proposed to Cindy that they dress and leave. They had, he said, promised to look in on some friends. "We won't be back for supper, Elaine. Perhaps you'll give us your decision tonight, sir."

FLETCHER AND ELAINE were left with the rest of the afternoon on their hands. They read the Sunday paper, dozed, got up and walked lethargically around the garden, returned to their chairs like animals trained to repetitive action. This lazy peace would have been disturbed by nothing more than the rising wind if Elaine had not forced herself to plead for Don.

She interrupted a daydream. The small dose of power had intoxicated Fletcher so that at last he permitted himself the luxury of illusion. *I am going back into business.* Here in California glittering opportunities awaited a man of Fletcher Strode's assets, experience, and cunning. As in the past he would buy moribund factories and shops, spend money in restoring them, profit through tax deductions, and sell gainfully.

"Only five thousand dollars," Elaine argued. "It's impractical for them, of course, but it could change their lives. Don needs an incentive."

The dream exploded. He returned to the present, looked down upon himself, saw the muscular arms, the powerful thighs of a useless man. The wind ruffled olive and live oak leaves. Insolent birds mocked human vanity. "Why are you so worried about Don?"

"Why, Fletch, he's Cindy's husband."

The answer had been too vehement.

"Is he your lover?"

The question sprang from sultry depths. Fletcher had seen them through the pantry window as they whispered over a tray of soft drinks; seen them in the pool, young bodies side by side; yesterday he had surprised them in his bedroom. Guilty looks had not gone unnoticed. Elaine always laughed at Don's jokes, admired his ties, offered solace when he doubted himself. Visions spun dizzily, lips locked, arms entwined, loins and bellies enjoyed intimacy. His own bed! The taste of sickness filled Fletcher's mouth, blood beat in his brain.

He barely heard Elaine's shocked responses. "Your son-in-law? Cindy's husband? Do you think I'd let him make love to me?"

The emphasis "Do you think I'd let *him* make love to me?"

scorned incest but condoned infidelity. She had betrayed herself innocently. Locked and naked bodies persisted in their ardors, but Fletcher saw them through a haze. The man's face was unclear.

Elaine fled. In her bedroom he found her standing motionless with drooping shoulders as though she were lost in a strange forest. The walls of her room were green, the curtains pale cream with a design of fruit and flowers, lutes and ribbons. She saw him but remained as motionless as a girl in a painting, big-eyed and vulnerable. He recognized heartbreaking beauty but was shaken by the fear that he was no longer the sole owner.

He seized her shoulders. "Have you cheated on me?"

The shoulders twisted away. As though this question were not worth an answer, she went about the business of selecting an outfit—blue trousers, a plaid blouse. Then the plaid did not please her and she chose stripes.

"Have you been unfaithful?"

On the hill an auto horn, some special imported siren, squawked impatiently, its distortion echo and mockery of Fletcher's voice. Anger mounted.

"Answer me, Elaine. I want the truth."

"Not with Don."

"With someone else?" He seized her wrists and jerked her toward him. "Look at me. Have you a lover?"

"Please, Fletch, you're hurting me."

She did not pull her wrists away, nor did he relax the pressure. So that she would not have to see his face she looked down at her long, pale feet. Knowing herself the betrayer, she felt betrayed, lost, and forlorn as a child. In her father's apartment on Morningside Drive where she had grown up among all the books and copies of famous paintings and omniscient grown people, the blackest sin had been untruth. *Be honest, child, be penitent, take your punishment.*

"Just once," she said.

Fletcher dropped her wrists, took a short step backward, clutched at a chair. The ground had dissolved under his feet. For all of his visions and suspicion, he had never thought . . .

no, no, impossible . . . Elaine! . . . the pure, the lovable . . . he could not, would not, believe it.

"Just once," she said again, humbly. "No more. And I never will again. Never!"

He had thought about it so much that revelation, the truth of the dream, numbed him. Her infidelity had been his own, exclusive, shaped by his creative mind, his secret work of art. All of those writhing bodies, naked limbs, shimmering breasts had been his indulgence, a collection of images conceived for the protection of his ego. Shaping and arranging them, giving life to monstrous visions, enduring self-made torments, he had been able to believe them untrue. Elaine's confession destroyed all of this. Truth was a shock to his ego. The dream was shattered, the dreamer forced to acknowledge creative forces outside of himself.

Over and over, looking down at her long toes, she repeated that it had not happened more than once, that she was sick with remorse, that never, never, never again would she allow the man to touch her. Fletcher tried for the sake of self-protection to reshape a vision, to see her and the man (whom she kept insisting was not Don) naked and together. The visions would not come alive. Fletcher's imagination, too, was impotent.

Her rueful voice pursued him down the corridor. He slammed his bedroom door behind him, slapped on trousers and a shirt, hurried to the garage, backed his car toward the road with the motor roaring like the voice of vengeance. He drove down the hill swiftly and without thought of destination.

"Forgive me," Elaine had begged, and "Please," and "Never again, believe me," before she had known he was gone. She had taken a few timid steps toward his bedroom, but when the knob turned, she had fled back to her room and closed her door. She had listened to the sound of the motor, watched the car back out of the driveway recklessly. His face came back to her in all of its sadness, and she knew that the truth had been a tragic mistake.

DON AND CINDY came back to the house reluctantly. Their friends had given them tea and cakes, then cocktails, olives, nuts, bits of cheese, and smoked meats on salted crackers, but had not invited them to stay for supper. They drove around aimlessly for a time and then went to the movies. Torn by hope and, at the same time, afraid to hear that Elaine had not been successful in pleading for the loan, they drove home slowly.

The house was dark. It was not much after ten o'clock, too early for everyone to be in bed. Perhaps Fletcher and Elaine had gone out to eat and see a picture, which, Don observed, was a good sign. Cindy's father never went anywhere unless he was in a generous and confident mood. Upon this assumption Don built a dazzling structure; owned the house, landed the job with Carter Consolidated, achieved promotion, became a member of the executive elite.

The doors were not locked. This was unusual. Cindy's father always checked the doors and windows before he left the house. "Still, if he took her out to dinner he must be feeling pretty good," reflected Don to reassure himself.

"Well, I'm not going to cook," announced Cindy and went to the refrigerator in search of something that could be eaten between slices of bread. They were eating when Elaine came into the kitchen. Her feet were bare, her hair untidy, her eyes moist. She said she had gone to bed with a wretched headache.

"Where's Daddy?"

"He went out."

"Not alone?"

"He didn't want to disturb me." The lie stood out like a fresh bruise. Elaine did not mind small social fibs. In the apartment on Morningside Drive these had not been considered sinful.

"Did you talk to him?"

"It didn't do much good."

"Why not? Did he refuse?"

"We got off the subject."

Don sensed evasion. Bright hopes faded. He saw his future as an unending hell of debt, of seedy jobs alternating with pitiful months of unemployment in which they would struggle to get along on his wife's income. Unpaid bills and unending worry had been the warp of his boyhood, stinginess and shame its woof. It was the sort of life he had hoped to avoid. Already he sensed in Cindy the middle-class woman's contempt for a husband who could not support her in style.

"We'll lose the house," she whimpered.

The easy assumption of failure angered Don. "Don't be so sure."

"But if we can't give them a thousand dollars tomorrow?"

He had to assert himself. "Don't you trust me to raise that kind of money?" He drank ginger ale in condescending sips.

"How?"

"Just leave it to me," he said haughtily.

Elaine poured a glass of milk but could not drink it. She told them her headache was worse and went off to bed.

"They must have had a terrible fight," Cindy said, not unhappily.

"Don't smirk. It may be the end for us. We might have to go back to New York."

"I thought you could raise that money so easily."

Don tried to recover bravado with lame argument. Cindy answered with the cruel logic of a child. They went on and on until fatigue sent them to their bedroom. Neither could sleep. From the peak of hope Don had sunk to the lowest pit of gloom. In every recollection of the day he found evil omens, and could see nothing ahead but a dismal repetition of his loathed boyhood.

Presently Cindy's voice drifted through the dark. "I wonder how much Daddy's really worth."

"What difference does it make? He's not going to let go of a nickel."

"You think he will leave it all to her?"

"Who knows?"

"She's just sitting and waiting. Anyone can see through that devotion act. Even Daddy, I think. Did you notice, Donnie? They're not nearly so lovey-dovey anymore."

Don had at last grown drowsy. He did not bother to speak. Cindy turned over in bed and gave herself to deeper thought. "At least I'm going to get a hundred thousand dollars. That's the very least."

Immediately Don was wide awake. "How do you know?"

"Insurance for me. He took out the policy when they got the divorce. A hundred thousand dollars to his daughter, Cynthia Kathryn." She clapped her hands and giggled with delight.

"You never told me."

"I didn't know it was that much. Mom wrote it in a letter."

"She did! When?"

"Just after we got here."

"Why didn't you tell me?"

"Mom said I shouldn't. She said Daddy wouldn't like you knowing."

The storm came closer. Wind rattled the Venetian blinds. Don got up to close the windows. "What difference does it make to me? *Daddy*," he mimicked her tone, "will probably live another thirty years."

"Mom was sure the cancer would come back," sighed Cindy. "She's surprised he's lived this long."

Don returned to his bed. "What's the use of thinking about it? Let's try to sleep." He was no longer drowsy.

Once more Cindy gave herself to thought. "What good's his life to him? He's living like a dead man. And all that money in the banks and stocks and stuff. When people could really enjoy it!"

Don was asleep in his own speculations. He made a noise that sounded like a snore. "All right, if you're not interested in our future," Cindy said and turned her back.

Outside, the wind howled in triumphant conquest over heat and fog. Trees were bent, flowers swept down. In her dark room Elaine listened for the sound of a car. The illuminated hands of the bedside clock dragged as though possessed of a human and malevolent will. She had no real cause for fear, but could not resist the ache for punishment. She knew that Fletcher had at last committed the act, smashed the car against a wall, plunged over a cliff, dived into the sea. She had sent him to his death. If he had not acted voluntarily, hurt and rage had blinded him to danger; the will to death had driven him involuntarily into a fatal collision. She waited for the phone to ring, sirens to sound, his broken body to be delivered on a stretcher.

The wind shrieked and died. In the hall Elaine heard heavy footsteps. She ran to her door, said timidly, "You're back?"

He nodded and walked past to his own bedroom.

"Good night," she called after him.

A rumble acknowledged her existence.

7
WHEN FLETCHER WOKE THE NEXT MORNING HIS head was clear, his temper even. His was not at all the mood of a man who has gone through a crisis. Incidents of the previous day returned in sharp focus: his blindly raging departure, horns bleating on the clogged highway, the sudden wind, an angry ocean, bright flags of bathing suits moving on the beach, lithe boys riding the waves; a world beyond his lonely pride. He had stood upon a bluff and watched the ocean hurl itself in senseless fury against the rocks. Sea birds had whirled above him in great arcs, dived into the water, rode back to shore like surf boys upon the foam. The air had a tang both sweet and salty that brought back pleasing memories of Coney Island, where he had first smelled the sea. Clouds hung low but the sun, fallen behind the western horizon, had tinted the sea with the gray-blue and rose-mauve of a dove's breast. The ocean took on a purple hue.

The colors of earth had never concerned Fletcher. His mind had always been fixed upon more immediate and personal matters. Were these, the wind and salt, changing colors, a charge of vitality, and the swift running of blood enough to keep a man alive? Five steps on the lonely bluff and it would all have been over. They would have found a body waterlogged and torn among the rocks.

The sky darkened, clouds turned leaden-blue, spume glowed white at the ocean's border. Fletcher had no wish to take the five steps. Men will themselves to death when the future holds no hope. For the first time since he had lost his voice, Fletcher's life promised power and drama. His circle was small, limited to three dependents, but his decision and activities could shape their future lives.

After a long drive in the windy night he came home, still unsure of his strategy with Elaine. She was not the first wife who had committed infidelity nor was he the world's first cuckold. He had lived for almost three years without a larynx. Compared with this, the loss of his so-called honor was a small thing. But he could not show that he condoned the sin by greeting her with open arms. A faithless wife deserved a sleepless night.

On the table beside his bed Elaine had left the usual two sleeping pills. In the morning they still lay there, and his first act was to add them to the hoard in the vial he kept hidden in the riding boot. The house was very quiet. Elaine had not stirred herself to make his breakfast. He would show her that he could get along very well without her. He made a pot of coffee, toasted bread, cut a melon, fried two eggs. His hunger was not appeased, and he fried a third egg. In the morning paper he read one paragraph about foreign loans, half a column about abandoned twins, a caption under the picture of a squirrel mother who had adopted an orphaned baby mouse, an editorial on the threat of Communism, the revelations of a columnist critical of the administration, and the meditations of a columnist who approved. Over a garish two-page advertisement of startling price cuts on electric appliances, he saw Elaine come into the kitchen.

They faced each other for a long moment. Elaine did not look well. Her ivory flesh had yellowed like meerschaum, her eyes were sunk into muddy pools. He wished her a good morning.

"Good morning. Did you sleep well?" She was cool in asking a question which had been the day's vital beginning since the only purpose of Fletcher's days had become the preparation for his night's slumber. He answered with a grunt. It would not do to let her know he had enjoyed a good night's rest.

"I had an awful night," she said; "didn't get to sleep until almost four o'clock. That's why I'm late. Oh, Fletch, you had to get your own breakfast. I'm so sorry."

She had said she was sorry when she confessed infidelity. Fletcher did not mention this. Until he had decided how to act toward her, the subject was better untouched. It shocked him to discover that he was moved by her wan look. The eloquent eyes showed the need of consolation. He had only to mention forgiveness to get his gay and loving girl back again.

"Would you like to go someplace today, Fletch? Dorine's coming."

The cleaning woman drove up in an ancient Cadillac. She was a lean, lively little creature with enormous energy and an overflowing heart. Among her numerous relations, friends, and employers she had known many fascinating maladies but none to equal poor Mr. Strode's affliction. She always spoke to him in a loud, compassionate voice as though he were deaf. Before she reached the kitchen door he had retreated to his den.

At his desk his first act each day was to turn the page of his desk calendar. Each page was divided into hours, every hour into fifteen-minute spaces that awaited notations of a busy man's appointments. The sterility of these spaces irritated Fletcher but he could not throw away the calendar which, bound in real leather stamped with his name, was the annual gift of his insurance agent. Today, importantly, two items appeared. The first reminded him to instruct his New York broker to report on the advisability of selling a thousand shares of a certain stock, which would bring him a handsome profit, enough to cover the down payment on that house Don and Cindy wanted so badly.

He heard their voices in the kitchen. How happy they would be if he summoned them to say that he had decided to let them have the money. He hesitated, not sure that he wanted to abet the foolhardy venture. It was not that he minded losing the sum so much as the prudence of a lender who could see nothing ahead but further indebtedness. His eyes were drawn to the picture of Cindy as a little girl. The face was tender, trusting, and vulnerable. He remembered the soapy smell of her youthful kisses. If only that husband of hers were not so smooth and lordly, so firm in his belief that the world owed him a living. At Don's age Fletcher Strode had supported a family and fought in a war. How would this soft generation sustain itself during a depression?

Cindy and Don went to the garage and got into the Jaguar. There was still time to summon them with the news that he would write a check for the thousand that would put the house in escrow, and when that was completed, let them have another four thousand. Why not? He could, if he wished, finance the deal, keep his daughter's husband from asking help of Nan Burke's father.

He saw them go off in the Jaguar. This gave him more time to consider the decision. For a few more hours his power was secure. He felt strong and independent, a man who operated with firmness and decision. Instead of asking Elaine to talk on the long-distance telephone to his broker, he wrote out a long telegram, decided to drive down to the Western Union office with it. On the way out he passed her in the hall and slapped her seat indulgently.

Her spirits rose. "Mr. Strode's in an awfully good mood this morning," she told the cleaning woman. "He ate an enormous breakfast."

"Let's hope it lasts. With the afflicted you can never be sure." While they cleaned Fletcher's closet, Dorine told Mrs. Strode about a lady she had worked for on alternate Thursdays. "Her son had a mental condition. Sometimes he was as gentle as a lamb, butter wouldn't melt in his mouth. But you never could tell. He'd get those whims. Like throwing eggs at the cat."

"Strictly fresh, I hope."

"It's nothing to laugh about, Mrs. Strode. The poor lady's heart was broken. He outlived her. What's this?" Something rattled in Mr. Strode's riding boot. Dorine pulled out the bottle of bright-colored pills.

Elaine had often blamed nervous imagination for her caution with the sleeping pills. Without asking its cause, Fletcher had agreed to her scheme of doling out two a night. Except on that spring afternoon when he had accused her of wishing that he was dead, there had been no mention of the subject. Now, thrusting out her hand for the vial, her fear took body.

"Is he addicted?" whispered Dorine.

"Please give me that."

"We had a neighbor once on West Adams, her niece used to hide stuff in her lipstick case. Pretty as a picture, too. You wouldn't believe it."

Elaine pressed the vial deep into her pocket. "Please don't talk about it, Dorine. Ever."

"They always hide it. Won't Mr. Strode be mad when he finds it gone?"

"They're only sleeping pills," Elaine said irritably.

"People kill themselves with 'em. Take that movie actress. That's why I won't work for movie people. You never know what you'll find in the morning."

Elaine retreated to her bedroom. She clutched the small bottle protectively as though someone threatened to take it away. What would Fletcher do when he discovered the pills gone from their hiding place? She counted them and realized with what self-control he must have resisted their use on sleepless nights. When she heard the car enter the driveway, she tightened all over as though she had been discovered in sin.

Feltcher was in a buoyant mood. "What have we got for lunch?"

He ate with good appetite. Cindy and Don had not come back, and it seemed natural for Fletcher and Elaine to enjoy a quiet meal on the terrace. A daring blue jay stole crumbs from Fletcher's plate.

"You know you're seeing Dr. Gentian this afternoon."

Fletcher nodded. This was the second important item on his calendar page. Elaine was pleased when she saw him drive off to keep the appointment. A man contemplating suicide would not suffer the pain and ignominy, the hammering and probing, the useless imprisonment, of the dentist's chair. A visit to the dentist is a gesture toward life. The bottle of sleeping pills made a bulge in the pocket of Elaine's tight trousers. She had kept them there because she could not decide what to do with them.

She decided to hide them in the kitchen cupboard, but Dorine was there frying herself a hamburger. At the bookshelves, looking over her shoulder to be sure she was not observed, Elaine thrust the vial behind her father's *Origin of the Species* in Italian. She felt as guilty as if she were involved in crime.

DR. GENTIAN HAD good news. His next patient had canceled, and he could give Mr. Strode an extra half hour. He drilled and talked, filled and talked, discussed with zest the city's most recent murder. The case interested Dr. Gentian because the victim was a dentist. Gagged and forced to listen, Fletcher sympathized with the assassin. "Am I hurting you?" asked the dentist. Without the slightest notice of Fletcher's grunt of assent, he went right on with his devilish work, adding pressure to the pointed instrument piercing his victim's gums. "Take it easy, Mr. Strode. Won't be long now."

Only longer than a lifetime. The ordeal became doubly excruciating because Fletcher suddenly remembered that he had left his diary exposed. He had been pondering over an entry when Elaine called him to lunch. She had had to shout for him three times, rather sharply, because she had cooked his favorite cheese soufflé, which could not be left standing. It had been careless of him to leave the diary exposed while he ate, unforgivable to have rushed off without locking it away. Oh, God, if she should find it!

"I'm not hurting you," Dr. Gentian said reproachfully.

Fletcher shook his head. He was all nerves and uncertainty. The telephone rang. The nurse hurried to the anteroom and came back to say that Mr. Strode's daughter had called to say she was shopping in the neighborhood and would meet her father in the parking lot.

At long last the ordeal was over, a new appointment written in the book, Fletcher free. Cindy was not at the parking lot when he got there. Tardiness was characteristic of his daughter but imprudent at a time when she was begging for favors. He walked up and down the street, wild with impatience, wondering how he would face Elaine if she had found the diary. While he tried to tell himself that it would serve her right for poking into his private papers, he could not accept the transparent excuse. She would consider him insane, consult a doctor; or worse, desert him altogether. He was in a frenzy of impatience. Small beads of cold sweat dotted his face. He returned to the parking lot. Cindy was still not there. To dull his nerves he went into a bar. Bourbon was his drink, but he ordered Scotch because the phonetics required less effort. The bartender was an idiot who asked questions framed so that they could not be answered with a nod or shake of the head. "Soda or water, sir?" "White Rock or Shasta?" "On the rocks or without ice?"

Fletcher's voice came out like the roar of a beast. Mangled sounds, exaggerated by an electronic device, caused an instant of shocked silence. At the end of the bar a couple of smart lads turned their heads to look, turned away too hastily. The bartender joined them in a whispered conference. He nodded toward the afflicted customer. Fletcher drank fast and returned to the parking lot. "Can I get your car, sir?" asked the imbecile attendant. "What kind, sir?" Fletcher walked away without bothering to answer.

Cindy appeared with her hair piled in such a heap that the contents of a pilfered safe might have been hidden beneath the mound of gilded straw. Busy with apologies and parcels, she paid no attention to the parking attendant's questions, so that Fletcher was forced to expose the crippled voice again.

His impatience was compounded by the tempo of traffic and Cindy's flow of talk. She was all afire about the movie premiere and the party at the oil millionaire's mansion. "With a marquee on the lawn and flaming shish kebab at midnight." Many of the women at the party would wear gowns that cost more than a thousand dollars. "Imagine, Daddy! Dresses that cost as much as twenty-five hundred. I'll never be in that class," she sighed. "Especially if we get the new house. I won't be able to buy a new dress for years." This was offered coyly. There was a pause while she waited for her father to say something about the loan. He said nothing. With a giggle Cindy explained that she indulged in the extravagance of new sandals. By shopping around she had saved four dollars.

An insolent driver tried to cut in ahead of the Lincoln. Fletcher sounded his horn.

"If you can't spend money you've got to spend time." Cindy giggled.

The insolent driver passed on the right and succeeded in sliding into the lane ahead. He turned and offered a triumphant grin. He was about Don's age, slender, clean-cut, with the same Ivy League complacence. Suddenly Fletcher's visions returned; the impudent grin over Elaine's bare shoulder. Fletcher pressed his foot upon the accelerator and all but jammed into the fellow's car.

"Daddy, watch it! You may not care about your own life but I'm too young to die."

Fletcher blew his horn viciously. No one had tried to cut in, but the noise relieved his tension. Traffic moved at an agonizing pace, drivers swore and glared. The road ascended a hill which gave a long view of the dreary line of cars ahead. Afternoon sun assaulted their eyes and miniature suns attacked from the enameled bodies of all the other cars. Gas fumes fouled the air. Eyes burned, noses clogged. Last night for a short time Fletcher had been revived by the lively wind; at the seashore he had enjoyed the simple act of breathing. Now the lack of fresh air brought back the familiar sense of smothering.

All of the day's irritations came to a climax in the frustration of a traffic jam. A prisoner confined in a metal box, he saw the waiting agony (motors throbbing, gas fumes, thickening, nerves tightening) as a symbol of his living days. All about him in these polished metal prisons the drivers sweated and cursed. What for? Striving to achieve what Fletcher Strode's labors had brought; useless leisure, a costly home, a powerful car, financial ease, a daughter he could not love, a young wife too lovable. The men in the other cars had certain consolations, the excitement of work, the enjoyment of small triumphs, the hope of future achievements. The smog brought tears to his eyes.

In the next lane of traffic the Ivy League fellow tried to flirt with Cindy. She smiled archly and fondled the structure of bright hair. To show disinterest in the stranger, Cindy turned to her father and once more gave voice to her opinions. Wasn't it a pity that Daddy hadn't accepted the tickets for tonight's affair? Really, Nan had offered them with the best of intentions. She was a kindhearted girl, almost too generous. And Daddy would have loved the movie premiere. The picture was supposed to be super, made from a best-selling novel with the most atrocious sex scenes. And afterward that divine party with the flaming shish kebab at midnight. "You ought to go out more, Daddy. Mix with people. They wouldn't mind your voice if—"

"Stop chattering."

"I'm sorry, Daddy, I didn't mean . . ." She let the sentence trail off. Her father looked as if he were ready to hit someone or drive his car into a post.

Traffic had begun to move a bit faster on the clogged road. Fletcher's hands ached on the wheel. More tears gathered, but his eyeballs were not cooled. "God damned smog." The climate would have to change drastically, he decided, before he could make a five-thousand-dollar gift to this silly girl and her fool husband.

RESIDENTS OF LOS ANGELES look curiously at people who walk in the hills. Twice drivers had stopped to ask whether Elaine would like a lift. When she said she wanted to walk, they regarded her as a foreigner or an eccentric. She had grown up in a world where one opened a door and walked on a street, where an errand could become an adventure. Condemned to the motorcar, she often felt herself a prisoner in a cell of metal and glass. Her mood today was wayward. The discovery of the sleeping pills had unnerved her. "Let him! If he's so crazy to die!"

The road twisted between shady gardens, but there was little pleasure in walking. She constantly had to jump aside to let a car pass. In the long, costly motors, women were more highly polished than their fenders. In this neighborhood wives lived idly, in suspension, remote from reality. They drove these vast, shining monsters, they wore costly clothes, wrapped themselves in lavish fur coats to shop in supermarkets, spent their days wandering in shops, buying or coveting things they did not need. In the monotonous sunshine they dried up and grew old, well-kept, sheltered, proud of having achieved the status of idleness, the privilege of affluent decay. "Not for me, thank you," she declared and plunged into another sinful dream of freedom.

"I love him." The words were uttered piously as exorcism against an evil wish. She had thought enough about divorce to know it unthinkable. A marriage begun with all the panache of romantic love, flags flying, bands playing, kisses, flowers, gaiety, and gifts, had become a dreary chore. "I love him." But love, too stridently asserted, is not love but protest, a seedy thing, an itch too easily irritated, a gaunt skeleton of robust reality. Now that she had betrayed love, there was only duty ahead, the penance of abstinence and devotion.

Having acknowledged guilt and vowed resignation, she allowed herself to view the dark future; caught glimpses of boredom, contemplated sterility, foresaw a life that was not life at all, but a never-ending rehearsal for death's arrival. In spite of dutiful vows she fell into another dream of liberty, met old friends, attended parties, laughed, skipped along the city's crowded sidewalks, saw plays, heard music, knew ardor, flirted with virile young men. A Thunderbird tooted at her. "I hate you," she informed its shining rear.

A glance at her watch brought back reality. It was late. Fletcher would be annoyed if he did not find her when he got home. "As if I lived in a harem," she told a passing truck. "And the rajah is also the eunuch." The truck driver backed up to ask if she needed a ride. He enjoyed nothing more, he said, than helping a lady. She told him he was gallant, and he tried to prolong gallantry. The man's crude flattery pleased and troubled her. She scolded herself for the reluctance to return to her husband. Penitently, "I love him," she told the treetops.

She came into the house through the back door, walked like

a trespasser through the hall. Against the glare of a west window she saw a dark silhouette at Fletcher's desk. "Oh, darling, you're back early." Her laughter, designated to show him that she was glad to find him there, had an artificial ring. "I just went out for a little walk."

"Hi, sweet." It was Don, not Fletcher, at the desk. He seemed put out with her for coming into her own house. His expression was strange, as though he were looking at someone he had never before seen. Nervously he ruffled papers on the desk.

"Are you looking for something?"

"Writing paper. I've got an important letter to get off and I've run out."

"In the middle drawer. Didn't you see it?"

"How stupid of me. I thought Dad kept private stuff in there and didn't even look." He opened the drawer with his right hand while his left lay firm upon the papers he had rearranged.

Don had been reading Fletcher's diary.

He was baffled by the contents. Elaine did not look at all like a woman planning a murder. With sweet concern she asked about Don's luck at the Carter office. He was so bemused that he forgot what he had told them about the situation. "I only got a few minutes with old Carter."

"I didn't know you expected an interview with him. I thought it was some executive, that bastard you said . . ." Elaine laughed.

Don echoed the mirth, falsely. "I saw the bastard too. And turned down the job." He had become so entangled that he could not make a statement without adding a new lie to bolster up the old ones. This morning, after almost an hour on the edge of a chair in an assistant bastard's outer office, he had been told that the job they had practically offered him had been given to another man.

"You turned it down? Was that wise? Even if they won't pay the salary you want, you've got to start somewhere."

She spoke so gently that Don, his arm still tight upon the papers that covered the diary, wondered if there was any substance to Fletcher's fears. Could this soft creature actually be contriving, with household implements and garden poisons, the death of her husband?

"Fletcher thinks so, too. He took all kinds of loathsome jobs to get his start in business. I think he'd be more likely to let you have the money for the house if he were convinced of your"— she sought the right word and used it delicately—"stability."

"You don't think I'm unstable, do you, love?"

"I'm serious, Don. Maybe you oughtn't to buy a house now. It's such a responsibility and if you don't have a steady income—"

"We've got to live somewhere." Anger rose. Forgetful, he raised his hand and smote the desk so that the papers were disturbed and a bit of the diary exposed. He covered it hastily. "It's easy for you to talk. With a setup like this." He glanced around the room, which was fitted with fine rugs and gleaming wood. As dramatically as hope could raise him to the highest peaks of optimism, he could be sunk to the darkest caverns of despair. The Carter job, which he had affected to scorn, had been his last chance. Now that he had lost it he saw, too clearly, that it could have saved him, convinced Fletcher of his stability, got him the loan and the house, and started him on a new life. He had no more contacts in Los Angeles, no other fraternity brothers to introduce him to important people.

"You can stay here. We've got loads of room," Elaine said and let a comforting hand fall upon his shoulder.

"And have Dad act as if he were giving charity to his own daughter?"

"You're too sensitive. He only fusses because he's so miserable. I think he loves Cindy, but he's been so hurt himself that he's unable to show affection."

Don looked up gratefully and let his free right hand cover hers. She backed away.

"We'd better not be too friendly."

"Why? What's up?"

"I told you. He's jealous."

"Of me?"

"Of everyone."

Don sprang up with only a quick glance to see that the diary was properly shielded. "Has he any cause to be jealous of me?"

"Don't be silly. You're his daughter's husband."

"And if I weren't?"

"I love my husband. Other men don't interest me." Immediately her mind was filled with the image of Ralph Julian. With the excuse that she had to prepare dinner, she hurried to the kitchen.

Don left the desk just as he had found it, with the papers in place and the diary uncovered. For no reason at all he felt better. At the bar he helped himself to a slug of Fletcher's twelve-year-old Bourbon. With a final glance at the desk to be sure he had left the diary open at the proper page, he returned to his room to dress for the gala evening.

In the kitchen Elaine beat eggs and cut up vegetables, but her mind was not on the chores and when sirens shrieked on the hill, she stabbed a paring knife into her thumb. Before she had gone out for her walk she had twice found new hiding places for the sleeping pills. Now the vial lay at the bottom of her jewel case.

Blood from her thumb stained the cucumber. "Damn you, damn, damn, damn!" she shouted at the retreating sirens and beat her heels upon the tiled floor. Don raced into the kitchen in a robe of Paisley silk. He made much of the cut finger, washed and bandaged it. Fletcher and Cindy walked in while he was fastening the adhesive tape. Elaine pulled away too quickly.

Don took a cautious step backward. "She's cut her finger."

"Don's been giving me first aid."

Fletcher hurried to the den. Cindy went away, pulling at her zipper and begging Don to hurry so that they would be at the theater early enough for her to enjoy the arrival of celebrities. Don lingered to ask whether Elaine thought Fletcher was angry.

"He obviously didn't like finding us together. You'd better not stay here."

"Oh, for heaven's sake, I was just bandaging your finger. You don't think that would keep him from lending us the money?"

"Better not ask any favors tonight. I've forgotten the ice

again. He'll be furious." She filled the ice bucket awkwardly. Her thumb throbbed. She would have liked to send Don into the den with the ice, but it would not do with his robe flying open and his loins exposed. She hoped Fletcher would not make an issue of Don's having been only half-dressed when he found them in the kitchen. At lunch there had been a kind of armistice. Fletcher had been awkwardly tender. Perhaps he did not know how to act the betrayed husband any more than she knew the proper behavior of an unfaithful wife. After Don and Cindy were out of the house, she and Fletcher might talk over the situation and come to terms.

She carried the ice bucket, announcing herself with little noises, coughing lightly, rattling the ice, swishing the petticoat under her skirt. If only she could please Fletcher, belong to him again. She had committed the unholiest sin, not with the act of infidelity, but with the act of confession. Absolution could be gained only by making sure of her love.

He was writing in the diary and did not look up when she crossed the room. She set the ice bucket down upon the bar and walked out quietly, like a servant.

THE DIARY HAD been on the desk, open and in plain sight, but did not look as if anyone had touched it. Fletcher was relieved, for he had seen himself unmasked, shamed, and confronted with all sorts of questions and accusations. In his anxiety he had known the diary for what it was, the pitiful plaything of a man bereft of physical and moral power. Belief had been shattered. He had vowed to destroy the wretched book. Once he had found it, apparently untouched, relief turned to irritation. His wife did not care enough to examine his diary and learn his secret thoughts. She had given it to him, often teased him for being so secretive about his diary, put on an act of interest. That's all it was, a pretty feminine act. She cared more about that half-naked fellow in the kitchen. How had those two spent the afternoon?

He brought out his best twelve-year-old Bourbon. The act of pouring brought back the searing memory of the latest humiliation, the bartender's masked curiosity, the whispering group at the end of the bar. He turned to the diary, read and relished an item written that morning:

> Yesterday she hit me with the news she had a lover. How much can a man take? No matter what schemes are in her mind she ought to be loyal while I am alive. Maybe she is too passionate to control herself. But what a shock to a loving husband. I drove to the ocean and stood on those steep rocks and looked down at the water and was tempted. Then a terrible thought came to my mind. I saw through her devious plans. She may not be brave enough to strike the blow herself so she is trying to provoke me to do it myself. This thought saved my life. I refuse to make it easy for her.

The entry showed rare insight. Fletcher poured another Bourbon, and thought about the incident in the kitchen. "She flaunts her . . ." he wrote, but got no farther because Elaine came in to tell him the soup was on the table.

"I made you minestrone." Her tone was humble.

This time Fletcher was careful about locking up the diary before he left the room. Don came to dinner in black trousers and a white dinner jacket, which gave brilliant contrast to his dark eyes and ruddy skin. "Don't you look distinguished!" cried Elaine.

Fletcher said the soup was too salty and pushed his plate away.

Cindy floated in late but grand in her beige organza, new sandals, green paste on her eyelids, pearly tips to her fingers, and the hauteur of a young empress. One would think she was a member of the two-thousand-dollar-gown class. She was piqued because Don had not noticed her new hairdo.

"But I did, love. Indeed I did. The moment you got home."

"Why didn't you say so?"

He had been binding Elaine's thumb when Cindy and her father came into the house.

"It's very becoming, dear," said Elaine, who wondered if she sounded like a mother-in-law. "Don't you think so, Fletch?"

"Looks like a haystack."

"But Daddy, it's supposed . . . I mean . . . it's casual. Bouffant casual. Really. All the girls are doing it now."

"Your father doesn't see many girls." Elaine spoke slowly as to a backward child. "He's not used to these new styles."

"I'm used to them, and I agree with Dad, that hairdo's downright ugly. How much prettier Elaine is without makeup and her hair natural." The remark was ill-timed. Don had meant to show agreement with Fletcher, but he had made the error of praising Elaine. He saw that she had gone rigid and looked away lest Fletcher, aware of every glance and inflection, might misinterpret the flattery.

Cindy noticed nothing. She was all wrapped up in her glamour and the anticipation of the party. Again she chattered about the affair, showing condescension to the pitiful older people who had to stay home and watch TV while gay youth mingled with the rich and famous, danced to irresistible rhythms. Smugly she offered compassion.

Fletcher became more and more irritated by the arrogance. All that fed his daughter's pride, the filmy dress, the new sandals, the pearls at her throat, the hideous arrangement of her expensively tinted hair, even the good-looking husband, had come from her father's labors. The silly girl had neither gratitude nor humility, not even the grace to keep quiet about his affliction. On and on she went reminding him that he, too, might have caught a glimpse of this night's glory if he had not been so rude to Nan Burke.

"Go stick your flaming shish kebab!" His anger rose like the belch that it was, a sickening excrement of sound.

"What, Daddy?"

"We're just a bit bored with the flaming shish kebab," Elaine said with determined joviality.

"You're jealous," Cindy teased, "because you're not going to the party."

"Not at all," Don put in quickly. "Different people have different tastes."

"Shut up, you phony!"

This, too, erupted like vomit. Fletcher found it humiliating to have Elaine speak for him, but Don's taking on the role of interpreter was galling beyond endurance. No doubt he and Elaine had discussed "poor Fletcher," had agreed on a technique for handling the deluded, disabled husband. At one moment they exchanged conspiratorial glances, at the next avoided each other with conspiratorial indifference. It was quite obvious that Elaine admired the young man in his white dinner jacket. As though her husband did not own three white tuxedoes; as though he had not taken her to Bermuda and Jamaica and Palm Beach for winter holidays and in the summer brought her to parties in Greenwich and Oyster Bay.

"Sorry, sir."

Was that the best reply Don could offer? With all of his prep school and university and family background, he showed no more spirit than a kindergartner. If anyone had ever called Fletcher Strode a phony—and at Don's age—the answer would have been a fast one in the puss. At twenty-nine Fletcher Strode had not owned a white dinner jacket, but he had supported his mother and sister, married a demanding woman, made and lost a fortune, and started a second. Until he was laid low by illness he had worked for every dollar he had ever spent. He did not deserve to be patronized by his daughter, pitied by a punk, deceived by his wife.

Elaine and Don tried to cover the empty silence with chit-chat. It was hardly better than Cindy's nonsense. For want of something more intelligent, these college graduates discussed the movie that was to have its first showing that night. Elaine hoped it would be good. She did so admire the star. "He has such unique male vitality."

"Terrific. Loads of sex appeal," cried Cindy. "Almost as much as Don."

What the hell was so unique about it? Fletcher's mouth opened in preparation for a lion's roar. Not even a mouse's squeak emerged. Fury jagged through his body in electric flashes. He struck the table. Silver and dishes rattled. He raised his fist again, pulled back in a mighty effort at control. With the correct technique, a long intake of air into the esophagus and his tongue in position, he prepared for speech.

"I can't let you have the money."

The words came out clearly yet the faces of his audience were as blank as if he had not articulated each syllable. Once more he went through the routine and this time, since the tones were all equal and could not show feeling, he used gesture and facial contortions for emphasis. His fist swung up once more, his eyes narrowed, a fierce scowl wrinkled his brow. "I am not giving you that five thousand dollars."

They understood. "Oh, Daddy." Cindy winked back tears that threatened her mascara. Elaine spoke as tragically as if her dearest wish had been denied. "Can't you possibly? Five thousand isn't so much to you." She turned, soft-eyed, to spend her sympathy upon the younger man.

Breeding and discipline showed in the composure with which Don accepted disappointment. The stoic silence enraged Fletcher. At Don's age, possessed of a healthy voice, he would have shouted and fought back. With all the force he could command, he committed speech:

"You think I've got money to throw around? Let him go out and earn it like I did. Or do you girls think he deserves it for his unique sex appeal?" Without inflection, the voice failed in irony. His audience faced him blankly. One would think the words had not been uttered.

"God damn you . . . parasites."

Fletcher's ear, tuned to the voice of his mind, caught it. The others heard nothing. No sound had come out. Emotion had destroyed control. They saw his writhing lips and waited.

Dumb anger whipped up fury. Why had he been so cursed? He, Fletcher Strode, who had worked hard all his life, taken responsibility, proved his usefulness on earth? The three of them stared like hicks before a sideshow freak. He tried again. His heart pounded, his head throbbed, his throat ached with the strangled sense of helplessness. Tears welled up. Before they could gape at the final disgrace, he sprang up and left them.

Elaine did not hurry to offer comfort. Probably she preferred to console Don. From the den Fletcher heard guarded mur-murs. Shortly afterward Don and Cindy drove off in the car that Fletcher Strode's generosity had provided. The rattle of china, followed by an avalanche pouring through the dishwasher, told him that Elaine was in the kitchen. Once more Fletcher turned to his diary. He read words, but the phrases and thoughts that had filled him with pride had become meaningless marks on paper. Where was Elaine? Time had passed, the dishwasher had quit churning, but she had not come to find him. The house had never been so quiet. Outside, a rising fog had silenced birds and crickets. A strange weight pressed upon him, the sense of mute-ness. To hear sound he beat both fists upon the desk. He was neither deaf nor dead. Death is silence. He beat the desk again with the fury of relief.

Life returned with the rustle of silk in the hall. He pulled himself up in the desk chair, seized his pen, and pretended to be busy. "Fletch, dear." She had painted her mouth and contrived a smile. "What did I hear? I was afraid you'd become angry again. Please, darling," she used the word shyly, "don't keep hurting yourself."

Don't be angry! Why not, for God's sake? You tell me he's not your lover, but I've got eyes in my head. And a good pair of ears. What am I to think when I hear you bragging about his sex appeal, showing off your shameless passion? Expect me to support him, don't you? Reproach me for not showering money on your gigolo. All in his mind. From his lips came only broken sound. He had lost control, become as mute as when he lay in the hospital bound down by clamps and tubes, helpless.

Elaine hurried around the desk to touch him with gentle hands. "Darling, please, please don't try so hard. Just relax and—"

He pushed her off. *"Don't touch me, you whore."*

This, too, was merely mouthed. She did not hear the words. Only his movements rebuffed her. Just the same, she tried to soothe him. "Don't get panicky. You're too emotional. When you've calmed down a bit, you'll be able to talk."

He seized her shoulders and whirled her around so that she

could see his lips. Their movement and a nasal whisper brought forth a word.

"Whore!"

She had come to offer remorse, to soothe him with tenderness. Instead she flared, "If that's how you feel, I'm leaving. I've withstood enough, I'm through." At its peak, her fury collapsed. His wounded animal look defeated her. "Tell me you didn't mean that." She offered the memo pad and a pencil.

He backed away.

She went on, "You can't believe it's Don. Your daughter's husband. You know I'd have nothing to do with him. Tell me you didn't mean that." Once again she thrust the memo pad toward him.

He made no effort to answer. The silence was piercing and endless, like acute pain. She thought of the pills hidden in her jewel case. "All right, it's my fault. I hurt you. Unforgivably. But please," she begged as for a small favor, "believe me, Don was never my lover."

Fletcher took hold of her shoulders, his fingers like hot claws digging into her flesh. He jerked her close to him. His lips moved but no sound came forth.

Elaine read the question in his face. "He wasn't important. Someone you don't know. Just a terrible moment, an impulse. I never want to see the man again as long as I live." Guilt compounded the lies. Her flesh betrayed her by turning red. She twisted out of the mental claws. Fletcher caught her in flight and struck out with his fist. She reeled backward, recovered balance and, mute too, stared at him in shock. Both hands protected the injured jaw.

He was paralyzed, his body no less impotent than his voice. Often, when his heavy hand had come down upon her in the play of love, Elaine had protested that he did not know his own strength. Fletcher Strode had made many mistakes in his life, committed not a few sins, but he had never before struck a woman. He knew that there were men, many wellborn and educated, who habitually beat up women. He had always thanked God that he was not that type. He could not look at Elaine, who stood there with both hands protecting the injury and her eyes flashing with justified fury. He wanted to speak, to say he had not meant to hurt her, to beg her not to leave him. It was less the physical handicap that kept him from it than his stubborn, rockbound pride.

She ran off. The rustle of her silk petticoat died away. Fletcher barely noticed. To appease his conscience he grasped at the vision which did not, this time, show the face of the unimportant lover, but only the tangle of limbs accompanied by sighs and purrs, blended gasps, the outcry of consummation.

Tears moistened burning eyes. He was crying. It was unthinkable . . . he, Fletcher Strode. He tried to exorcise self-pity by thinking of sums added daily—stocks, real estate holdings, industrial investments, bonds, and bank accounts. Bitterness would not be bribed. *Elaine, the fair, Elaine, the lovable.* He heard his voice, the old strong voice of Fletcher Strode, heard echoes of raucous laughter, and deliberately revived the vision, watched the embrace tighten, heard the sighing, moaning, singing out of joy in love. He knew the name of her unimportant man. There were not many lovers in Elaine's life these days. Surely she would not squander herself upon the delivery boys who came to the door, not the clerks with whom she flirted while she questioned the ripeness of melons. The red-haired doctor was not an unimportant lover; he was pale, stringy, thin, Jewish, but not unattractive, and what was more important to Elaine, he was a man who could talk to her about things that were Gothic or ambivalent or nonobjective. Irrelevantly Fletcher recalled a night, shortly after he had started his diary, when he had asked Elaine if she had ever questioned the meaning of life. "Doesn't everyone?" Her tone had snubbed him. "When you're a sophomore it's the burning question."

Fletcher Strode had never been a sophomore. At sixteen he had left school and become an errand boy, at eighteen he was a salesman, at twenty-three a success. His mind had been filled with schemes and tactics. He had never questioned his purpose in life because he had known it was to make money. Profit had been habit and reflex. His mind had not been permitted the luxury of abstract thought. And his reward was a wife who snubbed him as though he were no more than a sophomore. How much did the red-haired doctor make a year when he was twenty-two? Could that skinny highbrow, with all of his education, think more deeply than Fletcher Strode? If Elaine were to read her husband's diary, she would recognize the quality of his meditations.

He returned to his desk, found his favorite entry:

Evil is in the air around us. Look at those nearest you. Every soul contains every sin. In the hidden self a murderer waits . . .

And:

When I used to sing in church I believed in good and evil. Nowadays it is the style to say evil is sickness. Where has goodness gone to? Is the modern world just a big hospital?

And:

When you defend what's yours you have got to destroy something. It can be the very thing you are trying to defend.

He could no longer hypnotize himself by rereading his profoundest ideas. Pride had deserted, too. The diary provided no more solace than the Bourbon. Nothing could console him. There was no peace on earth for Fletcher Strode.

It would not do to let her see him with red eyes and moist cheeks. He rubbed at his face, refolded his handkerchief, thrust it back into his pocket neatly, locked away the diary, turned out the lights, checked the doors. Performing these small duties, he became himself again, master of the house, and reflected upon his thoughtfulness in leaving a light lit in the hall for Don and Cindy.

He walked along the corridor aggressively so that Elaine would hear him. Her door was shut. Underneath he saw a pencil of light. He stopped there, waiting to be asked to come in. In other days after disagreement and a loss of temper, they had both shown contrition, sought forgiveness, and found it in each other's arms. No quarrel had been allowed to last beyond bedtime. His standing there, meekly waiting for her invitation, showed the depth to which Fletcher Strode had fallen. "I am a cuckold," he cackled, "I am a cuckold. Fletcher Strode!"

His voice had returned, but he was too involved in contradictions to notice this minor miracle. He loved her, he hated her, he needed her, he never wanted to look into her eyes again. Certainly she had heard his footsteps, had noted the pause, had deliberately ignored his presence at her door. She would never forgive the blow, would forever loathe the sight . . . and the *sound* . . . of him. Since he had been forced to give up so much else, she was all he had, the only thing that made his life endurable.

She had threatened to leave him. If, by God, she deserted him, he would end it now. There would be no more vacillation. Every day he counted the pills hidden in the riding boot.

On the other side of the door Elaine waited, knowing that he stood there, humble and indecisive, this man who had never in his life wavered in decision. She had but to speak a word and he would open the door, bare his remorse, reaffirm love. She was afraid. Of what? "I love him." The words had no power. Her jaw throbbed, every nerve end twitched. After a while she heard him walk away. His steps were slow and heavy as though he carried a great load.

8 THE SKY RUMBLED, THE HOUSE QUIVERED, THE earth shook, windows rattled. Elaine was awakened but not alarmed; the breaking of the sound barrier was no more startling than any other of the daily shocks. Fire and police sirens, bloody accidents and hairbreadth escapes on the highways, the testing of civil defense alarms, motor horns, and Muzak had become the ordinary sounds of modern living. The explosion shuddered to silence. In its wake Elaine heard a voice. Or was the sudden frantic cry a fragment of a dream so terrifying that consciousness had driven it back into the cave of the unremembered? She felt bound to the bed, sodden. Last

night, in despair, she had swallowed two sleeping pills from Fletcher's hoard. Her limbs seemed not to belong to her body. Her jaw throbbed.

"Elaine!" The voice was Cindy's. She flung herself into the room. "Something terrible. Daddy—"

Elaine threw off the blankets, leaped out of bed. Cindy followed her along the hall, saying that the telephone had wakened her, that no one had answered until she had dragged herself out of bed. It had been a long-distance call from Daddy's broker in New York. He had commanded her to wake her father. "Some stuff about stocks, he wanted to answer a wire Daddy sent yesterday. He said it was more important than letting Daddy sleep." By prattling about details, Cindy avoided the unspeakable truth.

In Fletcher's room the curtains were still drawn. Cindy had switched on the ceiling lamp. It threw cruel light upon the bed. Fletcher lay on his back. The body was covered to the hips with a sheet. His powerful, tanned torso was bare. White against the dark flesh was the triangle of porous cloth that protected the opening at the base of his throat.

Elaine walked as if in a trance, her hand stretched out like a blind woman's. The sight of death so frankly uncovered caused a kind of paralysis. Fletcher was no less rigid than the woman standing with her hand extended above his body. At the door, like a lost child in her ruffled, baby doll nightgown, Cindy sobbed.

"He must have killed himself," Elaine said and stared at her hand as though she were surprised by her ability to move it. She looked about the room like a stranger who had never seen it before. And her hand dropped heavily, brushing the edge of the mattress.

No longer a desolate child, Cindy had become an old woman with a hag's jutted chin, fierce eyes, hard cords in her neck. "Why do you say that? How do you know?"

Elaine pushed her aside and went to the telephone. Cindy had left the handset dangling. Elaine hung up and waited for the dialing tone. The first name that came to her mind was Ralph's. She looked up his number and called his office. An operator's stilted voice asked if this was an emergency call. "Yes," Elaine said. "My husband's dead. This is Mrs. Fletcher Strode."

"How can you?" wailed Cindy.

If the girl had not been sniffling behind her, Elaine might have let go herself. It was safer, she felt, to force herself to immediate tasks. "We'd better have some coffee." She measured it out and poured water into the pot as though this were an ordinary day and she were preparing her husband's breakfast. Her eyes were dry. "You'd better wake Don."

"He's not here."

"What! He's gone out? So early?"

"He had a very early appointment. About a job," Cindy said between sobs. Don wanted to be away from the house in case the real estate agent called. He had given her instructions carefully. "He thought the conference might last all morning, and he has a lunch date, too."

"Can't you get in touch with him?"

"I don't know where he is," wept the girl.

"You'd better lie down and try to pull yourself together. I'll take care of things," Elaine said.

She forced herself to go back to Fletcher's room. There was a bluish cast to his flesh, and his face was expressionless as stone. He did not look like a man who had tumbled a girl about on beds and couches, on the back seat of a car, on the sand at the beach and, one crazy night in Kentucky (he had just won nine hundred dollars at the races) on the bathroom floor. She could not recall shared laughter, the touch of his hand, the scent of his flesh, the quarrels and the fun. Nothing; not even the fury of last night's insult, the hurt they had given each other. Upon the bed she saw, not her husband, not her lover, not her man—death lay there. "I'm sorry, Fletch," she said in a voice directed at nothing and with no life in it.

THE MORNING FOG had lifted. Watery sunshine shimmered on the hill while the streets below lay drowned in warm mist. The temperature rose. Sweating in a wool jacket, Ralph wished that doctors could dress as comfortably as truck drivers. He rang the Strodes' bell several times before the door was opened. The daughter stood there. She wore a dark robe that gave the correct note of mourning. Her fair hair had been combed, but lay limp about her face. "In there," she said through a damp handkerchief pressed to her lips.

Elaine stood beside the bed. Ralph took her hands. They were cold and dry. She wore a transparent nightgown with only spaghetti straps over her shoulders. Ralph was embarrassed by the lightly shrouded nudity, so that he could not offer the comfort of an embrace. Her quiet manner seemed sadder than a teary display of grief. "What happened?"

She nodded toward the bed.

"I mean this." He raised his hand toward her bruised face.

She shuddered as though he had touched a sharp instrument to an open wound. "It's nothing."

It was clear that she did not want to speak ill of the dead. While Ralph began his examination of the body, she stood motionless with bowed head.

"Put on some clothes. You're disgusting!" cried Cindy.

"Excuse me." Elaine used the tone of a minor social error. She hurried out of the room.

There was nothing for Ralph to do but inform the coroner's office. He used the kitchen phone so that he could make a report without adding to the distress of Fletcher Strode's women. He had barely hung up when the telephone rang. Elaine hurried to answer. She was covered from chin to instep by a flowing robe of a soft moss-green fabric. The call was from New York. Mr. Stoner said he had called before but been disconnected, and had tried for half an hour to get a connection. He had profitable information for Fletcher and wanted to tell him immediately.

Elaine could not blurt out the news that her husband was dead. "Sorry, he can't come to the phone now. He's not feeling well. I don't want to disturb him. You might call back later in the day."

"How can she?" wailed Cindy. "She hasn't shed a tear."

"Shock affects some people that way. They cut off all feeling, but later they suffer in other ways." Ralph spoke curtly. He had already noted Cindy's intolerance of her stepmother, but wondered at the vindictiveness in this hour of grief.

Like a simple housewife on an uneventful day, Elaine carried in the tray with coffee. Finally, when she had poured out three cups and asked about cream and sugar, she spoke of Fletcher. "Did he suffer?"

"I can't say. It doesn't look that way, but I've only made a superficial examination. I should say he became unconscious quickly. There's nothing in his face nor the position of the body to show that he struggled."

"I'm glad."

"We'll know more after the autopsy."

Cindy sprang up as though she had been catapulted out of her chair. "There's not going to be any autopsy on my father."

"My dear," Ralph used his smoothest bedside tone, "you've got nothing to be alarmed about. It's the regular routine of the coroner's office."

"What do we want a coroner for?"

In a voice sharpened by the strain of self-control Elaine said, "Let the doctor do what he has to."

"It's the law, Mrs . . ." For the life of him Ralph could not remember the girl's married name. "When a doctor's called in after death has occurred, he may not sign a death certificate unless he's seen the patient within three weeks or has been treating him for a condition that might cause mortality. Let's not get upset. It's quite natural, I assure you."

All the color had been drained from Cindy's face. She trembled violently. "You weren't my father's doctor. Why did she call you?"

"He's my doctor. I thought of him first," Elaine said.

"You should have called Daddy's doctor. Now there'll be all kinds of fuss. Newspapers and stuff." Cindy fell back into her chair. She was not only frightened, but on the verge of sickness. At last night's party she had drunk too much. Champagne always made her sick, but it was so expensive and so correct to profess a love for *good* wine that she forced herself to live up to other people's taste.

"Was he like this . . . in this position . . . when you first found him? Has anyone touched him?" Ralph scanned both of their faces.

"Cindy found him."

"He was just like that."

Gingerly, with the tips of thumb and forefinger, Ralph lifted the triangular white bib that protected the wound. The opening was unobstructed. "Then the stoma wasn't covered?" Ralph said.

Neither girl spoke.

"Only with this bib?"

"Yes, that was all," Cindy said.

"You're sure there were no blankets or anything that you pulled off?"

"The blanket was just like that," Cindy said.

Ralph said, "It's obvious that he wasn't smothered by the blanket then. Nor by turning his head in his sleep, twisting his neck and blocking the stoma. Usually a patient in that condition," he tapped his own Adam's apple, "wakes up when the air is cut off, just as you and I would if our mouths and noses were covered. So it apparently wasn't that. Did he take sleeping pills?"

"Is that what it looks like? Can you tell?" asked Elaine.

"The color of the skin indicates anoxia."

"Why did you ask about sleeping pills?"

"They cause respiratory depression. Air doesn't get to the lungs and the brain is deprived of oxygen." Ralph used layman's language so that they would understand. "There could be various causes. Gas leaks, smoke, smothering. A blanket over the stoma, as I said, or if his head was in the wrong position and he was too heavily drugged to wake up. The stoma might also have been blocked by something else. But it isn't." He raised the bib to show them that the opening was unobstructed. "What about sleeping pills? Did he take them?"

Elaine sat like an ancient figure sculptured in marble upon a tomb. When she had worked as a model, she had learned to remain still until the photographer gave her permission to move. Such repose made the others nervous. They could not see that, under the exquisitely calm surface, her nerves were drawn tight. She rearranged a fold in her robe.

"I gave him two last night."

"Only two? Anything else? Had he been drinking?"

"My father didn't drink."

"No one said he did, Cindy dear. He had a couple before dinner. That could be dangerous, couldn't it, mixing alcohol and sleeping pills?" Elaine asked.

Her voice was too bland, her self-control almost abnormal.

Perhaps, thought Ralph, she was straining to make herself believe that her husband's death had been an accident. The wife of a suicide too often blames herself. Before he could comfort her, Ralph had to know more of the facts. "When and how much did he drink? Do you know?"

"Daddy wasn't a big drinker. He usually had one, maybe two at most, before dinner."

"What time was that?"

"We eat at seven-thirty," Elaine said.

"Six-thirty last night. Don and I wanted to leave early," Cindy explained.

Elaine fixed appealing eyes on Ralph. He said, "I don't know. A fatal dose would depend upon the quantity of alcohol—which was slight—the number of pills and how he reacted to the combination. Had he ever taken both before?"

"I gave him two pills every night."

"Were more available to him?"

"Wait," Elaine said and ran out of the room. A few seconds later she came back with a red lacquer box painted intricately in gold and black. From the largest drawer she took a vial of pills as brilliantly red as the Chinese box. "I found these in his closet yesterday. He'd been hiding them in an old riding boot. You see, he'd been planning . . ."

"You had the pills hidden, you say?"

"Yes. This box was in my dresser. He couldn't possibly have got hold of them without coming into my room and waking me up. Besides, they're all here."

"What about the pills you gave him every night? If these were hidden, there must have been others in the house."

"He couldn't have got those without waking me either. Let's look." She beckoned Ralph to follow her. Cindy came along sulkily. In Elaine's room stood an old cabinet filled with art books and portfolios of reproductions. Behind a fat volume on Leonardo da Vinci she found a second vial of pills. "I kept changing the places I hid them. This was the latest."

"That's why you were so nervous," said Ralph, remembering the hesitancy and flushes on the day he had examined her in his office. "You've been afraid of this all along?"

She nodded.

"Your husband must have known, since you were so cautious with the pills."

"We didn't talk about it directly. I said I didn't want Fletcher to get the habit, one more pill a night and then another. I said it was dangerous for a man who slept so badly to have the pills in his room." Her eyes begged for understanding.

"Do you know how many pills were left in this bottle?"

"Twelve. I counted them yesterday and figured that we had only a few more days before I'd have to call Dr. Wilson for a new prescription. That was before I found the ones he'd hidden."

"My father didn't commit suicide." Cindy began to retch.

"Come along, young lady, I'm giving you a shot and putting you to bed."

In spite of the sickness, Cindy clung to her chair like a child unwilling to be sent to her room while grown-ups carried on their mysterious affairs. It was not surprising that she had become hysterical, but it seemed to Ralph that there was a strange contradiction in her concern for exterior circumstances. He managed to get her out of the chair and to her bedroom. Elaine tried to take her other arm, but Cindy jerked her off. "I want my mother," she sobbed.

The bell rang and Elaine went to the door to admit a pair of detectives.

BEFORE AN AUTOPSY is performed upon the body of a person suspected of suicide, the police visit the premises and prepare a report for the coroner. This is mere routine. The detectives were very polite to the new widow. The older man, Redding, looked like a public accountant. The other, stocky and dark, was heroically named Juarez. He remained silent while Redding asked questions. Elaine repeated what she had told Ralph about the sleeping pills, showed the two small bottles, and told them about having found the hidden vial in the boot while she and Dorine were cleaning Fletcher's closet. Redding asked questions as if he were following instructions in a manual for detectives. Both men were as solemn as mechanics inspecting a faulty machine.

Redding wondered if Mr. Strode had not got his pills from another source. The whole town was crawling with lousy peddlers who sold barbiturates to kids and addicts. Fletcher Strode might easily have dealt with these crooks. Elaine doubted it. She told them of Fletcher's extraordinary sensitivity to strangers. "Even Dr. Wilson's prescriptions were taken to the drugstore by me. He was afraid the clerk might ask him if he liked the climate."

Had he been alive, Fletcher would be stamping about the house, intolerant of strangers who had invaded his privacy. Elaine shuddered. The memory of that voice was a ghost that threatened to roar garbled notes at the intruders. The voice became so real and so close that she was afraid the others might hear and remark upon the strangeness.

Ralph told the detectives about Fletcher's operation, explaining that the suicide urge was not uncommon in laryngectomy patients. "Mr. Strode seemed unwilling to cope with the disability. I suggest that you see Dr. Ira Wilson, who's been attending to Mr. Strode since he came to California. No doubt Dr. Wilson has the whole case history." And once again Ralph showed the stoma and explained its function.

Redding nodded agreement as though he were a specialist called in for consultation. Juarez, who had not said a word until now, asked if the opening could not be blocked by some object inserted into the tube.

"Almost anything of the right size—a cork, a wad of cleansing tissue, a piece of handkerchief," Ralph said. "But you see, the opening's clear. How could he have got rid of it?"

They looked around as if they expected to find the object beside the bed. If, in a final moment of panic, the dying man had discarded such an object, certainly it would have been there. He could not have got up, hidden, or destroyed the thing and returned to his deathbed.

"Then he wouldn't have died. If he'd had the strength to take it out, he'd have breathed in some air and stayed alive," Juarez said.

Ralph replied that it was not impossible for the dead man to have, at the end, regretted the suicidal act, managed to remove the obstruction, and fight for his life. "But too late. And you'll notice that neither his face nor posture indicates struggle."

Redding was sure it had been sleeping pills. "These barbiturate suicides are a dime a dozen." Hastily, "Excuse me, Mrs. Strode," he added, "but when you've seen as much as I have, and you put two and two together, cancer, insomnia, and a sleeping pill habit, it's pretty obvious, isn't it?"

They returned to the living room. Redding filled out the report. Ralph telephoned his office to say that he might be detained for an hour. Elaine stood at the window and looked out at the autumn flowers. A few marigolds still bloomed and the chrysanthemums were in full glory, russet, tawny, gold, and pure white. Chrysanthemums were one of the few flowers Fletcher had known by name. When her mother died, he had sent an extravagant white blanket of gigantic blossoms. A sudden vision came to her, Fletcher under a burden of flowers. She shut her mind to it and thought, instead, of her husband as he had been yesterday, marching about the house, issuing commands in that broken voice. It echoed again, clearer than Redding's announcement that an ambulance would come for the body.

The body. This is what Fletcher Strode had come to. A body, a thing to be picked up, cut up, probed by rubber-gloved hands as he lay upon a white slab. Elaine thought of the man's pride.

"We'll ask for immediate action on the autopsy. To make it a bit easier for you, Mrs. Strode. Waiting's hard on the family of a deceased. We'll let you know when you can have your own mortuary take him."

She dropped to the window seat. The detectives left, and Ralph came to sit beside her. His hand fell upon hers. She gave no sign of feeling. He moved closer. She edged away. After a while, her eyes fixed on the flowers. Elaine said, "There's something you ought to know."

He waited.

She picked at a bit of fluff on her robe. For all of her efforts at self-control, she gave signs of tension. Her hands could not be still, and her eyes avoided contact. "He knew I was unfaithful. But not with you. I never told him it was you."

"You feel guilty?"

"I shouldn't have told him."

"Why did you?"

"He asked me."

"And you told the truth?"

"Should I have lied?" Fury flashed out. There was a quivering in the air as when high-tension wires shiver in a strong wind. "He asked me! Would you have wanted me to lie?" She had never before been shrill. "I'm sorry I hurt him. But he asked and I told him. I said I'd been unfaithful once, only once, but I never said it was you."

When she turned toward Ralph her eyes were empty. The face whose mobility he had loved was a taut mask. He tried to soothe her, but she rejected comfort. "Infidelity is murder."

"You don't think that's why he did it?" Ralph asked, less to get an answer than to show disbelief.

"It's not that simple. He probably planned it for a long time and that was the last straw. I shouldn't have told him."

"Don't go on punishing yourself. You were very good to him and took plenty of punishment. Don't ask for more." He saw by her remote expression that she was not listening. Consolation was less important to her than suffering. They sat in silence until the doorbell rang. Ralph admitted two white-coated men with a wheeled stretcher.

"Do you want to see him again?"

Elaine stared at the flowers. For five years there had never been a conscious hour without thought of Fletcher. She had reckoned his comings and goings, his pleasures and prejudices, irascibility, generosity, his boredom, his love, and his cruelty. She had adored, endured, raged, lived in the necessity of his presence and dreamed of freedom from the tyranny of his adoration. The body on the stretcher was none of these things.

Ralph closed the door so that she would not have to see them roll the stretcher along the corridor. She sat curled up on the window seat and studied the flowers in her garden.

9 "HI, BEAUTY!" CALLED DON AS HE UNLOCKED THE front door. The salutation was for whichever of the two girls heard him first. "I'm back, sweet. Anyone call me?" The tone was loud and automatically cheerful. He had to force the appearance of high spirits. The morning had been spent drearily at a double-feature in a cheap movie theater. After a greasy lunch at a stinking drugstore counter, he had wandered among the downtown stores, looking at imported slacks and brass-buttoned blue jackets, which would have been correct and smart attire for the host of a beach house. He charged two ties and a blazer to Elaine's account, less because he wanted the things than for the psychological effect. It was important that he appear jaunty and unconcerned.

"Hey, where's everybody?"

At the end of the hall he saw a shape approaching, but it was his own image reflected in the mirror whose green and shadowed surface showed a dismal figure.

"Cindy!"

A silent house, a shadowed mirror, the echo of his own voice brought about a swift sinking of heart. Fletcher's bedroom door was closed, Elaine's, too. He burst into the guest room. "Good grief, you're not still sleeping." His wife stirred and moaned. "Don't tell me you've been in bed all day. It's half-past three."

She lay with open eyes, staring at the ceiling. "Where've you been all day?"

"I called up a chap I knew at college. Tony Buchanan, I don't think you ever met him. He's in oil, I thought maybe he'd have some good contacts for me." The explanation was swift and glib. "Just caught him before he left for Spain. I drove him to the airport and we had lunch. I ought've called you, oughtn't I?"

Cindy groaned.

"Are you sick? What's wrong? Didn't I tell you not to drink so much champagne?"

"Daddy's dead."

"No! I don't believe it. You're kidding. Sorry, dear. That was a hell of a thing to say. As if I'd kid about it. But the shock." He stretched out his arms, regarded the tremor of his hands. "Look how I'm shaking. How'd it happen? Suicide?"

Cindy jerked up like a puppet on wires. "No! No!"

Her temper showed more of resentment than grief. Don thought he knew all of her moods. The vehemence surprised him. "What was it? An accident?"

"They said sleeping pills. Why does everybody think that?"

"Who's everybody? Have a lot of people been here?" he asked nervously.

"The police. And the doctor, of course."

"Police?"

"Two detectives. It's the thing when somebody dies and they *think* it's suicide. Why do they, Don?"

"Elaine's been afraid of it for a long time. How's she taking it?"

"Cold as ice. I don't understand her at all." An abundance of tears showed Cindy's warmer nature. "Why are you so worried about her?"

"She's his wife."

"I'm his daughter. And I refuse to believe in any suicide."

In a cajoling tone Don asked what made her so certain. Her answer showed family loyalty, if not logic. A man like her father would never do a terrible thing like that. Besides, he had no reason to end his life. "He had everything he wanted, didn't he? Unless there was some trouble about his investments and he lost everything. There was a broker that called him from New York this morning. You don't think he's lost all his money, Don?" Grief at her father's death was overshadowed by deeper fear.

"I've heard nothing about it. The market's strong now. Everything seems in good shape financially."

"You see!" Cindy exclaimed. "I knew it wasn't anything like that . . . I mean . . . why should he? Disgrace himself and his family. I don't want my father remembered as a suicide."

"It's no disgrace."

"It's the coward's way out. I loved my father too much to believe that of him."

Don consoled her as best he could, petted her gently, said she ought to be glad her poor father had found peace, and that they ought not to question the will of God. He sat in the darkened room, holding her hand until she fell asleep again. There was only one idea in his mind, to get his hands on the diary. His fingers itched for the touch of that potent book, his eyes ached for the sight of Fletcher's handwriting. He dared not move until he was sure that Cindy was asleep. Fortunately, the house was quiet. He listened at Elaine's door before he went to Fletcher's bedroom.

On the dresser lay the things Fletcher had taken out of his pockets before he lay down for his final sleep; wallet, address book, keys, pencil, fountain pen. Don's hands trembled with the key ring. He had to wipe sweat from his fingers before he could unlock the drawer. He opened the diary at random, turned from one entry to another, finding in each some new excitement.

Elaine came into the room quietly.

Don managed to slide the diary into the top drawer before he rose and took her in his arms.

"I'm glad you're home," she said. "I've been sleeping so

hard that there could have been an earthquake and I wouldn't have known. Dr. Julian gave me a shot of something absolutely lethal."

"I'm so sorry, dear."

She patted his shoulder to show gratitude.

Don looked over his shoulder to be sure that the diary was safely out of sight.

Elaine was neat and severe in dark trousers and a white shirt. Untinted lips and shadowed eyes added to the look of austerity. A purple bruise scarred her jaw. "I can't believe it, Don . . . that he's . . . gone. Or maybe," she licked dry lips, "it's just that I don't want to. Don, do you think it was that awful fuss last night and his getting so furious and losing his voice? It made him so desperate. I feel that—" But she cut herself off and assumed a locked-away look that denied feeling.

"How awful it must have been for you this morning. What bad luck that I wasn't here to help you."

She caressed the bruised jaw. "I tripped in the kitchen last night and knocked my face against the edge of the sink. Dorine puts too much wax on the floor. Is it still so swollen? Fletcher put an icebag on it." An inexperienced liar, she added unnecessary detail.

Cindy drifted in like a sleepwalker, sipping instant coffee and saying she had not been able to sleep again. "Has anybody got a cigarette?" She looked around frantically, as if she could not live another ten seconds without one. "Donnie, I haven't told mom yet."

"Want me to?"

Don saw that Elaine had gone over to the desk. He came over quickly and touched the papers that lay there. "As a lawyer I can be a big help to you girls."

"I'd better tell Mom myself. After all, I am her daughter."

No one denied this, and Cindy took the telephone on the long wire into the hall where she could speak privately, but excitement raised her voice to such a pitch that the others heard every word. She broke the news with ecstatic importance.

The first Mrs. Strode was, of course, hideously shocked.

From time to time Cindy would put her hand over the instrument and call in to report that her mother who had, after all, lived with Daddy for so many years, did not believe he was a man who would kill himself in any circumstances. Every question and statement was repeated several times. Fletcher would have been irritated by the long conversation. Since she was a little girl, Cindy had been scolded for tying up the telephone. Now she was free to talk as long as she liked. They were all free to be themselves without considering the whims of a sick and surly man.

She was through at last. "My mother wants to know when we're having the funeral."

"That depends upon when they finish the autopsy," Elaine said. "That detective promised to ask them to rush it. I thought he might have tried to call while I was sleeping. And Dr. Julian said he'd help me with the arrangements."

"Why him?" demanded Don.

"He wants to be helpful, but if you'd prefer to take care of things, Don . . ." Elaine was on her way to the kitchen. "Is anyone hungry? We haven't eaten all day."

"Did you ever see anyone so heartless?" asked Cindy.

"We've got to go on living," Don said. When Cindy had left the room, he took out the diary, put it in his pocket, locked the desk drawer, and went to the bathroom because it was the only place he could be sure of privacy while he read what Fletcher Strode had written about his life, his wife, and his death.

AFTER HE MADE his last house call of the day, Ralph stopped at a delicatessen, bought noodle soup, roast chicken, ham, tongue, roast beef, corned beef, smoked salmon, coleslaw, pickles, potato salad, three kinds of cheese, rye and white breads, apple strudel, and chocolate cake.

The abundance delighted Elaine. "How he would have loved this. Fletcher. Delicatessen was his very favorite food. He was even more extravagant than you are." Such memories were tribute, a list of foods her service to the dead. "Smoked turkey, sturgeon, Nova Scotia Salmon, *fois gras*, Holland asparagus and caviar." Here she paused to recall a naughty evening when they had started with an early snack of caviar and vodka, made love, and forgotten a theater party. Wayward memories restored her. She moved about gracefully as she fetched plates and laid out cold cuts in rows between bouquets of parsley. "Roquefort was his favorite cheese, but it had to be real, French, first-class Roquefort."

He would never again ask her to mix Roquefort with sweet butter, never stand as Ralph stood now, watching while she flew from table to refrigerator, from stove to sink, never come bumbling into the kitchen to find out what they were having for dinner. Now, poignantly, because of this small thing, his pleasure in the flavor of cheese, she saw death—*his* death—as something more than an end to suffering, for there had also been an end to pleasure. The joys of an ordinary day are what give purpose, if not meaning, to being alive: a clear sky, breakfast coffee, a walk on the beach, the car humming along the open road, the change of seasons, a good joke, the surprising conduct of one's friends. The list is too long for recording. Even in the last sad years, after he had rejected gaudier activities, Fletcher had loved to lie back in his comfortable chair, drinking cold beer and watching a stiff fight, a close race, a tough game on TV. He enjoyed surprises and treats, like giving presents; no birthday or holiday had gone unmarked. Pretty women still fascinated him; he never failed to watch the sway of a firm buttocks under a tight skirt, considered himself a connoisseur of legs and breasts, and could never resist pinching or kissing her flesh when his wife came close. There were other things, indeed too many for recording, and now it would make no difference that the Mets won or lost a World Series.

They ate so solemnly that the food lost flavor. Ralph's efforts at lightness increased the weight of gloom. To divert them he talked about his boyhood in this house. Elaine's bright eyes were turned toward him, but Ralph could not tell whether she was far away or listening too attentively. Just the same, he tried to divert her. "My Aunt Cora may not have been the world's greatest cook, but she was tops with certain dishes. Her stuffed breast of veal was famous. She got the recipe from a Hungarian chef whom Uncle Jules treated for stomach ulcers."

"Do you think," asked Cindy, "it would be correct for my mother to come to the funeral?"

"If she wants to," Elaine said.

"Wouldn't it be embarrassing for you, dear?" asked Don.

Elaine shrugged. "For her, too, I imagine. With such a small and quiet funeral, we'd have to speak to each other."

"It won't be that small," declared Cindy. "There'll probably be a lot of people. I won't have you getting chintzy about my father's funeral."

"She doesn't mean it's to be cheap, love. Elaine feels that your father hadn't many friends here, and—"

"We've got friends, you and I, Donnie. Dozens of people have entertained us, and with your contacts and all. It's been bad enough, not being able to entertain, but the least we can do is give my father a proper funeral. He deserves it. He was an important man."

"Whatever you like. Please take care of it, Don. Let Cindy have whatever she thinks will impress her friends."

"I refuse to sit here and be insulted. With my father not cold in his grave." Cindy pushed back her chair. High heels clattered on the tiled floor.

Elaine said she was sorry. Don started after Cindy, but changed his mind and returned to his chair to remark that the poor kid seemed strangely obsessed with the notion that her father had not killed himself. "What's your opinion, Doctor?"

Ralph replied that he could not judge an act he had not witnessed. There could be no definite answer until the autopsy was done.

"Elaine oughtn't to be surprised. She's been expecting it for a long time, haven't you, dear?"

Elaine's face, which so frequently betrayed her with a rosy flush, had become bloodless, the ivory flesh as yellow as saffron. Her right hand protected the bruise.

"She told me so quite frankly. Out there in the pavilion."

Her eyelids flickered, her long neck bent in acquiescence.

"Yes, I did expect it. I was afraid for a long time." Each word came out separately, forced by a reluctant will.

"Not without cause," Ralph said. "When a man keeps a supply of drugs hidden, it's obvious what's on his mind."

"Hidden! And you found them?" Don sounded angry as though he had been cheated of important information.

"Yesterday. Before he died. Dorine and I were cleaning his closet. So I knew I'd been right about what I told you."

My wife, Fletcher Strode had written in his diary, *is a devious woman.*

"What did you do with the pills?"

"I hid them the way I hide the others."

"What others?" Don persisted.

"The prescription. I kept the bottle hidden and only gave him two a night. Didn't I tell you?"

"No, dear, you didn't. Probably forgot to mention it." Don threw her an indulgent smile. "Bit complicated, isn't it? Two hidden stores of pills. Did you remember to tell that to the detectives?"

"She did," Ralph said, "and we discussed it with them. It's not extraordinary. A potential suicide always complicates things. With all the vacillations—he's apt to change from hour to hour—and in the end, the act is triggered by an impulse."

"Impulse." The word hung in the air while Elaine's hand, bearing a fork, remained at the level of her chin.

"Don't you believe it was impulse? After all that storm and temperament last night," Don said. "An impulse of that kind would be very natural. On anybody's part." He turned to Ralph. "It's not good form to speak ill of the dead, but we have to be honest about it. He was beastly to her."

"He was so miserable," Elaine flared out. "You don't know. None of us will ever know how miserable. Desperate!" Her hand tightened on her jaw as though she cherished the hurt Fletcher had given her.

In a sudden fury she gathered up plates and coffee cups. "Are we finished?" Whether they were or not, she whisked their dishes off to the kitchen. They went after her, offered help, but proved a hindrance. She was nervous, declared they got in her way, that they would put things in the wrong places, clog the garbage disposal, let good food go to waste. "Please, may I do that?" and "Do let me pass," or, with a shriek, "No, no, not there!" Ralph retreated to the edge of the kitchen and Don kept saying, "Sorry . . . so sorry, dear," like a penitent schoolboy.

"You must think I'm an awful bitch," she said to Ralph when Don had gone off to his bedroom and she was finishing at the sink.

"I think you've had enough. You've behaved admirably, but you're worn out. I'm putting you to bed."

"And leaving?"

"I'll sit with you until you've relaxed."

"Not in there." She led him along the hall past the door of her bedroom. Even as a doctor he was not to be allowed that privilege. She did not want him to remember that he had entered the room as her lover.

He arranged pillows so that she could stretch comfortably upon the living room couch. They agreed not to talk about Fletcher's death and could find nothing else to talk about. Neither lovers nor friends now, they looked at each other like strangers, and at the room as though they had no right to be there. When he had come to this house as an adopted child, Ralph had been drawn irresistibly to the formal parlor with its silk drapes, waxed woods, glistening porcelains, its pretty little objects of ivory and silver. The room had been declared out of bounds to a clumsy boy. It was cozier now, less formal, yet with all of Elaine's books and lamps and pictures, he still felt himself an intruder.

Death had come between the lovers. In the silence Elaine grew restless. She was worn out but not sleepy after her long, drugged nap. She recalled those conversations she had planned but never held, confessions of her fears, and she wondered, looking at Ralph's somber, bony face, if his knowing could have prevented the final act. "I meant to tell you," she began. Her lips twitched and a nerve jumped on the left side below the eye. She wanted her face concealed from his pale and searching eyes. Once more at the window with her back to him, "I was afraid, I guess. It was on my mind all the time," she confessed.

"I knew."

"Then why didn't you say something?"

"I didn't want you to be frightened."

"I was. Terribly. All the time." Passionate hands were clasped before her breast as in prayer. "I used to go to his room nights"—she breathed in spasms between the phrases—"to listen and know that he was alive."

"If you'd gone to him last night, you might have been in time to save him."

She had no answer. Beyond the window there was no world. The sky had no color, the stars were hidden. Fog shut out the ocean and the lighted streets below the hill. Elaine did not know that she was crying. There were no sobs. Tears jetted out of her eyes and ran down her cheeks. They brought no relief.

THERE IS AN acute moment between sleep and thought when every sense becomes aware and the mind, free of daytime clutter, finds reality in illusion. Elaine heard Fletcher at her door again. She knew he was dead, yet felt the living presence. Waiting as she had waited last night (and on so many nights when he had come to her bed for consolation), her ear tuned itself for the whine of hinges, the weight of footsteps, the rhythm of his breathing. Every nerve and cell anticipated the touch of his flesh, her heart raced, temperature rose, and all the excitable muscles of loins and pelvis became clamorously alive. For an instant, only the slightest sliver of a second, she let the past return, the good past, the times that had been crazy with love and consummation. "Hi, lovable!" Through all of this she knew and accepted reality. "You're dead."

Time became infinity as she lay in passionate silence waiting for the nightmare, if it had been nightmare, to come to its crisis. "Oh Fletch, Fletch," she moaned, "why did it have to be like this?" She heard the answer as clearly as if he were in the room, heard the voice, mechanical, irate, the crippled ringmaster crying out his bitter commands to the mocking, stubborn animals. Over and over, like a faulty phonograph record, those sickening belches and cackles. She turned on the light, rejecting sleep. Sleep had become the enemy, admitting terror, distorting memory, revealing truth.

In the light he was there, too, inescapable in every object she looked at, touched, and felt against her body. All of her trinkets, her jewelry, many of her garments, had been chosen by him. "I like you in those colors, lovable." The robe she wrapped about her on chilly nights was one he had enjoyed. She could feel the big hand on the soft fabric.

She forced herself to enter his room. Scents of intimacy remained. She smelled toilet water, sniffed his shirts, touched his hairbrushes. Last night he had left his things upon the dresser—wallet, fountain pen, key ring, a scattering of small change. Jacket and trousers had been hung neatly upon the silent valet, socks and shirts and shorts placed upon the bench below the window. Everything as usual, except the man who had died in that bed. His head had left a hollow in the pillow, the sheets were wrinkled, the covers thrown back. She stood a few feet from the bed, frowning at the emptiness as though she sought some answer there. Vigorously then, she jerked off the sheets. The ease with which she handled the dead man's linens was astonishing.

"What are you doing at this hour?"

She whirled about, faced Don, and said, "I thought I'd clean up a bit. It's all such a mess." She jerked off the bedclothes and automatically, like a good housewife, folded them.

"It's quarter to three."

"What difference does it make? I couldn't sleep. It's better to keep busy." She went on with the tasks. A passion for tidiness had seized her. "If people come here, we'll want it to look nice." With the same energy she gave to the folding of sheets, she offered excuses. "Cindy expects people to call. You and she have made so many friends."

"Plenty of time tomorrow. No one knows about it yet."

"I suppose I do look silly in the middle of the night." She swept out of the room, carrying the linens to the hamper.

Don hurried ahead to switch on the lights. In the narrow corridor he turned and faced her. When she had got rid of the sheets and pillowcases, she laid her hand upon his shoulder. "I'm glad you're here, Don."

He had not seen her alone since he had read the entire diary. "Let me help you through this. Ask anything of me, tell me anything you want, trust me, beauty."

She was glad he was there because she had to keep busy, to move around, use her hands, occupy herself with small tasks. She made a pot of cocoa. Fletcher had always taken cocoa on sleepless nights. He said it soothed him.

"I hope you don't think I'm nosy asking you this, but how are you fixed for money?"

The milk in the pan required full attention. She had to watch carefully so that she could snatch it off the flame when it started to bubble. "That's one thing I don't have to worry about."

"At the moment, I mean. Cash on hand. The estate will be tied up. In probate for quite a while."

The milk began to boil. Elaine slid the pot off the burner. "We haven't a lot, Cindy and I, but if you need anything right away, just ask me. I'll be happy to do what I can." The offer was reckless. Don had little more than two hundred dollars of borrowed money in his bank account, and was at the end of his resources. But he felt the risk worthwhile if Elaine had confidence in him.

"You're sweet, Don. Will you hand me two cups? The big yellow ones. I don't need money, thank you. I've got two accounts, a checking and a savings, in my own name, Elaine Guardino Strode. In case anything ever happened to him, he said." She stirred the cocoa with the wooden spoon. "He probably planned this for a long time." She went on and on about Fletcher's desperate unhappiness and the suicide impulse, repeating everything she had told Don that afternoon in the pavilion.

Don listened attentively. No matter what tomorrow should bring, today's assets depended upon Elaine's goodwill. His offer of a loan had primed the pump. "And remember, if you need advice, I'm a lawyer. I want you to come to me with all your problems."

She thanked him absently. There were other things on her mind, "Do you feel any twinges of guilt?"

"Me?"

Elaine sat moodily over the steaming cocoa, her head bent above the cup like a gypsy brooding over tea leaves. A shadow had fallen across her face. "We tormented him."

"That's nonsense, ridiculous, an exaggeration. No one tortured him, he was the one who caused all the trouble."

"He thought we were lovers."

"He thought. Suspicion haunts the guilty mind." This was a direct quotation. Fletcher had used the old saw as though it had been an original, striking thought. Don had made notes on several items before he locked the book back into the desk. "It was his jealousy. Not only of me, of every man. You told me so yourself."

As Elaine raised her head the mysterious shadow vanished. She held her cup in both hands like a child. "It'll be strange without him. There's a kind of emptiness already. These past few years, every day, every hour, has been with him and for him, trying to keep him interested in living. Not that I was very successful."

"You're free now. It's all over, your life's your own, you can do what you like."

Fletcher had known that she dreamed of freedom; there had been mention of it in the diary.

"What do I want?" She set down the cup and held out both hands for freedom to be delivered into them. "Perhaps later I'll know. It's funny, I used to think about it, when I was bored sometimes and lonely for New York, I'd imagine . . ." She stopped, hugging her body, lowering her shoulders under the weight of freedom too suddenly achieved. "Sometimes I thought he knew. Once he heard me on the phone, I was talking to an old friend who'd just got a divorce. I said to her that she was free, her life was her own. He thought I was speaking of him and me and ever since I've felt so . . . so . . ." She raised dark lids, letting Don look into her eyes, letting him know she was not afraid of a word, "guilty."

"You take things too hard, you're too sensitive." It was to show his faith in her that Don spoke this way.

"It was wicked of me, with him so sick and unhappy and dependent. But I suppose one oughtn't to feel too responsible for every foolish and meaningless word. Or daydream. Perhaps I am too sensitive." This was accompanied by a flutter of self-conscious laughter. "Daydreams can be dangerous, can't they?"

"Not if they stay just dreams."

"I suppose."

"But dreams are the source of action." Don remembered some professor—of law, psychology, logic?—who had advised students to seek criminal motives in man's reveries. With every word Elaine made herself more vulnerable and more helpful to Don Hustings. He added quickly, "You need someone to look after you. I'm the man of the family now. Leave your problems to me, dear."

"You are a help, Don. I'm so glad you're here."

"I'm glad, too." Sympathy shone out of his dark eyes. A family pet could have shown no greater devotion.

"Perhaps it's better this way. For Fletcher. He was too proud, he couldn't ever be resigned. There was no real compensation for him, ever. Not one of your cheerful cripples." She wore a delicate, faraway expression that her husband might have called devious.

Such a woman, mused Don, unaware that expedience shaped his thinking, might well be judged as her husband had foreseen. She had changed in Don's eyes; her flesh had a different color. She had become dark, brooding, tragic, Italian, with black hair falling about her shoulders like a shawl. The electric clock ticked, the refrigerator rumbled, and below the hill, fire sirens shrieked. The very air seemed nervous.

Later, when Elaine had gone back to her room, Don reread an item copied from the diary:

When it is over and I am gone she will say she loved me and wanted me to live. She might even believe this is true because I have noticed that most people believe what they need to believe. Especially when desperate and trying to hide from the killer side of our souls. Believing is convenient when it helps us forget that our minds are like beasts in the jungle.

In the locked desk drawer Don had also found lists of properties, stock holdings, bonds, and investments. Although not yet a member of the bar there, he knew that in California, as in most states, a person convicted of murder cannot inherit the victim's property.

He returned to the bedroom quietly. Cindy heard him, turned toward the wall, and pretended to be asleep. She had been restless too, had got up twice, first to take a crumpled plastic bag from a hiding place behind the luggage in the closet, to fold it and place in her hatbox; then to remove it, shake it out, and place it over the beige organza dress she had worn to the party.

10

"SORRY," SAID CINDY, POKING HER HEAD IN, "but Don told me to wake you up. Those detectives are here again and a new man. He'll want to talk to you. Don's been with him for ages." She came into the room, watching herself in the mirror, arranging a lock of hair, smoothing her lip rouge with a caressing finger. She was correctly dressed for mourning, but wore too much eye makeup.

Elaine noted the time with horror. It was after eleven. "I didn't get to sleep until after five." She pushed herself up in the bed. "More detectives?"

"Sticking their noses into everything. People in mourning ought to be allowed some privacy." In the mirror Cindy saw drama. "Don's made breakfast for you. Everything's ready but the toast. Who do you think killed Daddy?"

She could not have asked more blandly about a yard of silk or a recipe for salad dressing.

"Cindy!"

"Well somebody did."

"That's ridiculous. We all know it was suicide."

"I never thought so. And the detectives don't either."

"I don't believe it."

Cindy came to the bed and bent over Elaine triumphantly. Superior because the police agreed with her, that it had not been suicide, she whispered, "I heard him tell Don, that new detective, he's from the Homicide Department, more important than those two from yesterday, and cute, too."

"What did he tell Don?"

"That it wasn't sleeping pills that killed him."

"Are you sure he said that?"

"I happened to be in the hall and I heard it with my own ears."

Elaine slid to the far side of the bed. She did not like the heat of Cindy's breath upon her face. "Did he have any idea what it was?"

"He'll talk to us when he's through with Don. Was that another car?" Cindy darted to the window. More men were coming toward the house. One carried a camera, the other a metal box. Off Cindy whirled to learn the newest developments.

Elaine chose a black dress for her interview with the detectives. Her mirror showed a wan face with deeply ringed eyes and skin as sallow as old soap. In the mirror she found another face behind her own.

The detective, Juarez, called through the screen, "Sorry, Mrs. Strode. We're just looking around. I hope I didn't frighten you."

Elaine was shaken. Her house had become possessed by strangers. Juarez retreated to the shed where the gardener kept his tools, seedlings, fertilizers, and insecticides. Defiant, Elaine clattered down the hall, tapping high heels firmly upon the floor as she passed the living room. A man who had been talking to Cindy sprang to greet her. "Good morning, Mrs. Strode. I deeply regret that I'm forced to intrude myself at this sad time, but I'm afraid it's necessary. We must get to know each other. I'm Curtis Knight."

"How do you do?"

"I'm having a chat with your charming stepdaughter. You won't mind if I finish with her first?" he asked archly, like a child's nurse withholding a treat. "Why don't you have a bite of breakfast before we talk?"

"Thank you."

She clattered on down the hall, Sergeant Curtis Knight popped back to Cindy. He had barely seated himself when the girl began looking about, frantically as always, for a cigarette. "May I?" Knight sprang up with an unopened pack from which he deftly tore the cellophane.

He was not at all like a detective. Agile movements, gallant manners, winning tones were exaggerated almost to a point of absurdity. The miming was deliberate. It diverted the attention of those he questioned so that, while playing cavalier, he watched and listened scrupulously. His admirers were disarmed by his tricks, his subordinates irritated, while those subjected to his interrogation became self-conscious. No one enjoyed his theatrics so much as Knight himself. He was thirty-eight years old, a bachelor, devoted to his mother, and said to have extraordinary ambitions.

Cindy was impressed. Despite protests against the presence of the detectives in a house of mourning, she respected an officer of the law and hoped her answers pleased him. Movies and TV had given her an exaggerated idea of intelligence and deductive powers of such men. With an air of girlish restraint and few well-timed tears, she hid her fear of certain questions. Everything she has said to Redding yesterday was said again.

Knight noted every inflection and gesture. "And what did you do when you went in the bedroom and saw you father lying there?"

Involuntarily Cindy's hand reached out. "I . . . I . . ."

The hand was pulled back.

"Felt to see if he was alive?"

She nodded gratefully. "I was scared. I began to shake. I forgot the phone call and everything."

"And then?"

"I called Elaine and told her."

"How did she take it?"

"Cold as ice. And not too terribly shocked." Lest the detective think her prejudiced, Cindy went on, "Of course she's a lot older and has terrific self-control. And she did expect him"—her voice took on an uncalculated note of harshness—"to take his own life, she says."

Knight did not subject her to any more questions about the discovery of her father's body. He was more interested in the events of the evening before the tragedy, particularly the scene at the dinner table. "Daddy wasn't in a good mood at all," Cindy did not think it necessary to add that she had contributed to her father's ill humor, "and when Elaine admired *my* husband," this with a wife's emphasis, "Daddy was terribly, terribly angry."

"Why? Was he jealous of your husband?"

All earnestness and inflection, "He has no *real* reason to be," Cindy said. "Don hasn't the slightest interest in a woman of her age, but when a girl like Elaine, married to a man *years* older than herself, and a *young* man as attractive as *my husband* is staying in the house, it's *obvious*, isn't it?" Riding high on a tandem of prejudice and conviction she prattled on. This had not been the *only* time her father had *exploded* in jealous rage, insulted his wife, made life *unbearable* for Elaine. There had been dozens of things, incidents too trivial to remember, like the time Daddy threw the chocolate mousse at Elaine's new dress. "And you know what she did? Oh, she took things meekly, butter wouldn't melt in her mouth when Daddy was around, but," Cindy drew a breath of anticipation, "she broke all the lunch dishes. Haviland. Daddy teased her about it later but," gravely Cindy stated, "still waters run deep you know. She tried to show us how brave and patient she was, but after all, with a sick husband. I mean . . . she'd made her bed, she had to lie on it."

"You said that she, Mrs. Strode, expected your father to," Knight chose his words with care, "take his own life. Did she ever mention this to you?"

"Not to me directly. I heard her say it afterward. Yesterday when those detectives were here. But she'd told Don before. If she expected poor Daddy to kill himself, why didn't she do something? She told Don last week."

Malice was not calculated. Abrasive self-interest had not rubbed away with finishing school varnish. The girl had not only to uphold family honor, but she had to protect herself. There were areas of inquiry she hoped the detective would not try to explore. But why should anyone suspect anything about a plastic bag hanging innocently over a party dress?

BUTTERY YELLOW SUNSHINE lay thick upon the breakfast table. Don had gone out to the garden to pick an October rose for the one-blossom silver vase Fletcher had given Elaine, with a spray of white cymbidium, on Valentine's Day. The coffee was strong, the toast was crisp. Don served her with the skill of a devoted butler.

"What a pleasant place to have breakfast. May I join you? I don't think you'd be accused of suborning an officer if you were to offer me a cup of coffee." Sergeant Knight praised the coffee, asked the brand and method of brewing, admired the house, commented favorably upon Mrs. Strode's talents as a decorator. The flattery was not insincere, the sergeant not the usual police detective. Although he had little use for women, he enjoyed their homage. In a jovial way he remarked that Mrs. Strode was indeed fortunate in having a lawyer in the house. "Mr. Hustings will be here while I question you. And, of course, you know you may refuse to answer if you wish."

"You don't mind? I want to help you as much as possible," Don said.

She shrugged. "I have nothing to hide."

"You see, Sergeant, we're going to make it all very easy for you." Don passed around his cigarette case. The intense yellow of the sunshine falling obliquely upon them gave the scene a theatrical air as if setting and light had been designed for a comedy of manners.

The scene began with explanation and apology. Knight was sure Mrs. Strode would not mind having her home searched; a mere matter of routine, quite ordinary in the circumstances.

"What circumstances?"

"The case of your husband's death has not been ascertained."

"Then it wasn't the sleeping pills?" Elaine had already got a hint of this from Cindy, but if she had betrayed the knowledge she would have cheated herself of a full explanation.

"Not according to the tests, Mrs. Strode. The level of barbiturates in the blood was not sufficient to cause death."

Elaine shook her head. "It's hard to believe. Especially since he had secret stores of pills hidden all over the place."

"The laboratory's going on with tests, and they're looking around the house for some other clue to the cause," Don said.

"Then why," asked Elaine, "did Dr. Julian say it was sleeping pill suicide?"

"Did he, Mrs. Strode? Or were you the one who suggested it?"

The telephone had been ringing. Cindy came in to say that Dr. Julian wanted to speak to Elaine. "Go right ahead," Knight said as if she had asked permission. In the hall she met a detective who had been looking in the linen closet. He jerked a bow.

Ralph wanted to know how she felt. He had called earlier and been told she was asleep. "No one mentioned it to me," Elaine said. Raising her voice in defense of anyone who might be listening on the extension, she said, "The house is crawling with detectives. They're looking for some mysterious clue. Do you know that it wasn't the sleeping pills?"

The Coroner's office had given Ralph this information earlier. He could not talk now, he said, because he had not finished his hospital rounds. Elaine felt that he was being cautious. She had hoped he would not be too busy to see her later that day.

"Nice talk?" asked Knight when she came back. He started at once to question her about the sleeping pills. She found the repetition irritating. "I told this to all the other detectives yesterday. Must we go over it again?"

"I'm sorry if it distressed you, Mrs. Strode." Solicitude was a bit too showy. "But I want to hear it again, and precisely from your own lips." Above the smile the eyes were shrewd. Knight asked many questions about the events that had preceded Fletcher's death, repeated what she had already told him, and popped from one subject to another so unexpectedly that sometimes Elaine answered too quickly and without sufficient thought. Many details seemed irrelevant, but Knight gave every trifle the utmost attention.

"I understand, Mrs. Strode, that you were in the habit of going to your husband's room at night while he was asleep."

"Yes."

"Every night?"

"Almost. Perhaps not every night." She did not recall having talked about this to any of the detectives, but thought it wiser not to ask how Knight had found it out.

"Do you mind if I ask the reason you did this?"

She answered softly and Knight, apologizing because he hadn't heard, said, "Speak a little louder, please." There was another pause. Elaine offered a conciliatory smile before she told him, her tone scarcely above a lover's whisper, that she has gone to her husband's room to make sure he was breathing properly. "He'd been so terribly sick, you know."

"You were worried about his breathing through that aperture in the neck? Afraid he might have covered it in his sleep?"

"He was very unhappy. Desperate. I knew . . ." She had told this to Don as well as Ralph. Either might have told Knight. "I knew he didn't want to live."

"And when you went into his room night before last?" asked Knight in an offhand way.

Although she was sure it was a guess since she has said nothing of this visit to Ralph or Don, she answered, "He seemed all right when I went in."

"Sleeping normally?"

"It seemed so."

"You're sure of that?"

She inclined her head. "If I hadn't been sure, don't you think I'd have done something? Called for help?"

"Was anyone in the house at the time?"

"There's always the telephone," she replied in a mocking tone.

"Do you know what time it was when you went into your husband's room?"

"I didn't look at the clock. I think it was before Don and Cindy got home from the party."

"We got in very late, after three. The house was completely quiet."

"Perhaps you'd like to tell me in your way what happened on Monday night. Had there been anything unusual between you and your husband? Harsh words? A quarrel?" This, in spite of the bruised jaw. Knight seemed blind to it. He was being gentle with the woman. A successful pediatrician could not have surpassed him in the bedside manner. Speaking as to a sick child, and wearing a look of tender patience, he urged, "Tell me just what happened that evening."

"Hasn't Don told you?"

"I wasn't here the whole time. Remember, dear, Cindy and I left before eight." Don's hand fell upon Elaine's. "But you don't have to answer, you know. You've got a legal right to refuse."

"Why shouldn't I answer? This is just as important to me as to anyone else." But she could not go on. Her mind wandered. What had the detective asked? A feeling of weakness came over her. She got up and walked away from them.

Don started to speak, but Knight held up his hand. He knew how to handle women. "Naturally you're distressed. It must be painful, after your shock and the loss of a loved one, to recall unpleasant occasions." He had gone to stand beside her, to soothe her with his sympathy. When she came back and slid into her chair docilely, he asked if there was anything she needed. A cigarette? Water? Another cup of coffee?

Elaine did not respond. Her nervousness was not, like Cindy's, loquacious. She attempted a wan smile.

"You can't believe your husband is gone? I know," Knight said, and to Don, confidentially, "It is difficult to accommodate oneself to the idea that a dear one will not return." He turned back to Elaine to say that he had suffered the loss of a sweetheart, a young lady just twenty years of age. "For months afterward, when I passed the corner where we used to meet, I'd look for her. Sometimes I'd think I saw her standing there." Whether this was true or not, he had found the device of personal recollection useful in drawing out the shy and reluctant.

Elaine's memories of her husband were too intimate to be shared with a stranger. It was true that she could not wholly believe that Fletcher would never stamp through the hall, never enter this room to demand attention and offer reassurance. He had not been the only one who had become dependent; every day, every hour, Fletcher's will, Fletcher's decisions, Fletcher's strength, had sustained her. Their lives had been too closely knit for the bond to be severed in a day.

The breakfast nook was now too sunny, heated like a greenhouse. Don suggested that they find a cooler place for their conversation. They chose the den. As soon as Elaine had seated herself, gingerly, upon a straight chair like a caller, she was sorry they had not gone into the living room. Fletcher had spent most of his time here: in that big chair, he had read the newspaper; at the game table, played solitaire; from the love seat, watched television. The lower shelves were filled with his paperback mystery novels.

Don had chosen to sit at the desk. "Well, sir, shall we go on? I'm sure, sweet," he offered a small bow to Elaine, "You're anxious to have this over with."

"You said yesterday that you lived in fear of your husband's taking his own life. That's true, isn't it?" To spare Elaine the bother of answering, Knight bobbed his own head. "And before that, last week, you spoke of it to Mr. Hustings?"

"Sergeant Knight asked me about it and I told him what you said," Don put in hastily.

"It's true," Elaine said.

"Didn't you also tell Mr. Hustings that your husband asked if you'd be afraid to put him out of his misery?"

"Did I?" How could she be sure of everything she had told Don? More vivid than the scene in the pavilion was the memory of a night when Fletcher had demanded an answer to the question. On the bloated convex surface of the TV they had watched—she and Fletcher hand in hand on the love seat—a drama in color. At the high point, when the actor had brought a velvet pillow from his invalid wife's favorite chair, the picture had dissolved into an advertisement for kitchen soap. While a troupe of beguiling boys tracked over linoleum and a happy mother informed the audience that a brand-new, scientific discovery made mopping up a pleasure, Fletcher had asked if she would have as much courage as the husband in the television play. Elaine's wrist remembered the sweat and pressure of his hand.

"Yes, love, you did," Don said with authority.

Meanwhile one of the lesser detectives had come in, excused himself for whispering, and conferred with Knight. It seemed that they wished to remove a few trivial household objects for examination. Everything would be returned and care would be taken so that nothing would be damaged. The detectives were given permission and went away. They left soon after. Knight stayed. He had settled himself on the love seat, cozily, like an old friend.

A new phase of the interrogation started. Questions concerned Elaine's relations with her husband. Elaine became fiercely loyal, refused to let the detective insinuate that Fletcher had caused her to suffer and rebel. Had he been alive, she could not have protected him with greater ardor. So there had been quarrels, insults, assault with pudding, broken dishes. In what family were there no arguments and misunderstandings? "Can you blame a sick man for being irritable at times?" Passion attacked smugness. "It was worse than just ordinary illness. His voice, it was terrible to hear, he couldn't bear listening to himself. He was desperate, he hated life." Intensity was so great that her own throat closed, she could barely use her voice, and she felt as maimed and mute as Fletcher. Huskily, "But he wasn't deliberately cruel. Ever! It wasn't in his soul to hurt me. My husband was kind and generous and he loved me," she argued as though those words alone answered all questions.

"Would you mind, Mrs. Strode, if I asked how you happened to get that bruise on your face?"

"She tripped in the kitchen and fell against the sink. The maid had used too much wax on the floor."

"I see." Knight's curtness was a declaration of disbelief.

"Perhaps you'll tell us the cause of that final quarrel on Monday night?"

"It's not necessary if you don't want to," Don warned. It was not surprising that he counseled silence. To say that the quarrels and tragedy had been brought about by his need for a thousand dollars would ravel threadbare pride. In Don's world, where people tossed about the names of millionaires, where association with the rich sustained frail pretenders, one thousand dollars was a poor excuse for all that fuss. The rings on Elaine's fingers, the rug under their feet, the fittings of the kitchen, had cost far more. To make public Don's poverty would utterly destroy him and would affirm Fletcher's cruelty to his family. Small wonder that Don's soft eyes were fixed in doglike appeal upon Elaine's face.

"It was nothing, Sergeant Knight, just a trifle, the usual family fuss."

"AND THIS SMALL thing, this trifle, an ordinary family fuss, drove your husband to suicide? You honestly believe that Mrs. Strode?"

"I told you, he was desperate!" She turned to Don for support. "You saw him those last few days, you know the state he was in. Tell him!"

"I've told him everything I know, dear."

"I take it that Mrs. Strode is unwilling to tell us about the final argument." Knight cajoled in the manner of a nurse who suggests punishment as an alternative to a treat.

"It's her right, if she doesn't want to answer certain questions." Don spoke to Knight, but looked to Elaine for approval.

"All I'm trying to do is make him understand how much Fletcher wanted to die. How he suffered, what hell he went through." Elaine was shaken. Tension raised her temperature, brought goose bumps on her arms, made her nipples thrust themselves in protest against the fabric of her dress. She needed to scream. "The last few days were just pure hell," she managed to say edgily. "And weeks. And months. A man like Fletcher. You don't know."

Don urged calm.

"I'm perfectly calm," she snapped back, and challenged Knight, "All right, let's get on with the inquisition."

"I'm sorry you take it in that spirit, Mrs. Strode. What I'm asking about are the matters we've discussed frankly. Perhaps if we'd get at details." But instead of asking questions he sat back and waited. Silence was another of his devices. Often, by wearing out a person's patience, he had been rewarded by a revealing outburst. No laxative had a greater purgative effect than fear.

Don said, "Perhaps you'll understand Mr. Strode's disposition better if you read his diary. That may answer all the questions."

Knight sucked his breath. "He kept a diary?"

"He was always writing in it, wasn't he Elaine?"

Elaine had been touched and pleased by Fletcher's enjoyment of her Christmas gift, amused by his tenacity in keeping it locked away. What secrets had the recluse to guard? No wife could suspect infidelity of a husband too sensitive to ask for a bill of fare. For a moment, reluctant to betray the secrets of his unhappiness—surely the diary must contain those—she held one of her statuesque poses.

"Well, Mrs. Strode?"

"It may be helpful to Sergeant Knight. Do you know where the keys are, Elaine?"

"Of course, of course," she answered, thinking that the diary might solve their problem and keep them from poking into her secrets. She hurried off in a fury of eagerness to find confirmation in Fletcher's writings, to have her statements proved, to look into the mind of the dead. Zealous and confused, she stared straight at the key ring without finding it until Don and Knight came into the bedroom, and Don pointed it out to her. It was in the most obvious place, of course, with his wallet and coins and fountain pen, just as Fletcher had left them when he emptied his pockets.

Knight could not repress a smile. The case was building and in it were the elements of public interest: sick husband, young and beautiful wife, cruelty, and best of all, wealth. Front-page notoriety was inevitable. Knight's mother often asked why he never got interesting cases in rich people's houses. "Curtis dear, you're so much smarter and more refined than those tough detectives they always have on the TV." Knight continued to smile as he followed Elaine and Don back to the den.

She unlocked the desk drawer, found and handed him the diary. "I hope this will help you."

"Have you read it?"

"No I haven't."

The answer did not convince Knight. In his opinion all women spied and all married women were without honor. From an early age he had been instructed and warned by a mother who knew the nature of females. "Have you read it?" he asked Don.

Don scoffed at the question. He had only caught sight of the diary when Fletcher Strode had been writing in it. "He was always quick to hide it when you came into the room. That's why I feel it must be important."

This Knight believed. He pocketed the diary, thanked Elaine for her cooperation, said that she'd be hearing from him shortly. He did not leave at once. From the living room window Elaine saw him in conversation with a couple of strange men. When at last the talk ended and Knight drove off and she turned from the window, she found the room barren. All the cushions had been removed. Bed pillows were gone, too, from her room and Fletcher's. The hamper in the hall had been ransacked, and from it the detectives had "borrowed" the linen she had stripped from Fletcher's bed shortly before three o'clock that morning.

THE MEN WHO had interviewed Sergeant Knight in the garden were reporters. Elaine would not talk to any of them. Don took over the painful duty, urged her to lie down and relax. Cindy hurried in to announce that the news was on the radio. According to the broadcast, the police suspected foul play in the alleged suicide of retired New York millionaire found dead in the bedroom of his Pacific Palisades mansion.

Ralph heard it on his car radio while he drove from the hospital. He was sour about it. Two members of the Homicide Squad had wasted over an hour of his morning. There was no doubt that the police believed, and hoped, that Fletcher Strode had been the victim of foul play. Ralph had sneered at the idea. The tendency to suicide was, he told them in technical language which always impresses officious laymen, common in post-laryngectomy patients. While he had not been Mr. Strode's doctor, Ralph had frequently visited the house and had observed the contradictions and vacillations that accompany a deep death wish. He had also given a lecture on the ease with which suffocation could be caused in a patient who breathed through an opening in the neck. A number of post-laryngectomy patients had, according to an authoritative paper on the subject, attempted suicide by obstructing the passage of air, but had failed to achieve death because the urge had ended when the struggle for breath began.

The detectives knew this, but were skeptical of the suicide theory. Their questions showed that they believed that someone had committed the deed and had later, stupidly, removed the object. Had it been left on the body, suicide would have been taken for granted. Later he heard all of this shouted from the car radio and in much more colorful language. The announcer's overdramatic voice irritated him, too.

Several cars were parked on the street before the Strode house, and the police car was still there. Don opened the door. "Elaine isn't seeing anyone," he said, but conceded that Ralph was not just anyone and could be admitted. There was an air of importance about Don; he strutted about like a civic official. Status had been acquired as he sat at Fletchers Strode's desk, offering drinks and information to reporters. The grateful audience built up his self-esteem. He told nothing but known facts, but his growing assurance gave truth a racy flavor.

Elaine had spent the afternoon pacing and studying the pattern of her bedroom rugs, and throwing herself upon the bed and watching leaf shadows on the wall. The doors of the old house were of heavy wood, the walls thick, but she could hear the murmur of voices. When Don said that Ralph had come, she combed her hair and touched up her face. In the hall a flash of light assaulted her. The shock sent her staggering back a few steps. Arms caught her. She felt his presence before she recognized her lover.

The camera was focused again.

"Get the hell out of here," Ralph snapped.

"Sorry, mister." While he apologized, the photographer took a second picture of the widow. "Thank you so much, Mrs. Strode," he said as he skipped out.

In the living room Ralph drew the curtains. Peeping Toms with cameras had infested the garden. "Those bastards," Ralph said, then turned to greet her. "Are you all right?"

"There've been detectives poking around here all morning. They don't believe it was suicide."

"Yes I know. They questioned me, too."

"Have you met Sergeant Knight?"

"No. A couple of other guys."

"What did they ask you about me?"

"Questions."

"Are you trying to keep something from me?"

"What's on your mind? Was Sergeant Knight tough?"

"He was the soul of gallantry. In a vicious way."

"Don't worry," Ralph said in a cajoling tone that might assure a moribund patient that the death pangs were no more than inflamed imagination. "In cases of this sort, where the cause of death isn't determined, they're always suspicious of the widow. Just the same, I think you ought to have a good lawyer."

"You think so? Wouldn't that make me look," she switched on a nervous smile, "as if I needed a lawyer?"

"You do. If for no more than protection against the gallantry of ambitious detectives." As an intern riding the ambulance of General Hospital, Ralph had learned a lot about the police. The courteous ones were invariably the most ruthless. Front-page crime, the appetite for notoriety, the uses of publicity, blinded men to compassion.

"Don's been helping me through the questioning. He's a lawyer, you know."

"Has he a license to practice here?"

"He hasn't taken his California bar examinations, but he expects to do one of those cram courses. They're nothing at all, he says, for a trained legal mind. Basically, the law's the same all over the country. And since he's just standing by and helping me with advice, I don't think I need anyone else."

Donald Hustings's efforts to impress new acquaintances had not impressed Ralph. Nevertheless he said, "If that's the way you want it," and let it go at that.

"I know it was suicide and I'm sure they'll find it out. Perhaps," Elaine said hopefully, "Fletcher wrote something about it in his diary. We gave them the diary this morning."

She went to him shyly. "One thing you can be sure of, Ralph. No one will ever know about us."

"I'm not worried."

"I am. Scared to death."

They stood apart as though the memory of the affair barred intimacy. Whatever urge had drawn them together was now so flavored with guilt that they shrank from each other. Their very looks seemed to have changed. She saw the jutted jaw, the flesh sparsely distributed over stern bones, the overwhite, freckled flesh, the dusty reddish hair. With a faint ghost of a smile she offered thanks for his faith in her. He regarded this effort as frailty, saw her parlor as ivory melted down to the texture of wax. Faint violet circles framed her eyes. Her beauty was over-refined, weary, scarcely alive.

Uncertainly Ralph extended his hand. Elaine took a few wary steps toward him. He folded an arm about her, then the other arm. This was no more than a gesture of consolation. She shuddered close, clung to him as to a rock in a treacherous current. Neither was aware that the door had opened.

Cindy had not thought of knocking. A living room is common ground for all members of the household. The girl was shocked, sincerely. Ralph and Elaine sprang apart as through the embrace had been of passion rather than compassion. They offered no excuses.

Shock waned as indignation took over. Fletcher's daughter wore a smirk that clearly asked, "What did I always say about this woman?" Ralph stood too straight. Elaine bowed under the weight of shame that rose, not from this, but the earlier situation; as though on that adulterous Thursday they had been discovered together in her bed. Her eyes sought a resting place, found the couch stripped of its pillows. It seemed unreal, contrived, a scene of drama arranged for action, absurd. But Fletcher was dead. The nonsense was tragic.

Ralph said, "I'm going back to the office. If you want anything, phone."

"Thanks for everything," Elaine said.

There were no farewells. The man marched out and Elaine stood there with an empty look in her eyes. Cindy waited for a word of excuse. Elaine did not bother to speak. She offered insult like a queen who knew it her privilege to ignore the feelings of a waiting woman.

In the bedroom Cindy found Don stretched out, enjoying secret thoughts. Her indignant version of the scene, "Daddy's not cold in his grave, it's absolutely brazen," encouraged a dream born of the study of Fletcher's diary and nourished by a quick computation of the Strode assets. Seeing himself like Gregory Peck (but younger), addressing a conference of elderly millionaires, Don Hustings informed the board of directors that Heatherington Industries was but one of the many organizations that sought the talents and investments of Donald Hustings. *"I happen to control considerable capital, gentlemen."*

"Why don't you say something?" demanded Cindy. "Why do you lie there looking mysterious? Did you hear what I said?"

"Yes, my sweet. Every fascinating word."

"Well, what do you think about it?"

"Elaine's a devious woman."

"We knew from the beginning she was no good. What did a girl her age want a man like Daddy for except his money?

It was in her mind when she picked him up in the restaurant."
Although Don often heard these grievances, Cindy could not
resist going through the catalogue again. It had always irked her
to hear her father brag about Elaine's intelligence, her honors at
college. Hunter College! Cindy had not stayed in school beyond
her sophomore year but she had, at least, gone to a respectable
college and belonged to a sorority that would never have admitted Elaine Guardino. "What was she but a common New York
working girl, a gold-digger from the start?"

Don let her rave. His dream had progressed to a conference
with Nan Burke's father, who had entreated him to accept the
title of vice-president. Cindy went on and on with her opinions
and her mother's complaints, including the theory that Fletcher's illness and operation that destroyed his voice had been visited upon him as punishment for the desertion of a loyal wife.
To hear Cindy, one would think Elaine had planted the cancer
in his throat.

"I wouldn't put anything past her. Not *anything*."

"What?" asked Don, reluctantly taking leave of the banker.

"You haven't been paying attention and," suddenly shy,
Cindy approached the bed like a virgin, "I've got something to
tell you. Important."

Don yawned. Although he had given only half an ear to her
raving, he felt that he would go mad if he had to hear any more.
"Yeah, I know."

"You don't know anything." She had become wildly agitated, clinging to the footboard with tight, white hands. "You're
going to be terribly, terribly, terribly angry, but I've simply got
to tell you. I'll die if I don't."

The doorbell rang. Cindy leaped as if she had been attacked
from behind. Her pallor took a greenish hue.

"Better pull yourself together before you talk to anyone,"
Don said. The guest room window showed a bit of the driveway, just enough for him to catch a glimpse of the car that had
just been parked there. He paused to straighten his shirt and run
a comb through his hair before he went to greet the visitor.

THE POLICEMAN ON guard asked no questions when the Rolls-Royce was driven in by a uniformed chauffeur. In visiting the death mansion, Nan Burke had felt the need for formality and had her houseman put on his peaked cap and drive her there. She had canceled a committee meeting for a concert to benefit talented children and had hurried to offer consolation to her bereaved friend. On the way she had stopped at a florist to pick up a bowl of white orchids. No relation could have shown more exquisite sympathy. At every meeting and each farewell, Nan and Cindy touched cheekbones, but upon this sad occasion, Nan pressed poor little Cindy to her ample breast.

"He was such a dear man," declared Nan passionately.

"He simply adored you," Cindy said.

"He only met me once."

"My father was a judge of character, and he knew what a wonderful friend you'd been to me."

Both girls cried copiously, Nan into a bit of Swiss linen edged with Valenciennes lace, Cindy into one of the paper handkerchiefs she had found it necessary to carry since tragedy struck.

"To think we were all together, and your father so lively last week. In this very room."

Cindy explained that the police had taken the cushions. "To examine in their laboratories," she whispered breathlessly. The police, it seems, had emptied all of the cigarette boxes, but not for examination. There was not one cigarette left in the house. Nan took a diamond-encrusted case from her polished crocodile bag. As she leaned close to touch Cindy's cigarette with her jeweled lighter, she whispered, "What really happened?"

"It wasn't suicide."

Both girls inhaled emotionally. Nan's whisper sank to a lower pitch. "Do they know who did it?"

"The police have a very good idea."

The odor of mystery increased Cindy's importance. Nan's awe was as clear as a newspaper headline. As the daughter of a famous mortgage and loan banker and philanthropist, and as a leader in social and charitable affairs, she had often been photographed for the society section of local newspapers, but Cindy's picture would probably appear on the front page.

Don too, showed a rise in status when he thanked Nan, sincerely but without too much effusion, for her sympathy.

"May I offer you a cup of tea? Or coffee? In the absence of our hostess."

"Where is Mrs. Strode?"

"In retreat," replied Don with a cryptic smile. "Would you prefer a drink?"

Nan thought a martini would be divine. "Very dry and without the olive. That's seventy-five calories I can't afford. Is Mrs. Strode prostrate?"

"I never saw anyone calmer in my life."

The girls went to the bar to keep Don company while he mixed their drinks. Nan admired his skill. "Rexie's all thumbs when it comes to anything slightly useful. So we have to depend on William." This was the houseman who had donned the uniform to drive her to their house. "What an utter cocktail, simply out of this world. I wish you'd teach William, but it's never the same with help, is it?" She had become merry, laughing as she added, "A good cocktail needs TLC as much as a baby. Tender, loving care."

Don acknowledged the wit with hearty laughter while Cindy, aware of the mourning mood, showed a demure smile. This changed to sly pleasure as she announced with deliberate hesitancy that she had another important bit of news.

"Tell me, I can't bear waiting."

"You're going to have new neighbors. Guess who."

Nan had hoped for further revelations about the tragedy. She made a noble effort to keep her disappointment from showing. "You, darling? Not really! How great!"

Cindy did not think it would show bad taste if she permitted enthusiasm in describing the house. She spoke modestly of the neighborhood and size, but used fancy decorating magazines phrases in telling about the ingenious architecture, the modern Old-World charm, the boundless view. She knew that

Nan would positively adore it and said they planned some wizard parties "after this is all over and we're in a fun mood again." In Cindy's mind, magically, it was all over, there was plenty of money for gracious living and Nan's friends thronged into the little house where a colored bartender in a white coat mixed cocktails while Cindy in a long hostess gown graciously received tributes to her cleverness in using genuine Pennsylvania antiques with modern Swedish.

"I'm not so sure about the house," Don said as he stirred a second cocktail for Nan.

"Donnie!" Cindy was stricken by the announcement. She could not, in Nan's presence, remind Don that her father's death would profit them so that the house would be no problem at all. "Just because my poor father's—I mean, it's terribly distressing and all that—but I mean—we mustn't give up." Raised eyebrows conveyed a message, which Don seemed not to notice. "My poor Donnie's been so . . . so . . . by this shock . . . I feel . . . well, he's positively not himself. But we mustn't lose interest in living, darling. Aren't you still mad, mad, mad about the house?"

"I'm not sure it's the right place for us."

"Why not? You said it was the dream of your life to have a house at the very spang edge of the ocean?"

"I still do, love. And no one can say that the house isn't as charming and picturesque as you say"—Don did not wish to denigrate his taste of the past week—"but don't you think it's a bit . . . unspacious?"

Cindy clung tenaciously to last week's paradise. "It isn't too small. For just two people."

Don had found statelier mansions for his soul, places closer to the status of the Burkes' crowd. "It just occurred to me sweet, that we might want to live more expansively." He spread his hands to measure the growing dream. "And a slightly more convenient neighborhood. Somewhere closer to your place, Nan."

"That would be just too lovely," Nan said without excessive enthusiasm.

"But," Cindy began again but Don, more and more enraptured by his visions, cut in with the modest news that he would not want a place quite as large as Nan's but one that, he implied, would be luxurious. "We really ought to have a pool. There are so many days out here when the surf's too high for comfortable swimming." He added a tennis court and covered patio for parties. At the same time Mr. Heatherington was pleading with him for extra capital and Nan's father was wondering whether young Hustings would consider a seat on the board of a complex of suburban banks.

Cindy could not easily accommodate herself to the larger dream. She parted reluctantly from the little house. Still considering herself a minor heiress, she had not yet raised herself to Nan's level. What put Cindy into a superior position today was her role in the mystery drama. She let drop deftly the information that Elaine had gone about telling the world she expected her husband's death, and in the very manner that it had happened. Cindy still balked at the mention of suicide.

"She actually talked about it? My God!" Nan's mind went to another committee meeting, a luncheon the next day, where guests were free to gossip until the coffee was served and the chairman called for silence. "Tell me more about it. Everything. Do the police know that? What do they think?"

"We ought to be more discreet, love," Don said reprovingly and shook his head at Cindy in the manner of a man who knew himself master of the house. "I don't think the police would like mere opinion broadcast."

"I only told Nan."

"And I won't say a word to anyone," Nan promised.

With the humility that only a big man can show, Don begged Nan to forgive his warning. He had not meant to rebuke the girls. "It's just that one has to be a bit cautious in these matters. It's safer on the prudent side." And he turned the conversation from this spicy subject by asking about her husband, her father, and the state of their health and business. Nan listened humbly as Don offered opinions about banking, letting fall the names of famous financiers and of stocks worthy of investment, speaking with authority of tax laws, interest rates, blue chip stocks. It was hard for Nan to keep from yawning. She might as well have been at home with her father, her husband, and their cronies. Her arrogance dwindled; she became a mere wife and daughter and soon afterward left, escorted to the Rolls by Don, who stepped aside to let the chauffeur open the door.

After she had gone he stayed in the driveway with the two policemen. Their conversation was unimportant. They spoke of baseball, their wives, and the weather. The sky had become clear, the memory of fog drifting off. "What a country this West is," Don said. "Still open to pioneer spirit. There's nothing a man can't accomplish out here if he's got the stuff in him." He tapped his chest vigorously.

"You got to get a chance out here like any place else," the older policeman said doubtfully.

"Every place in the world a man's got to get a chance. You've got to recognize the chance and seize it," cried Don.

"It's the way the cookie crumbles," the younger cop said.

"Right you are!" exclaimed Don and raced exuberantly back to the house.

11 THE EVENING PAPER WAS TOSSED UPON THE driveway by the middle-aged newsboy in a bright red convertible with a raucous radio. On the front page was a photograph stolen by an enterprising reporter. The snapshot, enlarged and framed in silver, had been taken in Jamaica during the honeymoon. Both Mr. and Mrs. Fletcher Strode wore jaunty tennis shorts. On the third page there was a two-column reproduction of an advertisement posed by Elaine before her marriage. In a chiffon nightgown and with outstretched arms, head thrown back, smile radiant, she demonstrated a girl's ecstasy at having found a deodorant that guaranteed underarm daintiness. A smaller photograph showed the "one-hundred-and-fifty-thousand-dollar death mansion" for which Fletcher had paid eighty-five thousand dollars.

Cindy said she thought it was awful, people's lives being exposed in that vulgar fashion. "Just listen to this, 'The beautiful blond daughter, New York debutante, here for a holiday with her lawyer husband . . .' Isn't it too silly?"

"You might just possibly have suggested it," remarked Elaine.

Don laughed. Cindy's mouth twisted. She went on reading the paper, aggressively rustling pages and reading aloud those passages which were most flattering to herself or most embarrassing to Elaine.

Elaine escaped to the garden. She was very nervous. The birds in the branches twittered restlessly. At this hour of the twilight— no matter how noisily they sang at night— they were quiet. Usually Elaine was not disturbed by natural sounds. This evening she felt positively ill with drowsiness. Fatigue lay upon her like a smothering weight. She had been neither able to sleep nor to arouse herself. Twice she had made coffee, twice let it grow cold in the cup. Once more the desert wind had conquered sea breezes and fog. There had been a three-day surcease and now the heat was upon them again. How Fletcher would have suffered! She felt now that she must find and comfort him.

Voices pursued her. Don and Cindy came out in bathing suits. "Do you think it's heartless of us?" Cindy asked. "But we've simply got to cool off."

She stood at the edge of the pool, but did not go in. Don dived with an enormous splash. Cindy shuddered away from the pool. "Come in, beauties, it's marvelous."

Elaine said she was too tired and returned to the house. She was afraid of what she might say if she remained in their nervous company. The scent of jasmine was too sweet, the fallen blossoms of red oleander like blood upon the grass. She had begun to hate her garden.

Cindy watched her go. She was tense and strung up, too. Since Nan had gone, Cindy had been flitting about like a moth under a lampshade. Don had asked about the important matter she had wanted to confide before her friend arrived. This had sent her into a twitter so that she could not keep her mind on any one thing. Don had thought a dip in the pool might soothe her.

"Aren't you coming in?" he called.

"I'm not in the mood." She looked over her left and right shoulders to be sure there were no more reporters waiting in the garden. The short twilight ended abruptly. Lights flashed frequently, for traffic had become heavy on the hill. Motorists came to gape at the death mansion, but were urged to keep moving by the two policemen in the car at the curb.

Don climbed out of the pool, shook himself like a terrier, and dried his face on his bathrobe.

"What's it all about? Tell me and get it over with."

Cindy ran ahead to the pavilion, looked about again, and drew a chair to the center. "You needn't be so cross. I'm terribly upset." Nan had emptied her cigarette case so that Cindy wouldn't be left stranded. Cindy lit one and held the burning match until it scorched her fingers.

The match dropped, flaming, to the floor. Don sprang to stamp it out, but remembered that he was barefoot and pulled away. "For God's sake, you could start a fire." He looked down for something to press down upon the flame, but there were no small objects about. All the ashtrays had been removed. Perhaps on Monday, when their lives were normal, Elaine had taken them to the kitchen to be washed; perhaps the police had "borrowed" them for examination in the laboratory. Every detail had significance.

The small flame flickered out. Don walked to the rail and looked down at the rows of asters and marigolds, remembered what he had read in Fletcher's diary about the poisons used in the garden.

"What happens to the people who hide things from the police?"

"Huh?"

"It's supposed to be a crime or something, isn't it?"

"What do you want to know for? Did you hide something?"

She was so slow about answering that Don had to snap at her again about dropping ashes on the dry wood. "We've had enough around here without a fire, too."

"If you're going to be nasty, I won't tell you." She joined him at the rail, flicked ashes into the flower bed.

"Concealing evidence in a criminal case makes a person an accessory after the fact. Have you concealed something?"

The cigarette was pressed out viciously against the wooden rail. She dropped the stub into the flower bed as slyly as if it were evidence of crime. "A plastic bag. The kind that comes over clothes from the cleaner's."

"Plastic bag? Where was it?"

Don touched her hand and Cindy shuddered away. She had neither the talent nor training for secrets. A child of the permissively bred generation to whom lies were unnecessary, she stated facts and feelings flatly and with little concern for effect. Her falsehoods had concerned clothing prices which she had inflated to improve her position with girlfriends. Otherwise she had always practiced easy honesty. Since Tuesday morning she had suffered a secret.

"On him. Daddy."

Don drummed on the rail. To Cindy it seemed that years passed while he stood there tapping his fingers and looking out at nothing. "Aren't you surprised?"

"You found the bag on your father?" His tone was measured.

"Yes. It was under that thing," she touched the base of her neck, "he breathed through."

"The bib?"

She nodded.

"Then it wasn't an accident," Don said. "And you pulled it off?"

"I didn't want people thinking Daddy committed suicide."

"For Christ's sake!"

"I couldn't bear it. People thinking . . . I mean . . . a girl at school, Martha Ann Lee, her name was, her father . . ." Confession felt like vomit rising. "It was terrible. All the girls whispered and we couldn't look at her without thinking. I mean . . . she had to leave school . . . Martha Ann Lee. The whole family was disgraced. I didn't want people thinking . . ." The taste of nausea filled her mouth. She couldn't go on.

"You little fool." Don's anger attacked her like a weapon. "Suicide's no disgrace."

"But it was. One day we met Martha Ann on the street. Nan and I. We couldn't forget. What could we say to her? People remember for the rest of your life."

"Front-page headlines are a hell of a lot worse than whispers."

She fought back sickness. "I never thought . . . the police and all that stuff. I mean . . . it could have been a heart attack if the people didn't know."

"Just when did that thought occur to you?"

"You needn't be so mean. People do die of heart attacks all the time at this age."

"Is that all there was to it? You didn't want it to look like suicide?"

"Suicide is the coward's way out. I was thinking of Daddy's reputation. How did I know there'd be all that fuss? Besides, Donnie, there's the insurance. A hundred thousand dollars, I told you the other day. And I thought of my mother's insurance, too."

"Did you think that they wouldn't pay if it was suicide?"

"They don't. Didn't you know that? I was thinking of you too, darling." She appealed like a child asking forgiveness of a father, and since she no longer had a father, elevating Don to that place. "We can't afford to lose all that money."

Don explained that she was mistaken about the insurance. Perhaps Martha Ann Lee's family had not received the benefits, but the father might have taken out the insurance just before he died. Fletcher Strode had been insured for many years, since before Cindy was born; at the time of the divorce he had increased his insurance for the protection of the child and his first wife. It was unlikely that after so many years the benefits would not be paid; unlikely, too, that Fletcher Strode's policies contained the suicide clause.

"How would I know that? I always heard they wouldn't pay a nickel if a person committed suicide. Was it so terribly wrong?"

"Not only wrong, criminal. It could get you into a hell of a lot of trouble."

"Oh, no!"

"It's a crime to conceal evidence. You could go to jail for it."

The sickness returned. Cindy raced to the edge of the pavilion and vomited into a bed of marigolds. Don came after her. "Take it easy," he said and led her to the long chair. She was as chilled and damp as if she had been fished out of the pool, as tremulous as if she had been rescued from death by drowning. Don offered to her a drink of water, some brandy or hot tea, but she refuted everything except a cigarette, which she reached for with such agitation that she grabbed at the air.

"Do we have to tell them?"

"It'd certainly change the case. I don't think Sergeant Knight would welcome the information."

"Why not?" Cindy breathed more easily.

"It's big opportunity for him. He can get a lot of publicity out of a murder case, make himself a big man. How do you think he's going to take it if his murder turns out to be an ordinary suicide?"

"You see!" cried Cindy, who saw this reasoning as vindication.

"On the other hand, what does it prove? Only that there was a plastic bag and that it caused death by suffocation. He might well have done it himself."

"Why do you keep saying that? Do you know anything special?" She dropped her burning cigarette onto dry wood.

Don did not notice. He had become the defense attorney, finding arguments to protect the client. "You might have saved your father's life by pulling off that bag. You'd had no experience with death. How did you know when you came into the room that he wasn't alive?"

"You're right. That's what I thought," she cried eagerly. "That's why I did it. Honestly, Don."

As defense attorney he felt it his duty to be objective considering the case from all angles. "It was a bit late for that."

"How did I know? You just said, Don, that I didn't have any experience with death. You make me feel that I did something terrible."

"You did something foolish. If you'd confessed to the detectives right away, your action wouldn't be questioned." It was necessary for the attorney to let the bewildered client know both the hazards and the hopeful aspects of the case. "The bag might be significant as evidence if it could be produced without incriminating you."

"Can't you do something to fix it up? You're a lawyer."

"Where is the bag? What did you do with it?"

"It's in my closet. Over my beige organza." She dared a small chuckle. "At first I hid it on the floor behind our bags, but when those detectives started snooping around, I hung it over my dress. What could be more natural? A light dress like that ought to be kept covered. One of those men," she said almost gaily, "looked straight at it. He opened my closet door and there it was, over my dress."

"They came into our room?"

"Just for a couple minutes. Looked around without much interest. Of course there was nothing to suspect us of."

"Of course not."

"There was the bag right over my dress. I don't have to tell them about it, do I?"

"You're not to mention it to anyone. Let me think about it."

"I had to tell you. I couldn't hold it in any longer."

"If I thought it'd help, I'd advise you to let Knight know right away. But," The pause was calculated, "Speaking as your lawyer, I want to give you this advice. Don't breathe this to anyone unless I advise it."

"Suppose they find it?"

"It's just as you said dear, a plastic bag over a party dress is the most usual thing in the world." A second and more ponderous pause was aimed at intimidation. "Is there anything else you think you ought to tell me?"

"Why . . . why should there be?"

"I'm asking."

They went into the house. In their bedroom the sudden glare of electric light caused embarrassment, strangely, for they had lived together for almost a year. Cindy became as modest as if the sight of her body would expose something she wished to hide. Don went into the bathroom to take off his bathing trunks.

He came out in pajamas. Cindy had put on a long, opaque night-gown. They faced each other warily.

"You know what I think, Donnie?"

Don was far off, in the courtroom, hearing the monotonous voice of the clerk reading from Fletcher Strode's diary. When a man has written, not once but many times, that he suspects his wife of planning murder and murder is done, a jury cannot have much doubt.

"I spoke to you, Donnie."

"Yes, dear."

"Whoever put that bag over Daddy wanted it to look like suicide."

"Obviously."

"You don't have to bite my head off. I was just figuring things out. Why are you so snappy about it?"

"Sorry," he answered curtly. "I was thinking about some-thing else."

"You know what you sound like? Like you're scared."

"I have nothing to be afraid of," Don said loftily. "Only for you, my sweet."

"Oh, now! They wouldn't put me in jail for hiding the bag. I don't believe it."

"You've got to be mighty careful. People get strange ideas. You know of course, that a person convicted of murder can't inherit the victim's property. That's the law in most states."

"Why should that bother me?" She gave him her most wide-eyed stare.

Like a cautious attorney giving advice across the width of a desk, he lowered his voice. "I don't think for a minute that you've got anything of that sort to worry about, dear, but we do have to be careful about what we say since we . . . that is, you . . . are next in line for the inheritance of the property."

"You're the only one who knows."

"Weren't you a bit indiscreet this afternoon? It may have impressed Nan, but it might look to outsiders as if you wished to cast suspicion on someone else."

Watching the blond girl in the mirror, Cindy rearranged a

stray lock. "Don't you trust me, darling?" And she enjoyed the reflection of a subtle smile.

"Naturally, darling. But it's only that sometimes you're," he could not tell her she was crude and, instead, chose, "impulsive."

"I can keep things to myself. You'd be surprised," she told him with hauteur. "I may be thinking of something terrible right at this moment. And I won't tell you."

"By all means, keep your thoughts to yourself. It's the safest way."

In the mirror their eyes met. Cindy stared into his face with fixed zeal. Don wheeled around and looked at her directly. She moved toward him. In their eyes were understanding and promise. Cindy felt subtle. Don nodded delicately. Never in the wildest moments of love had they been closer in spirit. "Oh, Donnie, oh, darling." It was like the final sigh upon a pillow.

THE NEXT MORNING, while Cindy was in the shower, Don took the party dress from its hanger. The almost inaudible rustle of the plastic stuff brought to mind the moment when he had kissed Elaine over a bundle of plastic-covered suits at the door of Fletcher's closet. WARNING: TO AVOID DANGER OF SUFFOCATION KEEP AWAY FROM BABIES AND CHILDREN. DO NOT USE IN CRIBS, CARRIAGES, BEDS, OR PLAYPENS. THIS BAG IS NOT A TOY. A shadow passed the window. Instinct commanded Don to jump back and slam the closet door. Second thought told him that such precipitate action might arouse the curiosity of anyone looking through the windows. In a leisurely way he selected a linen jacket and dark slacks, moving as carelessly as a man whose mind is on nothing more than the selection of an outfit for the day.

He found Elaine in the garden. When he laid his hand upon her arm she jumped like a cat. "It's only me, beauty. Nothing to get nervous about, is there?"

"This heat again. It tightens me up. And Sergeant Knight yesterday." A delicate tremor possessed her. "I hardly slept at all. And even here, in bright daylight, I hear footsteps behind me. People jump out of bushes. I'm a mess."

"You've handled yourself wonderfully. Few women would have such courage."

She shook away from the light contact of his hand. "Ralph says I ought to have a lawyer." Lest his pride be hurt by this, she hurried to say, "A local lawyer, someone who practices in California. What do you think?"

"Let's wait and see how things shape up. Leave it to me, I'll find you the best man in the state." Don took her arm again, masterfully. When he had first heard about Fletcher's wife from Cindy and her mother, he had been charmed by their vindictive descriptions of the siren who had stolen the doting father and husband, and had thought of his father-in-law's young wife as one of the those lovely, unattainable New York girls who enter exclusive restaurants on the arms of wealthy older men or rich young playboys. Once Cindy had shown him a photograph in an old copy of a fashion magazine, Elaine wrapped in furs, stepping haughtily into a limousine. The lovely dream had become human, attainable, dependent upon Don Hustings. He wished the circumstances were different.

"Is it terribly serious, Don? Am I just being hysterical or do you think they really believe—"

There was a sudden flash of light. Someone jumped out from behind the row of oleander bushes. "Thank you, Mrs. Strode." It was a thin girl with a leather case strapped over her shoulder and a camera in her hand. She scurried around the house to the driveway.

"There *was* someone in the bushes." A trace of hysteria colored her laughter. "What were you saying, Don?"

He held more firmly to Elaine's arm. "What a pity," he sighed, "that innocence can't be proved."

FROM A BOOTH that smelled of old sweat and cigarettes, Don spoke to Sergeant Knight, "May I come and talk to you, sir? I've come across some information that might interest you."

"Good. I'll be out there this afternoon."

"I'm not home. As a matter of fact, I happen to be downtown, right in your neighborhood. You don't mind my leaving the house, do you?"

"You weren't stopped," Knight said. "But I'm afraid I can't see you this morning. I'm just leaving for Lowell Hanley's office." He pronounced the name of the District Attorney with reverence. "Can you call me back in an hour?"

The meeting in the District Attorney's office was a long one. When Don called back, he was told that Knight was tied up. Don was restless. It was impossible for him to sit among the bums at a morning movie and among well-dressed idlers before the board in the broker's office. He wandered into a couple of shops, but found nothing to interest him in the way of Parisian ties, English macintoshes, Italian shoes. In hot sunlight he tramped without direction along ugly streets, among tawdry buildings, moldy movie theaters, appalling souvenir shops, cut-rate drugstores, employment agencies, and cafés that poisoned the air with fumes of cooking fat too often heated. From time to time he paused, purposelessly, and found himself studying displays of secondhand furniture, Chinese vegetables, tropical fish, trusses, and artificial legs. Dispirited people shuffled past, ashamed to be walking in a city where self-respect is determined by the possession of a car, where the major pursuit is the car just ahead, and a pedestrian is looked down upon as a pauper.

The people who moved listlessly in the hot noon glare were poor and disenchanted, with shapeless clothes over coarsened bodies, dirty hair, and eyes that looked at nothing.

Sweating in a glass phone booth that caught and held the insufferable glare, Don began to doubt the wisdom of his latest move. He was certain that Knight would be grateful for his assistance and appreciate his honesty, but there was the possibility that the facts might be unpleasantly interpreted. While he wavered, Knight's voice came through. The meeting was over and he was ready, in fact anxious, to hear the important revelation. How soon could Don get to his office?

On impulse, Don suggested that Knight meet him for lunch, named an expensive restaurant with a cuisine that would sooth the spirit of a curmudgeon, and give pleasure to a dyspeptic. Knight's enthusiasm was disarming.

They had no sooner met and been led, like the blind, through dark caverns to their table when Knight said, "Well, what's the earthshaking information?"

"Let's order our drinks first. You'll want to relax after that long conference."

Although Knight was somewhat tense after an argument that had lasted more than two hours, he would take nothing stronger than a double tomato juice without Worcestershire sauce or Tabasco. Nor would he, although Don set a generous example by ordering the most expensive steak on the bill of fare, eat anything more extravagant than a vegetable plate with two poached eggs. Knight was no gourmet; he relished the restaurant's extravagance for snobbish rather than epicurean reasons. At some time he would let drop, "Now at Ticino's they really know how to poach an egg."

"In dietetic habits I'm a Spartan. At home we eat only organically grown foods. My only weakness is coffee. A bad habit, but I need the stimulation in my work. But I limit my cigarettes. Most of the time I smoke to put other people at ease. They tend toward nervousness during an interrogation. Even the innocent wince when a member of the department asks a question. A cigarette gives them something to do with their hands. Let's get down to business. What's on your mind?"

"I'd like to ask you one question first, if I may, sir?"

"Go ahead."

"You've read the diary?"

Knight's hand fell upon the briefcase lying beside him on the banquette. In it was a copy of the diary reproduced by a new machine so accurately that every stoke of Fletcher's ballpoint, every deviation in the flow of ink, every heavily stressed punctuation mark, showed clearly. The original was now locked away in Lowell Hanley's safe. The meeting in Mr. Hanley's office had concerned this subject. Discussion had been heated. The District Attorney had, in general, taken Knight's view of the case while the Chief of Police had been skeptical about several important points. The department's chief psychologist had given his opinion in words of four syllables. No agreement had been reached, and Knight had been instructed to go on with the investigation, but with discretion.

"Indeed I've read it. Very interesting."

Don saw that the detective was not prepared to let him know how they meant to use the information Fletcher Strode had provided. "May I ask," Don, too, exercised discretion, "if there were any references to suicide, overt or otherwise?"

"You haven't read it?"

Don had told Knight yesterday, when the diary was brought out, that he had not read it. He knew, too, that Knight had not forgotten, but was also playing a discreet game. Instead of making an issue of it, he said, "All I know is that Dad wrote in it a lot. And if he was plotting suicide, there might have been some indication in a concealed journal. And," he took out a cigarette and felt in his pockets for his lighter, which was there but which he pretended not to find because he knew that Knight liked to render small services, "some interesting stuff about the circumstances that preceded his death."

Knight leaned over to touch his lighter to Don's cigarette. He used a lemon-flavored cologne, but too profusely to be in good taste. Don drew back. Knight noted tension in the hand that held the cigarette, tautness in the flesh around the eyes.

He said, "Yes, the events of the poor fellow's last days were given in some detail." He waited. Since Don did not ask questions, Knight went on provocatively, "You lived in the house, you must have noticed that Mr. Strode was in a state of mental and emotional distress. Wasn't it noticeable?"

"It was hell. Sheer hell for all of us, but particularly for Elaine."

"Would you say that his wife was the cause of this condition?"

"More the victim." Don observed a grim silence, sighed, added, "I hate to speak ill of the dead, but at times he was brutal to her." His hand flew, as though self-impelled, to the place where the bruise stained Elaine's jaw.

Knight sipped tomato juice.

"You don't believe that cock-and-bull story about her slipping against the kitchen sink? Elaine'd die before she'd say he hit her. Especially now that he's dead."

Knight gave Don no encouragement.

"What I wanted to ask you, sir, was there anything in the diary about finding me in Mr. Strode's bedroom with Elaine?"

"In his bedroom?"

Don's smile dismissed implications of incest. "I was afraid he might have made something of it, although it was really innocent. The cleaner's boy delivered a bundle when Elaine and I were alone, and I offered to carry it to his room for her. There were several of his suits in those plastic bags the cleaners use—"

He used a diversion to heighten Knight's curiosity. Having finished his martini, he signaled the waiter. "You don't mind if I indulge in my bad habit?"

"It's your own liver," Knight said. "I can tell you this much, there was nothing in the diary about that incident in the bedroom. Why does it bother you so much?"

"I was afraid that Dad might have made something of it. And I wouldn't like anything of that sort to get out. Especially in the newspapers. People have nasty minds, and I have a wife to think of. I'm glad he didn't mention it in the diary."

"Is that incident the important information you had for me?" Knight asked sternly. "It was my impression that you knew something more."

If he had noticed the mention of plastic bags, he preferred not to heed it.

"I know what caused Mr. Strode's death."

They had to sit silent while the waiter slid their plates into place. A silver cover was removed from a silver platter, vegetables and poached eggs exhibited. A chateaubriand stuffed with caviar could not have been more elaborately served. Knight nodded approval. When the waiter had gone, he poked at the vegetables with his fork. "Now this is a correctly cooked string bean. Not overdone, the vitamins are preserved. How did Mr. Strode die?"

"He was smothered with a plastic bag."

Knight went on eating. His face showed neither pleasure nor surprise. Only a slight twitch of the nostrils betrayed excitement. "How do you know that?"

Like a defense attorney who has spent many hours preparing his arguments, Don gave facts. Even the mood has been considered: compassion for the sorrowing daughter, indulgence of Cindy's mistake. Like a father speaking of an adored brat, he explained, "She had no idea that it was incorrect to keep the bag hidden."

"Stupid," was Knight's word. Without compassion. "Just stupid."

"She was trying to be gallant. In her own way. Protecting the family name. She believes that suicide is disgraceful. Her father's reputation is very dear to her."

Knight sniffed. He could understand Mrs. Hustings's having snatched the bag away and, in the first moments of shock, hidden it away, but once an investigation was under way, she ought to have performed her legal duty.

"I'm afraid my wife isn't too familiar with the law. She's led a sheltered life."

"Don't they teach them anything in those fancy girls' colleges?"

"Not such masculine subjects as the law," retorted Don with a challenging glance.

Knight gave attention to the business of isolating the lima beans, carrots, and corn kernels from the beets and potatoes, which he pushed to the far side of his plate. As though it were a mere aside, less important than the string bean that now claimed his attention, he murmured, "Must be a lot of life insurance, huh?"

"None of us knows how much," Don answered, "but does that mean much to your investigation? Even if the coroner's verdict is suicide, I'm sure the benefits will be paid. Mr. Strode held his policies for a long time."

"A lot of people, most of them, think the companies won't pay in suicide cases."

"I don't think my wife knows anything about that."

"Where's the bag?"

"At the house. Over a dress in our closet. Your assistant looked straight at it and asked no questions."

"I see." What Knight saw were headlines and news photographs: *Sergeant Curtis Knight who discovered the vital clue in the mystery death of the New York millionaire.* He thought of the morning's angry meeting, of the war between the District Attorney and the Police Chief, of ambition rampant and caution couchant, of the polysyllables offered by the psychologist. How would the introduction of the plastic bag affect the present situation and Knight's future career? The whole thing might blow up in his face. "Of course," he said thoughtfully, "this may change the entire aspect of the case."

"In what way, sir?"

"The use of the plastic bag nearly always indicates suicide."

"Nearly but not always?"

Knight pointed his fork at Don's face. "Have you any good reason for believing this wasn't?"

"I'm thinking of possibilities. Infants smothered in cribs are usually the victims of their mothers' carelessness, but suppose, sir, that a parent finds a child a burden and wants to be free? You see the point, don't you?" Again Don played lawyer, tried to impress jury and judge with logical theory. "A man drugged with sleeping pills is just as helpless as a sleeping child. That's only an illustration, but certainly possible."

A conical green lampshade protected a meager bulb in the small lamp set upon their table. The dusky ray, slanting upward from a circular opening, etched in Don's face. Knight tilted the shade so that further light was shed upon his companion. The scrutiny was disconcerting to Don, who signaled the waiter for another drink. Knight cautioned him against it.

"If you're going to drive home, it's not safe."

"Nor legal," said Don with a wry grin. He changed the order to coffee, and tried a new strategy. "If you were to search the house again, sir, you might find the bag hanging over a tan party dress in my wife's closet. And ask a few pertinent questions which, of course, would bring out the truth—"

"Allow us to handle it in our own way," Knight said, stressing plural pronouns so that the young man could see he was not to be got around by any scheme to further his own career.

"You realize, of course, that my wife's handled the bag and I'm afraid I touched it myself, inadvertently, when I looked at it."

"Fingerprints don't often show up on that plastic. Rarely. If that's what worries you."

"Why should I worry? So long as you don't punish poor Cindy for her gallantry." Don cast a smile of understanding at Knight to show tolerance of female foibles.

"I'll want a written confession from your wife."

"That'll be very hard for her."

"Gallantry requires a bit of hardship." Knight grimaced.

"You haven't mentioned this to anyone else?"

"No."

"Does Mrs. Strode know anything about it?"

"Not that I know of, sir."

Knight said nothing more until he had finished his coffee. In parting he offered a grateful hand. "You were right to tell me about this. Otherwise your wife might be in a lot of trouble. As things stand, I don't think the delay in her confession will amount to much. I'll talk to Lowell Hanley about it."

Nothing more was said of the new clue, but the handshake was a gesture of tacit cooperation. Don drove home at an illegal speed. In midafternoon the freeway was fairly empty—a good omen. Cindy heard his car and ran to meet him at the door.

"I've got a surprise for you."

"What is it?" He threw the question over his shoulder as he hurried to the bedroom closet to have a quick look at the sight which would soon greet the eyes of Sergeant Knight.

"Looking for something?" Cindy asked with feigned ignorance.

"Where is it?"

"Where's what, Donnie?"

He closed the bedroom door before he spoke of the bag.

"It's gone." Cindy beamed.

"Where? Who took it? Was anyone here?"

"I burned it"

"You . . . what?"

"Out there." She tilted her head toward the window that looked toward the garden. "No one saw. It only burned for a few seconds, that stuff goes up in a flash. There were hardly any ashes and I put them in the dirt where the gardener puts all the old raked leaves and dead flowers and stuff. I mixed it all up with dirt and that guck."

She waited for praise. Don grunted.

"No one will ever know now." She smiled at the girl in the mirror. Don came up behind her. She saw him in the mirror, too. His hands rose so that she expected an embrace. Instead she was whirled around and shaken like a wet dishrag. "Donnie! What's wrong now? I thought you'd be glad."

He jerked her close and looked down into her face. "Why should I be glad?"

"I just thought you would."

"Cindy, is there anything else you ought to tell me?"

"What do you mean?"

"You've acted very strangely since your father died."

"Me?" She wriggled out of his grasp and backed away. "You're the one who's acted funny. Really weird."

"I was trying to protect you."

"Don't you think I was trying to help you?"

"Thanks, don't bother." He flung himself upon the bed.

Cindy turned to the mirror, trying on a haughty expression but finding it difficult while she winked and screwed up her eyes in the process of putting on makeup.

Don watched. "What's all that for? You don't think you're going to a party tonight?"

"Have you forgotten? We've got to go and arrange for the funeral. Elaine said we could spend as much as we wanted."

"You have to make yourself up like a tart to go to a mortuary!"

He was impossible. Cindy gathered up her little pots and pencils, flung herself into the bathroom, closed the door with a bang. She spent a long time on her face, for her hand was unsteady with the brushes. When she came out her eyes were bare of the usual black rims and she had penciled her brows with a faint line. "I won't wear any makeup if you don't like it, darling."

Don was in a better mood, too. The radio was on. An old-time combo played Dixieland. Don open the closet door. "Behold, milady." The beige organza was enveloped in a plastic bag.

Cindy squealed.

"After the mortuary we're going downtown and telling the truth to Sergeant Knight. They'll make a recording and you'll sign it."

"No!"

"Yes you will. You've got nothing to worry about. I'll be with you, and on the way I'll coach you for the confession."

"I'll die."

Once more he pulled her toward him. This time he was tender. "You're okay, sweet. Remember, you've got me to take care of everything for you. Your very own personal, private lawyer." Don was blithe again, sure of himself. In the pocket of his jacket was a plastic bag, the third one which had been hanging over Fletcher Strode's cashmere jacket. There were no other bags in Fletcher's closet now and Don, as always secure with a strong lie in him, felt that the future held good fortune.

12

THE FASCINATION OF MYSTERIOUS DEATH VARies with the size of the victim's income. In slums people barely turn their heads to look at the tenement where a brutal slaying took place, while in the neighborhood of expensive houses they throng to stare at the walls and roof of what newspapers call "the murder mansion." Many cars ascended the hill, turned at the dead end, and drove down again. Their occupants saw a garden, a wall, a house, curtained windows, closed doors, but enjoyed, no doubt, the same illusory thrills as those tourists who travel thousands of miles to look at houses in which movie stars once lived. Only one visitor was admitted. Ralph Julian was greeted like a star at the stage door. "Go right in, Doctor." He belonged to the drama, his name had been in the papers.

He brought an arrangement of flowers, which he held awkwardly while he greeted Elaine. Roses, daisies, asters, and chrysanthemums became a barrier between them. Ralph greeted her with restraint. Over his hasty lunch he had read of the latest developments in the mystery death of the wealthy recluse. From unnamed sources reporters had learned that new and conclusive evidence had been discovered by the Sergeant Curtis Knight of the Homicide Squad. The head of that department had expressed the belief that the mystery would be solved within twenty-four hours.

Several other pictures of Elaine had been dug up. One was the advertisement Ralph had found in an old magazine and brought to show her the day they became lovers. Her white, filmy dress and her hair were tossed gracefully by a breeze and she carried a basket of daisies. Another picture, blown up large, made her an adventuress with hair piled high, gems in her ears, black gloves above her elbows. Who was she? Over a barrier of flowers Ralph looked at her and found himself wavering. He could not believe in the cunning bitch whose female grace disguised a soul of blackest evil, but she was surely not the modest young housewife he had discovered on her knees, uprooting irises.

"I'm sorry I couldn't come over and see you last night. I meant to but I was held up"—he decided not to alarm her by speaking of that private and shocking conference with a man close to the Chief of Police, and ended up with the doctor's infallible excuse—"by an emergency."

"Of course." She understood about doctors. "Can I give you anything? Coffee? A cold drink?"

They were alone in the house. Don and Cindy, she said, had gone to the undertaker's to discuss arrangements for the funeral. Fletcher's body had been released, "borrowed" household articles brought back.

"Nothing was discovered. They didn't find anything that

explains anything." She sank down limply on the cushions that had been restored to the couch. All the starch had gone out of her.

It was the heat, she said, that lifeless dry heat that destroyed her. She could barely move or think, and nothing mattered. Ralph took her pulse, measured heartbeat and blood pressure. When she held out her hands, there were tremors. "Delayed shock," he said. A sudden death was enough to unsettle the healthiest woman and she had, in addition, to endure the nasty business of investigation. Most girls would have gone to pieces. Elaine had changed in other ways. All the lightness and mobility had gone out of her. Ralph could not tell whether the lassitude was caused by sorrow, fear, or caution. Contemptuous as he was of the opinions he had heard and read, he could not help being affected. Most of all he was scornful of himself for the wavering. As though questioning an invalid, he asked, with forced cheeriness, "Will it upset you if Sergeant Knight comes to question you again?"

Quickly, almost too quickly, she came out of her trance. "Is he coming? How do you know?"

"Since they discovered nothing from the autopsy, they'll certainly go on with the investigation."

"It's become such a public thing," Elaine said.

From the street came the rumble of the sightseers' cars. Elaine got up and walked about the room as if she were in search of something, a voice, an answer, tranquility. Bare-legged and bare-armed in the short dress, she looked like a frightened waif.

"Don begged me not to read the newspapers. He said they'd upset me."

Ralph pushed aside the curtain. The plants in the garden had been sprayed that day and they gave off a sweetly poisonous odor. "They'll say anything to get sensational headlines. Didn't I tell you yesterday that it's customary to cast suspicion on the widow?"

"Don said something else this morning." She strained to keep her tone light. "He said there's no proof of innocence." The bluff failed. She was sodden with fear.

"I wouldn't pay too much attention to Don if I were you."

"He's been awfully kind. I don't know how I'd have got along without him."

"He shouldn't have said that to you," Ralph had become harsh. "You've got nothing to be afraid of."

"Haven't I?" She steadied herself against the arm of a chair. "All that questioning and poking about in our affairs. Every little moment of our lives." She beat at the upholstery. "There are lots of things about my life with Fletcher that I don't care to discuss with the police. Or anybody else." She raised her hand against the chair again, but let it fall like an unbearable weight. "Sometimes, quite often lately, I'd dream about his death." She waited for a shocked response.

"A common enough dream."

"Not night dreams, a daydream. I thought about Fletcher dying. Although I suppose," she left the support of the chair, "it isn't too extraordinary to think about your future when you live with someone who expects to die."

"You don't have to tell the police about your dreams."

"Do you think people give themselves away without consciously wanting to?"

"I wouldn't worry too much about it. They're cops, not psychoanalysts."

"I loved him. Dearly." She tried to recapture the sense of love, tried to see Fletcher here, now, in this room. He had never been able to resist touching her when she passed; even when she was rushing about at her chores, he would reach out and pinch her gently, stroke her bare arm or cup his big hand over one of her breasts. Had she honestly longed for freedom? "It disturbs me, remembering. I feel . . . unfaithful."

Her flesh, so given to blushes, grew rosy. The very word, unfaithful, gave life to another memory. Vitality returned to her unexpectedly, that sense and memory were aroused in Ralph. Both drew back. Such heat and challenge were unfitting, uncomfortable, and perverse. The moment was wrong. She and Ralph dared not look at each other. They became interested in furniture, concerned with lamps, aware of the pattern of the carpet, drawn by a bloated silver dish like a giant egg on legs, an absurd antique sent by one of Fletcher's business associates when he married Elaine.

Silence was pricked by small confusions. They listened to the birds beyond drawn curtains, to tires whining at the turn of the road, the throbbing of the refrigerator, the beating of their hearts. Elaine had come alive, Ralph was unfrozen. No climax had occurred, no communion of flesh, but both were forced to recognize heat and immediacy. And these fools allowed their eyes to meet and share the moment. They could think of nothing to say. Ralph did not want to think of her impossible situation, Elaine could not go on talking about shame and fear. The walls bore down upon them, the clock, the birds, the refrigerator, they asserted their right to make themselves heard. Backing away slowly, Ralph and Elaine created distance, rejected feeling, tried to tell themselves the moment had been illusion. There remained the bitter flavor of guilt.

Don and Cindy burst in, full of news. The funeral was to be tomorrow, late in the afternoon, so that the first Mrs. Strode could get there comfortably. It was to be strictly private, with guards to keep out strangers and busybodies, but dignified so that their friends could honor Cindy's father. They had chosen a coffin of solid bronze.

"It's the least we can do for Daddy."

"We hope it's all right with you, Elaine," added Don with the pompous gravity of the man of the family.

The doorbell rang. "I hope I'm not disturbing anyone," said Sergeant Knight, "but I happen to have a few more questions to ask Mrs. Strode if I may." He bobbed his head in a gesture of courtesy. "I'd like all of you to stay here, if you will. It'll expedite matters to have everyone present." He used the melting tones of an actor who creates emphasis by understatement. "You, too, Doctor."

"Please do," Elaine whispered.

The intimacy was not lost on Knight.

They went into the den, the coolest room in the house. Fletcher had put in an air conditioner of the latest and most expensive kind, advertised as silent. Its muted roar never ceased. Had this been his home, Sergeant Knight could not have assumed the role of host with greater urbanity. All tact and gentleness, "I think you'll be comfortable here, Mrs. Strode," he said and pulled out Fletcher's big leather chair, pushed up the ottoman, urged her to stretch out and relax. Rebelling, Elaine obeyed. She distrusted him implicitly.

In a straight chair by the door sat a stalwart young man who had come with Knight. This Mr. Corbin had a set of teeth that gleamed like costume jewelry. He took notes swiftly with his left hand, and paused only to wipe sweat from his face with a crumpled handkerchief. From time to time Knight directed a meaningful glance toward Corbin. These signals seemed no more than theatrical effect since they seldom occurred when anything important was discussed. The atmosphere was somber and contrived, thickened by smoke from Cindy's endless chain of cigarettes which Don and Knight, in endless competition, hurried to light.

Knight had brought a briefcase filled with pertinent information, copies of laboratory reports, notes on the conversations between Detectives Redding and Juarez with the family of Fletcher Strode immediately after the death was reported; his treasured copy of the diary; and transcripts of notes concerning his conversation with the family, with Dr. Ralph Julian, and with Dorine Henshaw, the domestic who had discovered the secret hoard of sleeping pills in Fletcher's boot. In a formal opening speech Knight said that he would not bore them with these reports since the important facts were known to all. Immediately afterward he stated these facts in his own words and full detail. The air conditioner roared as if a sleeping lion were held captive behind the grill.

The coroner's inquest, Knight informed them, would take place the following Monday at ten a.m. He believed the means of death would be known to them all at that time, and he hoped, for the sake of all present, that suicide could be proved. As Dr. Julian had clearly stated, death could easily be accomplished by a man in Mr. Strode's physical condition by closing the aperture in his neck with a small object. No such object had been discovered. "Nor do we believe it possible that a man could remove a cork, a wadded handkerchief, tissue or some similar article at the moment of death. But there are other ways . . ." He paused to look into each of their faces and, when his glance was met, to offer a smile of calculated sincerity.

Cindy started to speak, but Don shook his head at her. "I wish, Donnie," she murmured, "you wouldn't always do that to me."

"Do what, love?"

"Whenever I start to say something . . ." She stopped in confusion because Don looked at her so severely that she felt a cold shiver pass through her body.

"What was it you wished to say, Mrs. Hustings?"

She dared not look at Don. He was angry and cautious about many things, which he had not fully explained. "I don't remember," she said.

Probably she had meant to deny her father's suicide again, thought Ralph, and wondered if Knight had taken notice of the hysteria and frequency of these protests.

Knight went on with his speech. "There are other ways to suffocate a man in deep, drug-induced sleep. If one had a strong enough will, the human hand could be held there until the victim passed away." He held his hand over his throat to illustrate the act. "Or a blanket or pillow, the classical method used in Shakespeare's *Othello*." He enjoyed his phrasing and looked obliquely at Elaine.

"Did my pillows and sheets prove anything, Sergeant Knight?" Her voice had too keen an edge.

"I don't mean to distress you, Mrs. Strode. In these unhappy hours you've borne yourself extremely well. So let's try and keep our tempers now." This was in a confidential whisper, a delicate rebuke that all of them could hear. "Please remember that I don't enjoy this any more than you. But unfortunately, one must do one's job in this world." After a sigh that deplored cruel necessity, Knight proceeded with gusto to repeat questions and arguments and to consult his notes as though he did not know precisely what they told. Using a low register that strained everyone's hearing, he referred to contradictions in Elaine's actions and answers. His questions were framed for simple yes and no replies. "Didn't you tell Mr. Hustings last week, on Thursday, four days before your husband's death, that you knew he contemplated suicide?"

"Must we go over all of this again? I told you everything already," she reminded him fretfully.

"Can you deny that after your husband's death you said you felt guilty?"

Boredom ended. They all sat up straight or slid forward in their chairs.

"Did you?" demanded Ralph.

Elaine lay back against the leather cushions, regarded the long tanned legs stretched out upon the ottoman. "Did I?" Her voice sounded feathery, careless, without substance.

"You did." Knight shuffled his papers again.

"Perhaps I did." Elaine kept them waiting while she thought about it. "I don't remember, but how can one remember every word one's ever said?"

Ralph leaped up. "So what?" he cried. "Suppose she did say she felt guilty? A person can feel guilty about picking his nose."

Cindy's hand dropped. She looked wildly around for a cigarette.

"I'm afraid, Doctor, this did concern her husband's death. She said it to Mr. Hustings while"—Knight had leaped like a ballet dancer to offer Cindy his cigarette case and his back was toward Elaine as he tossed the tidbit—"she was changing her husband's bed linen at three o'clock in the morning."

Don said, "I hope you're not vexed at me, love. Sergeant Knight asked me a lot of questions and I simply told him what you told me."

"I'm not angry at all," Elaine replied with acid sweetness, "but I am wondering what this is all about. You told us you weren't going to repeat what we all know, Sergeant Knight, and you've spent an hour doing nothing but that. Is it a trick of some sort? Are you trying to trap one of us into saying something that might be useful to you?"

Ralph shot her a look of warning. In her situation it was injudicious to offend the detective. Knight's vanity was obvious. Ordinarily Elaine would have been sensitive to the nature of the man, shown appreciation of his little tricks of charm. Ralph could understand her not liking Knight, but knew it unwise of her to bait him in this way.

All of Knight's attention was given to his right thumbnail. He studied it as scrupulously as if he were doing research on cuticles. "Perhaps one of you is waiting," he bent closer over his thumb, "to be trapped. Deviously."

A nervous smile crossed Elaine's face. She had become rigid. Everyone, even Cindy, had become aware of the extraordinary tension. To those who had read the diary the word was potent; *devious*. Fletcher had learned it from Elaine and used it often. *My wife is a devious creature.* The word was ammunition and Knight had fired it, deviously.

WHEN SHE HAD given him the diary, Elaine said she had not read what her husband had written. Knight had not believed her. But now that he knew the contents, he conceded (as he had in that dreary session in District Attorney Hanley's office) that Mrs. Strode had been truthful about it. No sane woman, however innocent, would have allowed that document to fall into the hands of the police. Knight had read and reread, memorized and indexed important entries. The fact that Elaine knew nothing about the fears and prophecies recorded by her late husband was helpful to Knight. He intended to keep secret the source of his information until its exposure could profit him.

"I'd like to remind you of something, Mrs. Strode. A certain conversation with your husband."

The telephone interrupted. Don answered and summoned Ralph. The exchange gave him the telephone number of an anxious patient. The call took a long time. Ralph's absence pleased Knight. In asking Ralph to stay, he had in mind the possibility of catching him and Elaine in some revealing lie or inconsistency, but he found the doctor too alert to reveal himself or to allow indiscretion.

Don had gone to the bar. "How about something cool, sir? You won't think we're trying to suborn the police if we offer you a fruit juice?"

"I see," said Knight with an appreciative wink, "that you remember my addiction."

Corbin looked wistfully at the Bourbon poured out for Cindy and Don, but had to content himself with a ginger ale. Elaine sipped ice water.

Knight did not wait for Ralph to come back, but went on glibly, "You had a conversation with your husband about the poisons in the garden shed." He waited. At last his patience was gone and he said sharply, "Didn't you?"

She answered like someone who had been napping. "Didn't I what?"

Knight repeated the question with emphatic pauses between words. He saw her hesitancy as a stall to keep him waiting while she formulated an evasive answer.

Elaine was honestly confused. "Poisons in the garden shed?" she repeated like a student who ponders a question too difficult for a prompt answer.

"Don't you recall the conversation?"

She had kicked off her high-heeled slippers, which she left on the ottoman as she ran across the room in bare feet. "I know I didn't like having all those Danger and Beware bottles in the shed. When you live with someone like he was, my husband, you're naturally," she passed a limp hand across her forehead, "frightened. Who wouldn't be?"

"What does that mean, someone like your husband?"

"I was afraid he . . . that is, I knew . . . he thought about committing suicide."

"And you were so frightened that you called these poisons to his attention?"

Elaine did not remember mentioning the poisons to Fletcher although she knew, definitely, that she had told the gardener to take them out of the shed. And he did. He kept them in his truck and only brought them out when he had to get rid of snails and slugs and aphids. "Did I talk about it to Fletcher?"

"Last June," Knight said.

"How do you know?"

"Not long afterward you spoke to a girl on the long-distance phone. About being free. You said a girl ought to be ecstatically happy to have her freedom."

"I remember that. It was Joyce Kilburn, she'd just got her divorce. I wanted to console her. But how—"

Knight cut in. "You thought a lot about being free again. You dreamed about being free and living in New York like you did before you met Mr. Strode."

There was no denying this. She had already confessed guilt. Color jetted up from the richest, darkening face and neck. Her voice coarsened. "What are you trying to do, convict me for my dreams?" Whirling about, "Why don't you say something, Don? You're supposed to be a lawyer. I thought you wanted to help me. Has he any right to ask me these questions?"

Don raced to her side. "Easy now, sweet. It won't help to lose our tempers. I'd have advised you if you'd been willing, but you said you wanted to tell the truth."

"He's right, Mrs. Strode. You offered cooperation to the fullest extent." Knight's amiable tone gave contrast to Elaine's shrillness. "Please don't be distressed if I ask a few more questions about your private life."

Don tried to lead her to a chair. She brushed him off and ran out to the hall. At the telephone Ralph was telling a patient that laxatives were not the answer. She raced back into the room, saw Knight in Fletcher's chair at Fletcher's desk where Fletcher used to sit when he kept his accounts, considered his investments, paid his bills, and wrote in his diary.

Knight inclined his head.

"Fletcher wrote those things!" Belief gathered slowly. "About the poisons in the shed and what I told Joyce and all the crazy, trivial things that happen in a house?"

"I hardly think you'd consider them crazy and trivial if you had read your husband's diary."

"He didn't think I meant to poison him?"

"No such accusation has been made, Mrs. Strode."

"Why did he put such things into his diary?"

"You ought to know better than anyone else."

"It's a trick," she said, "I don't believe a word," but knew, while she denied it, that there could be no other source of information so crazy, so trivial, and so true. "I'd like to see the diary."

"Sorry, Mrs. Strode, I am not at liberty to show it to you."

"Why not?"

"You gave it to me of your own free will."

"You asked if I'd read it and I said I hadn't. Now I want to. I have a right to know what my husband wrote about me."

A soldier does not yield his gun so readily. The diary was more than a weapon to Knight; it was also his shield, and more, a walking stick to help him up the steep climb, a magic wand to waft him to a place among the mighty. "I'm afraid I can't give it to you right now."

"Is that right, Don? Is it legal for him to keep it from me?"

"I'm not sure of the law in this state. It's not a matter that comes up every day," Don answered smoothly, "but for the moment, let's not make an issue of it. It's as much to your advantage as anyone else's to get this ugly mess cleaned up."

"But why won't he let me see it?" She had become fretful. Narrowed eyes, locked muscles, the darkness of her face destroyed her beauty. She had run her hands through her hair so that it was as wild as a witch's. "It looks like a trick to persecute me."

"Careful, dear," Don murmured, "it can never be more than circumstantial evidence. You have no reason to be so agitated, sweet."

"Please don't blame me, Mrs. Strode. I'm only trying to understand the things your husband wrote in his diary."

"But Fletcher wouldn't have, he couldn't believe"—she rubbed her hands and bent her head and moaned because she could not bear to voice the hideous thought—"such stuff. He loved me."

"He thought you were trying to provoke him to suicide when you told him you'd taken a lover."

Shock was intended. Knight allowed himself the luxury of a glance at his audience. Corbin bared his teeth at the juicy information that the drama had included adultery when only murder had been expected. Cindy's chest and shoulders rose with every breath. An irrelevant stream of giggles escaped. Don tried to look grave. He dared not show pleasure in a statement that sent warm blood racing through his body and filled his head with visions of prosperity.

Elaine had regained a measure of calm. Anger remained, but at a lower temperature. Rigid, head high, she asked, "Is that what my husband wrote or your own interpretation, Sergeant Knight?"

"What was your reason for telling him about your *lover*?" Delicate inflection gave the word an obscene sound.

What reason? Like acute pain the scene returned. Elaine saw her husband stamping into her bedroom, his body bare and brown above the shorts, a bandanna tied about his neck. He had smelled and shone with sweat.

"He asked me."

"Asked if you had a lover?" Knight kept the question hanging in the air until Elaine assented with a nod. "And you told him that you had?"

"What does that prove?" she demanded.

"Will you allow me to read what your husband wrote about that incident?" Of course she would; how could she disallow it? Knight riffled through pages, but only for effect. "Ah," he breathed and began to read slowly and with emphasis like a student of elocution:

"Yesterday she hit me with the news she had a lover. How much can a man take? No matter what plans are in her head she ought to be loyal while I am still alive. Maybe she is too passionate to control herself—"

"You see," squealed Cindy, "Mom knew, she always said a girl like that couldn't behave decently." Don commanded her to shut up, but she had to express superiority with another trill of proud laughter before she settled down to listen to Knight declaim:

> "What a shock to a husband. I drove to the ocean and stood on those high rocks and looked down at the water and was tempted. Then a terrible thought came to my mind. I saw through her devious plan. She may not be brave enough to strike so she is trying to provoke me to do it myself. I refuse to make it easy for her."

Elaine had gone back to the leather chair. Moaning softly, she sank onto the ottoman and covered her face with both hands.

"Sorry, Mrs. Strode, I didn't hear what you said. Could you speak a bit louder, please?"

More to herself than to the others, "Poor Fletch, he was so sick," she said. Her hands fell from her eyes. She raised her head and saw that Ralph had come into the room. Conflict tore her to bits. She thought of too many things at the same time; of the terrible agony which had driven Fletcher to these accusations, of the shame of the cuckold, and of the way it had all ended. At the same time she wondered how much of this Ralph had heard and how he must feel at having their affair exposed to this vulgar group, with Knight so righteous, Don so smug, with Cindy sniffling happily, and Corbin grinning so that each of his pearls glowed separately.

"It seems my husband kept a diary," she tried to explain to Ralph calmly. "He had some sort of idea, a crazy obsession," but she could not name the nature of it. "Sergeant Knight read some of it to us, but he won't let me see it."

Knight sensed accusation. "I'm very sorry."

"Don says I haven't the legal right to demand it."

"I didn't say that, dear." To Ralph with one of his candid, boyish glances Don explained, "I told her I wasn't familiar with the California law in regard to that special request."

"Why can't you show it to her, Sergeant Knight?"

Knight's hand tightened on it as though the reproduced diary were an amulet. He beheld himself with it in court, envisioned the explosive effect of entries such as the one he had just read, saw his name and picture in the papers, considered the effect on his career of a front-page trial, foresaw the pleasure of his mother. Since he had first read Fletcher Strode's prophecies, he had dwelt in a dream.

The head of the Homicide Department, Knight's boss, had been skeptical about the diary. The Chief had been in agreement. The department's head psychologist had been consulted. In the conference with Lowell Hanley, these three had argued with dark cynicism. The District Attorney had been inclined toward Knight's viewpoint. No one realized more acutely than this ambitious man that the diary could be a publicity bombshell, but he was too experienced not to reckon that a bomb can explode in more than one direction. The District Attorney's ambitions were of no lesser intensity than Knight's, but on a higher level, and handled with subtler tactics. After a hot argument, it had been decided that Knight was to pursue the investigation, using the diary's contents as a means of obtaining more solid evidence. Discretion had been commanded. Privately, Knight had been informed that Mr. Hanley was one hundred percent behind him and that his personal cooperation would be given freely at any hour of the day or night.

Knight's answer showed both discretion and a tolerant spirit. "If you knew the full contents of the diary, Doctor, you wouldn't want her to read it."

"I know them."

"I beg your pardon."

"I've read the diary."

"That's impossible." Knight's urbanity showed a raveled edge. "You don't mean to say that Mr. Strode allowed you to . . ."

"Dr. McIntosh asked my advice."

Knight's nod showed recognition of the name while Ralph explained to the others that McIntosh, an old schoolmate, was chief psychologist to the Police Department. "Since I knew Mr. Strode, he asked my opinion of the validity."

"And what did you make of it?"

"Bullshit."

Cindy gurgled.

"No apologies," Ralph said.

"You're honestly convinced of that?" fretted Knight.

"I have no doubts whatsoever."

"Mr. Hanley was much impressed by the diary."

"The diary, if valid, would serve our District Attorney well. In court and the newspapers," Ralph said drily.

"One would expect a more considered opinion from you, Doctor." Knight paused like a political speaker about to make a point. "It's obvious that you're prejudiced in favor of the lady, but I should think that your conclusions, as a man of science, would be more objective."

"Objectively and scientifically, I think the diary from beginning to end is plain bullshit."

"Doctor, there are ladies present."

"I chose my words with the ladies in mind. To dispel fear," he cast a veiled glance toward Elaine, and with a direct stare at Cindy, added, "and destroy any illusions they may cherish."

"Please answer one question for me. Objectively. As a man of science."

"I promise not to use dirty words."

Knight let the levity pass. "What I want is your frank opinion as to the reason a man of Mr. Strode's intelligence," Knight raised his hand in warning against interruption, "and you surely won't deny that Mr. Strode had considerable mentality to have reached a high point of financial success. Then why should a brilliant man think he could deceive us all, the police as well as those nearest and dearest, with statements he knew to be false? If they were false!"

"I doubt that he considered them false."

"But, Doctor, you just said—"

"I said I didn't believe the hogwash in that diary, but that doesn't mean that the writer wasn't convinced."

"Which means, I take it, that you believe Mr. Strode was not sane?"

Cindy tried to speak, but Don prevented it.

"I think he had become more and more disturbed. If you read the diary carefully, you'll notice a definite deterioration in his reasoning. I went over it carefully last night and looked through it again, superficially, this morning. It seems to me that the fantasies grew stronger and that he had come to believe them."

"Nonsense." Don was on his feet. "Shit, if you prefer the doctor's language. I lived in the house with him all summer and if I ever saw a sane and strong-minded character, it was Fletcher Strode."

"That's for sure. My father was perfectly sane."

"Let's say he was sick. That's the popular term now," Ralph said. "A sick man who hated and distrusted himself and who'd lost the desire to go on living, but hadn't the will to kill himself."

"You've certainly changed your opinion." Don aimed his forefinger at Ralph's temple. "You were so sure it was suicide."

"I'm still sure. I've done some reading since this happened, and find that the publications confirm my opinion. The suicide urge is common in laryngectomy patients. That diary was a symbol, a direct invitation to death by a man afraid to commit the final act."

"Do you mean he wanted his wife to kill him?"

"Let's say he wanted to think he wanted it."

Knight stalked over to Elaine. "How do you feel about it? You knew him best. Do you believe he wanted you to kill him?"

"I don't know," she said in a flat voice.

"Don't know!" Don had come to stand beside Knight. The three men surrounded the crouching figure. "You must certainly know what you told me so confidentially last week."

Elaine answered with a quick dip of her head. Don spoke in the manner of a prosecuting attorney. "You told me very clearly that you were afraid he'd kill himself. Is that all you were afraid of?"

"I don't understand you, Don." Crouched on the ottoman in the classic pose of despair, she spoke without looking up at him.

"What don't you understand? Have you forgotten telling me about some TV show you and he saw together? About a mercy killing? And the question he asked afterward?" Don spoke with the objectivity of a man sure of his facts. "The thought's been on your mind ever since, hasn't it?"

Elaine gave no sign of having heard. Even when he demanded, less objectively, "Can't you answer the question, Elaine?" she remained silent. Don's authoritative, prosecuting attorney voice had not reached her. "Lovable," she heard in broken tones. Her hands protected a wound in her own neck; her eyes sought him where the other man sat at his desk. The diary had been a refuge, solace for the maimed ego, a substitute for the lost voice.

"You don't deny it?"

Don had become querulous.

Knight sat still, fingertips pressed together, hands forming a steeple. Through experience he had learned that passion reveals more truth than the most thorough and ruthless interrogation. He had made no accusations, taken no action that could cause criticism of police tactics. He had only to sit back and let the Strode family do the job for him.

"She can't deny anything. She killed my father."

"Cindy, my dear," admonished Don, "you have no right to make such an accusation. Nothing's been proved, has it, sir?" With charming deference of a prep school boy trying to please a master, he strolled toward Knight. Although his wife was vindictive, Don Hustings showed decent objectivity. Pockets hid hands clenched as passionately as if they already protected the Strode fortune.

Suddenly he felt himself seized by the shoulder, whirled about, and made to confront Ralph Julian's fury. There was no color in the lean face, no tremors in the hands that gripped his shoulders.

"What the hell is this all about? Do you want to find Elaine guilty?"

Knight and Corbin leaped at them. "Easy, lad," Knight said. Corbin seized Ralph from behind.

Ralph let go.

Don smiled sadly. "I've been trying to guard Elaine's interests, sir. Sincerely." Once again appealing to the headmaster, the boy showed respect. "We're all interested in the same thing, aren't we? To get at the truth."

"Seems to me you and your wife are more interested in getting her hanged."

"He's the crazy one," said Cindy with a hollow laugh.

"I resent that," replied Don with dignity. "Though I do understand wanting to protect his own interests. Since you were mentioned in the diary as her lover."

"Fletcher couldn't have written that." Elaine dared not look at Ralph. She had told him with conviction that Fletcher had not known the lover's identity.

And Ralph said, "I must have missed the name."

"Perhaps you overlooked an embarrassing item," Don said, "but if you went over it twice, I don't see how you could have missed the bit about the redheaded doctor. How many redheaded doctors does Elaine have?"

Elaine sprang to life, flaming. "You said you hadn't read the diary, Don."

"I did?"

"You know you did." Fury flamed her cheeks, hardened her voice, caused every nerve to twitch. "When we gave Sergeant Knight the diary. You said you hadn't read it. Didn't he?" She ran over to accost Knight with her question.

"Let's try to keep calm, Mrs. Strode."

"I don't seem to remember." Don spoke in the lofty tone of a man who could not be bothered by the trivialities cherished by women.

Don had told Knight at lunch that he had not read the diary. Nothing was said of this. A slight pursing of the lips gave the only indication that Knight was aware of the falsehood.

"You lied. Why, Don? Why can't you tell the truth about it?" Elaine's questions were rhetorical, more the expression of scorn than a demand for reason. "You knew what the diary said and you told Sergeant Knight that it might be useful. It was you who told him that Fletcher kept a diary."

"If I did," Don fixed earnest, schoolboy eyes on Knight, "it doesn't change anything. None of the facts are the least bit altered."

"There are other things in the diary. Perhaps Don overlooked them," Ralph said and coolly took the document from the desk. "There's an item that might answer your question, Elaine."

"Unless it's relevant, let's not waste Sergeant Knight's time," Don said.

"It's relevant," said Ralph, peering at the pages.

"Read it," said Knight.

Ralph read dully and without inflection:

"I always believed that a man ought to be ready when opportunity knocks at his door. I still think it is a good idea except that nowadays a lot of young men are so busy waiting for the knock that they forget about the real hard work that invites opportunity to come in. The way the world is getting now a young man would just as soon knock down old ladies and push baby buggies in front of speeding trucks if he thought he saw opportunity across the street. An A-1 genuine door-watcher has moved into my house and I hope no old ladies or baby buggies get in his way."

The air conditioner groaned. Cindy yawned. Knight considered Don's profile, the curve of sculptured lips, the elegantly cut features, the smooth forehead, and melting eyes. Don listened with the superior expression of a man forced to sit through a dull play.

Ralph finished and told Knight, "Mr. Strode would have recognized the motive behind Don's lies."

Knight had a question. "But if he was not, according to your diagnosis, in his right mind, why do you make so much of his observations about life in general?"

"A person who is paranoid on one subject may see other things with complete clarity."

"Was there anything in the diary about me?" put in Cindy.

"Speaking of opportunities—" Knight crossed the room as silently as a cat, pounced down upon Ralph, and said, "May I?"

The request for permission was not necessary. He had already taken the pages from Ralph's hand. "I won't waste your time reading all of Mr. Strode's clear and relevant observations, Doctor, because you've probably noticed certain entries about opportunities in common household objects, but here's an idea we haven't considered." With a flourish that might have drawn from its scabbard, he took a pair of heavily rimmed spectacles from a monogrammed leather case, adjusted them on his nose, and read:

"Why does she always place temptation in my way? All over this house are dangerous objects. Many are even marked with warnings. If I resist too long, she may become impatient and take the fatal step herself. On the surface she is sweet and soft but underneath there's the deadly will of a woman who will get her own way at all costs."

"As you'll notice, no specific object is named." Knight looked at Corbin, nodding briefly. "But there were—and probably still are—warnings placed most conveniently close to Mr. Strode. Corbin, will you get the article we placed in the car?"

Corbin was already on his way.

"I took the liberty of making a search of your house," Knight told Elaine. "I didn't ask permission this time because I thought you'd rather not have your conversation with the doctor disturbed. You two seemed very absorbed."

"Thanks." Elaine tried not to show annoyance, but she was uncomfortable at the discovery that she and Ralph had been watched. What had they said? Nothing that could be useful to Knight, she was sure, yet the knowledge irritated her. She sat erect, folded her hands in her lap, and waited attentively.

Don and Cindy were not surprised to see Corbin carry in Cindy's beige organza dress in a plastic bag. After their visit to the undertaker's, they had gone downtown to Police Headquarters where Cindy had signed a confession stating that she had found the bag on her father's body, removed and hidden it. She had been assured that by this voluntary act she would escape punishment, but now, although she might have expected it, the sight of the bag affected her nerves. She began to tremble.

Like an actor playing detective, Knight examined the bag, slipped it off the hanger, held it up for them to look at, shook it, listened to the faint rustle, brought it closer, and read aloud: "Top Drawer Cleaners. Ladies' and Gentlemen's Fine Custom Cleaning." And in lower pitch, "Warning: To avoid danger of suffocation keep away from babies and small children. Do not use in cribs, carriages, beds, or playpens. This bag is not a toy."

Everyone was silent. There were no human noises in the room, no sounds of breathing, no sniffles, no sighs, no tap of fingers, no creaking of chairs under nervous buttocks.

"A medical question, Dr. Julian. Could such a bag smother"—Knight held on to the word while darting a veiled look at Elaine—"a man in Mr. Strode's condition?" He touched his throat as people always did when they spoke of Fletcher's wound.

"It could kill an ox," Ralph said.

"We call it the cheap suicide," put in Corbin.

The word was unfortunate. Knight winced. And Cindy looked angry.

"It would have to be placed over the nose and mouth in a way to prevent inhalation of air," said Knight and drew from his pocket a square of the thin plastic material of which such bags are made. "Allow me to demonstrate." He held the stuff over his face and breathed in. The plastic clung to his mouth and nostrils. "In the same way," he said, pulling it off, "it would adhere to the opening in Mr. Strode's neck, sealing it tight so that no air could enter. And since we know, both by his wife's statement and our laboratory tests, that he had taken barbiturates, there is no doubt that he was in a deep sleep so that the bag could be fixed firmly over the throat without his knowing. And that he did not wake and push it off as people do when blankets interfere with their breathing."

"For a man speaking of possibilities, you seem very sure of your facts," remarked Ralph.

"They are facts. We know positively that Mr. Strode died

of suffocation caused by this bag." With a brief smile Knight added, "You seem astonished, Doctor. I don't wonder, since you were the first to examine the body."

"There was no sign of a bag when I got there."

"It had been removed and concealed."

"Is that true?" Ralph turned toward Elaine.

"I didn't hide it."

"Mrs. Hustings," announced Knight with a nod toward Cindy, "has confessed that she removed the bag."

"What the hell for?" asked Ralph.

"To protect her father's memory against the disgrace of suicide." This time Knight bowed as though he honored Cindy for the act.

She failed to recognize the chivalry, but sat like a mute or a dreamer. Don spoke for her. "Thank you, sir."

Too acutely Elaine remembered the moment when Don, holding the bundle from the cleaner's, had kissed her. The bags had been a wall between their bodies. When Fletcher walked in, the bags had slipped to the floor. Fletcher had helped pick them up without a word of reproach, but Elaine had felt guilty and tried to excuse herself.

"So we know what caused Mr. Strode's death," Ralph said, "but can his loyal daughter tell us who put the bag over him?"

"I didn't want people to think my father—"

"*Sh-sh*," commanded Don. His fists were clenched, his jaws jutted.

"Let's keep our heads. I'm sure Dr. Julian did not mean to infer anything derogatory to your wife," Knight said.

"I agree with her. The diagnosis was correct, I'm sure. The plastic bag points definitely to suicide." Ralph nodded at Corbin. "Cheap suicide."

"We have no proof of that," Knight argued.

"We have no proof that it wasn't. And since the only person who would know definitely will never be able to tell us—"

Ralph stopped dead. A car horn, raucous and unexpected, struck their ears like an echo of the maimed voice. Elaine's back arched like a cat's. Don turned toward the window as though he expected to see the curtains parted by a ghostly hand. Cindy groped for her package of paper handkerchiefs.

"I am forced to disagree with you, Dr. Julian. There *may* be one person who knows definitely how that bag happened to be on the body. Do I make myself clear?"

"Almost too clear," Ralph answered. "Clearer than you know. I hope your bosses appreciate your zeal."

Knight's urbanity was not disturbed. He studied the plastic bag as though he had never before seen such a thing, then held it up for them all to see again. "Do you recognize this bag, Mrs. Strode?"

"It's like all the others. They all look alike."

"You recognize the name on it?"

"Certainly. We always send our things to the Top Drawer."

"Are there any other such bags in the house?"

Elaine answered scornfully, "You ought to know, you've made a thorough search."

"Please answer my question."

"Yes, there are. Some in my husband's closet and perhaps in Cindy's and Don's room, too."

"No, not in our room! You can look if you want," Cindy said feverently.

With the diffident laugh that accompanies a confession of economy, Don admitted, "We use a cheaper cleaner. Top Drawer's a bit out of our class."

"Mrs. Strode, didn't you mention the fact that the cleaner's boy delivered some of those bags recently?" Knight erred deliberately. He saw Elaine stiffen and scowl as she looked at Don.

"He must have told you."

Smiling ruefully, "I did," he said. "After Cindy confessed to Sergeant Knight about finding and hiding it, he asked if I'd seen the bag before, and I told him how I'd helped you hang up several of them."

"I see," Knight said slowly as if pondering a difficult problem. "Do you remember when that was, Mrs. Strode?"

"Why don't you ask Don? He remembers everything."

Don reminded her that they had been in the pavilion together when they heard the truck stop in the driveway. It was no wonder, he told Knight, that Elaine was not too clear about it because she had been rather distraught at the time.

Knight wanted to know what had upset her, and Don said that it was just when she was telling him that she feared Fletcher would kill himself.

"I see. Naturally she'd be upset. Naturally," Knight said as though this were all new to him. "And what did you do with the bags, Mrs. Strode?"

"You've heard it all from Don. We hung them up."

"In Mr. Strode's closet?"

"They were over his suits."

"Tell me why"—Knight's softest tone was most menacing, his slow and sensuous walk a threat in pantomime—"when you believed your husband suicidal, you hung those dangerous bags in his bedroom."

Her head went up, her eyes met Knight's in challenge. "Why don't you read the diary again? You've got such faith in it, perhaps you'll find your answer there." Insolence was deliberate. She was worn out, emotionally drained and, like a weary child, wayward and bent upon opening herself to attack.

Ralph sprang toward her. "Don't say any more. You don't have to, you know. Let me get you a good lawyer."

Don looked supremely indifferent.

"One more question, Mrs. Strode." Knight made a statement of it, rather than a question. "Do you remember how many suits covered with plastic bags the cleaner delivered that afternoon?"

"Two. And the cashmere jacket."

"Three?"

Don confirmed this with a nod.

"Are those three bags still there, over the garments, Mrs. Strode?"

"You've made a thorough search. Don't you know?" A mask had formed, giving her face a remote and haughty expression.

"Shall we go and look?" Knight stepped aside so that Elaine could precede him. The others followed in a straggling procession and formed a tight group beside the bedroom door.

The air conditioner in Fletcher's room had not been turned on. Heat assaulted them. Light from the ceiling lamp struck their faces. Knight created dramatic effects by underplaying. He opened the closet door quietly. No plastic gleamed over the suits. He asked Elaine to identify the two which had been delivered by the cleaner, and the cashmere jacket. They all hung uncovered.

"Where are those three bags?" Knight asked.

Elaine walked toward the closet stiffly, looked inside, and then back at Knight. "I don't know."

"You don't know? But I thought you hung them in here a few days ago. Did you remove them?"

Elaine seemed not to be with them in the hot, bright room. Rapt, controlled, driven by some force beneath her dark look, she stood alone and remote. Ralph, aware of all the shards of tension, every flick of an eyelid, each startled glance, all the twitches and tremors, saw her as a stranger.

"I asked a question, Mrs. Strode. I'd appreciate an answer." Urbanity had collapsed. Knight used a brusque tone.

"What was your question?"

"What became of the three plastic bags? One, we know, was found on your husband's body and was removed by Mrs. Hustings. We've got that one. But the other two? Why were they removed? So the absence of the third wouldn't be noticed?"

Cindy dropped her cigarette. It lay smoldering on the carpet. Elaine said, "What became of them, Don?"

Don favored Knight with his frankest youthful expression.

"I've told you everything I know, sir."

"I asked you, Mrs. Strode, why those bags were removed."

Corbin leaped to stamp out the small flame. The carpet was singed and gave off a rancid smell. Elaine kept them waiting. The others showed their feelings more clearly: Cindy's tremors, Don's deceptive charm, Ralph's ill-contained anger, the zest and suspense Knight could no longer keep hidden.

Ralph took Elaine's arm. "Don't say any more. Try to control yourself before you speak." To Knight he barked, "She doesn't have to answer. Quit tormenting her."

"She knows that," Don hastened to put in. "I've advised her several times. There's no reason to get so excited. It's only circumstantial evidence."

"Evidence, hell! What are you trying to do to her?"

"Keep out of this, Doctor," ordered Knight, who had become more and more the cop. "Mr. Hustings is trying to help her."

"What's your game?" Ralph took off his glasses as though, by uncovering his eyes, he could penetrate deeper into the detective's mind. "Why are you straining so hard to turn a simple suicide into murder? Publicity? Your career? Advancement? Is Lowell Hanley behind this? Big stuff for you boys, mysterious death, sensational diary, beautiful girl—"

Pale with fury, shaken, Knight snapped, "I'd advise you to keep your prejudices to yourself. They won't do your girl friend any good."

"Please, please, Ralph, let me speak for myself." No longer icy and remote, Elaine had become herself again, graceful in the pride of her carriage as she shook off his hand and moved toward Knight. She had made a decision, was free of uncertainty, spoke in a silky, provocative voice. "I've decided not to say any more without my own lawyer."

Knight looked down at the diamonds and arabesques of the carpet and at Elaine's long, bare feet and painted toenails. Sadly, and courteous again, he said, "Then I'm afraid I'll have to ask you to come downtown for further questioning."

"Now?" cried Ralph.

"I'm afraid that's necessary, Doctor."

"But it's getting late. Why not tomorrow? She's exhausted. This has been a long ordeal."

"Those were my instructions."

"Why didn't you mention them earlier?"

"I'm allowed to exercise my own judgment. After obtaining certain answers to certain questions. Or failing to obtain them."

"Don't worry about me, Ralph. I'm perfectly willing to go."

"I'll come along."

"A doctor isn't necessary. The young lady appears to be in good health."

"Do you want me, Elaine? I think we can arrange to overcome Sergeant Knight's objections."

"You, too, Mr. Hustings. They may want to ask you a few questions."

"Of course, sir." Don turned to Cindy. "Will you be all right, dear?"

"Don't they want me?"

"Thanks for offering to cooperate, Mrs. Hustings, but your signed confession is sufficient. Try to get a bit of rest," said Knight and blessed her with a smile. "You've been through enough today."

"What about Mrs. Strode? She's been through plenty, too." Ralph persisted.

Elaine said, "Thank you, Ralph, but if you really want to help me I'd like you to get me a good lawyer. May I change my clothes, Sergeant Knight? This dress doesn't seem quite correct for the police station."

WHILE THEY WATCHED, she had kept up the appearance of calm, but once she had shut herself into a lonely room, feeling was permitted. Her hands were clumsy. No matter how she tried to hurry—and she felt it important to get done—she fumbled. Choice was impossible. She changed three times, went back to the dress she had first selected. It was too heavy for the weather, but proper with long sleeves and a decently mature hemline. Her hair was wound into a demure knot at the nape. The occasion demanded stockings, a girdle, gloves. White or black? She was not on her way to the funeral, but would certainly be photographed as a widow.

Everybody was busy, Ralph and Knight competing for the telephone, Don changing his clothes and comforting his wife with another drink. Corbin had carried out the beige dress in the plastic bag, also the uncovered suits and cashmere coat. He put them on the backseat of Knight's unmarked car. The two cops in the black-and-white police car watched with curiosity and asked questions, which Corbin refused to answer.

Softly, so that none of them should notice, Elaine went to Fletcher's room. Windows were open, the air heavy with twilight heat. "The smog will be terrible," Elaine said aloud, tragically, as though bad air were the worst she had to face. She studied furniture, drapes, the uncovered mattress, small trinkets Fletcher had cherished, leather boxes, a pair of brushes, a shell shoehorn an old girl friend had brought him from Naples, and her own picture in a leather frame beside his bed. She thought of him stumbling in here on Monday night after he had waited so long and humbly at her door. What a comedown it had been, what a slackening of pride after he had cursed and struck her, to come begging alms of tenderness. She had been cold and deaf to his need, had indulged the spiteful need to punish him. If she had opened her door and her arms, if they had (without hope of fulfillment) been content to give each other warmth and physical reassurance, to grow drowsy in sweet intimacy, Monday night would have been like any other and she would have been up early on Tuesday to cook his breakfast.

She forced herself to recognize truth, to see it all again, contrition and impulse, instant and movement. No matter how people probed and bullied, there would be questions to answer. "I did love him," she said aloud and as dully as she had spoken of the smog.

Ralph waited in the living room. There was no air conditioner to shut out the sounds of life. Twilight noises entered, the humming and buzzing, the wind in the olive tree, and the endless rumble of cars. At the touch of a hand Ralph whirled about. A dark woman looked at him out of shadowed eyes. She rose upon the balls of her feet to touch his cheek with her lips, then drew away as though such liberties had already been denied her.

"Ralph, dear, you've been so good to me. Far too good."

"We're getting you Peter Albi. A patient of mine is one of his partners, they're both going to meet you downtown. You know who Albi is?"

"I'm sure he'll be just fine." Elaine looked out at the garden, watching a pair of rabbits as if their nibbling at her plants meant more than the reputation of her lawyer.

"How do you feel? Are you alright?"

"Fine. Much better now."

"Better?" Ralph squinted at her skeptically.

"Yes indeed. I won't have to tell a lot of lies. I'm no good at it. It was the lies that wrecked me."

"You lied?" He retreated to the impersonal manner of the consulting room. "You lied?" he said as if he had asked, "You bled?"

"It wouldn't have been necessary if that little idiot hadn't taken the bag away. A cheap suicide," she said bitterly. "That's what everyone would have believed, the suicide of a man who wanted passionately," the word affected her, she clasped her hands under her chin, "to die." Sharply, as if Ralph had contradicted this, she demanded, "Doesn't the diary prove it?"

"You said you hadn't read the diary."

"No, I hadn't. At first, when I gave it to him, I asked Fletcher what he was writing, but he became so mysterious about it that I knew . . ." She stopped to shake off a painful thought. "No, I didn't know he thought I *wanted* to kill him. But the diary, you said it yourself, was an invitation to death. It must have been in both of us, deep down, hidden, for all that time. Oh, God!"

"I thought that Don," Ralph said, seizing the thought that he had heard incorrectly or misinterpreted the confession, "Don . . . such an opportunist. I thought . . ."

"You're not listening. I've been trying to tell you, Ralph. Please listen."

An hour before—or was it a month? a year? centuries?—there had been a madness drawing them together. Now, it seemed, they lived in different countries and spoke languages that could not be translated. "You don't want to know. But it's true. He knew how it would be. Fletcher!" She softened at the name. "He wanted so much to die. I knew. For such a long time, Ralph. I knew at night when I'd go in and look at him asleep. He didn't want to wake up. Ever!"

Ralph was frozen, incapable of speech or direct thinking. He dwelt in a vacuum. A sudden silence had shut out all of the living world: centuries had become mute; household appliances had quit moaning; no planes flew overhead; no cars rumbled on the hill road.

Elaine's voice crashed into the silence. A whisper assaulted reluctant ears. Lamely at first, "I told him that I was leaving him. Fletcher! I said I couldn't take any more," she said, and then in a great rush, added, "I meant it. I wanted to be free. I wanted to go away, far . . ." The pause was too abrupt. She choked back memory, but found herself unable to exorcise a scene from her wicked dream—a ship, the man, infidelity as evil and more enduring than the moment of physical sin. She closed her eyes and turned her head away as though she could draw a curtain on the past. "But I knew I couldn't. Ever. I could never leave him, and it would go on and on like that. And on and on, forever." She tried to walk away from herself, moving about the room, and in her restlessness going faster and faster so that she seemed to be running toward some far-off goal. And spoke to the air, to a vision, to someone who was not there. "He cried that night. Imagine! Fletcher! Crying." She paused, listening. Illusion, a motor horn, an echo?

"You'll tell this to your lawyer?" Ralph's throat was affected. He spoke thickly.

"I wanted to be free."

The far-off cry sounded again, but whether it was in her head or on a street below the hill, she could not tell. Free? This, too, was illusion. No matter what her lawyer pleaded, a jury decided, a judge decreed, there would never be a day without memory, nor a night free of his ghost. Fletcher Strode would always possess her.

"Are you cold?" Ralph asked, for she was shivering in the hot room.

The world was again filled with the small noises of living. Ralph heard crickets, the first night bird's note, a cough somewhere in the house, a voice in another room, the pounding of his heart. On one level of his mind, the habitual and professional, he considered symptoms, the thunder of blood in his head, rapid pulse, chill, the death of sensation in his hands; on another plane, bemused by the discovery of her other nature, he wondered how he felt about her. He could find no words of comfort, could not will himself to speak, nor offer a gesture of affection.

Elaine had gone back to the window. In the swift twilight the marigolds were turning gray, the white chrysanthemums had become lavender. "It was a lovely garden," she said and sighed. "I suppose Mr. Albi will want to use the mercy killing argument." Her eyes found the climbing rose that she and Fletcher had bought the week they moved into the house. It was Fletcher's flower, the only one he had ever planted. "Perhaps it was. Perhaps."

"Of course," Ralph said. "It couldn't have been anything else."

"I wonder."

Knight came into the room. "Are we ready?" He asked with a jovial smile as if they were going out together on a date.